A SCANDALOUS AFFAIR

- A notorious noblewoman with an assortment of husbands

- A defiant young lord with bizarre enthusiasms

- Mad revelry, hidden loves, untimely condolence notes—and a brutally mangled corpse. . . .

Suspicion runs rampant among the gentry of an English village, as Inspector Alleyn tries to find a method in murder—before a crafty killer can strike again!

HAND IN GLOVE

Ngaio Marsh

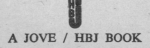

A JOVE / HBJ BOOK

Five previous printings
First Jove/HBJ edition published April 1978
Second printing January 1979

Library of Congress Catalog Card Number: 62-12371

Printed in the United States of America

Jove/HBJ books are published by Jove Publications, Inc.
(Harcourt Brace Jovanovich),
757 Third Avenue, New York, N.Y. 10017

FOR
JONATHAN ELSOM

Contents

Cast of Characters

Alfred Belt	*Manservant to Mr. Period*
Mrs. Mitchell	*Cook to Mr. Period*
Mr. Percival Pyke Period	
Nicola Maitland-Mayne	
Désirée, Lady Bantling	*Now Mrs. Bimbo Dodds, formerly Mrs. Harold Cartell. Née Désirée Ormsbury*
Andrew Bantling	*Her son by her first marriage*
Bimbo Dodds	*Her third and present husband*
Mr. Harold Cartell	*Her second husband*
Constance Cartell	*His sister*
Trudi	*Her maid*
Mary Ralston ("Moppett")	*Her adopted niece*
Leonard Leiss	
George Copper	*Garage proprietor*
Mrs. Nicholls	*Wife of Vicar of Ribblethorpe.*
Superintendent Williams	*Little Codling constabulary*
Sergeant Noakes	*Little Codling constabulary*
A foreman drainlayer	
Superintendent Roderick Alleyn	*C.I.D. New Scotland Yard*
Agatha Troy Alleyn	*Wife of Superintendent Alleyn*
Inspector Fox	*C.I.D. New Scotland Yard*
Detective Sergeant Thompson	*C.I.D. New Scotland Yard*
Detective Sergeant Bailey	*C.I.D. New Scotland Yard*
Sir James Curtis	*Pathologist*
Dr. Elkington	

HAND IN GLOVE

CHAPTER ONE

Mr. Pyke Period

While he waited for the water to boil, Alfred Belt stared absently at the kitchen calendar: WITH THE COMPLIMENTS OF THE LITTLE CODLING GARAGE. SERVICE WITH A SMILE. GEO. COPPER. Below this legend was a coloured photograph of a kitten in a boot and below that the month of March. Alfred removed them and exposed a coloured photograph of a little girl smirking through apple blossoms.

He warmed a silver teapot engraved on its belly with Mr. Pyke Period's crest: a fish. He re-folded the *Daily Telegraph* and placed it on the breakfast tray. The toaster sprang open, the electric kettle shrieked. Alfred made tea, put the toast in a silver rack, transferred bacon and eggs from pan to crested entrée dish, and carried the whole upstairs.

He tapped at his employer's door and entered. Mr. Pyke Period, a silver-haired bachelor with a fresh complexion, stirred in his bed, gave a little snort, opened his large brown eyes, mumbled his lips, and blushed.

Alfred said: "Good morning, sir." He placed the tray and turned away, in order that Mr. Period could assume his teeth in privacy. He drew back the curtains. The Village Green looked fresh in the early light. Decorous groups of trees, already burgeoning, showed fragile against distant hills. Woodsmoke rose delicately from several chimneys, and in Miss Cartell's house, across the Green, her Austrian maid shook a duster out of an upstairs window. In the field beyond, Miss Cartell's mare grazed peacefully.

"Good morning, Alfred," Mr. Period responded, now fully articulate.

Alfred drew back the curtains from the side window, exposing a small walled garden, a gardener's shed, a path, and a gate into a lane. Beyond the gate was a trench, bridged with planks and flanked by piled-up earth. Three labourers had assembled beside it.

"Those chaps still at it in the lane, sir," said Alfred, returning to the bedside. He placed Mr. Period's spectacles on his tray and poured his tea.

"Damn' tedious of them, I must say. However! Good God!" Mr. Period mildly ejaculated. He had opened his paper and was reading the obituary notices. Alfred waited.

"Lord Ormsbury's gone," Mr. Period informed him.

"Gone, sir?"

"Died. Yesterday, it seems. Motor accident. Terrible thing. Fifty-two, it gives here. One never knows. 'Survived by his sister . . .' " He made a small sound of displeasure.

"That would be Désirée, Lady Bantling, sir, wouldn't it," Alfred ventured, "at Baynesholme?"

"Exactly, Alfred. Precisely. And what must these fellows do but call her 'The Dowager'! She hates it. Always has. And not even correct, if it comes to that. One would have expected the *Telegraph* to know better." He read on. A preoccupied look, indeed one might almost have said a look of pleasurable anticipation, settled about his rather babyish mouth.

Below, in the garden, a dog began to bark hysterically.

"Good God!" Mr. Period said quietly and closed his eyes.

"I'll attend to her, sir."

"I cannot for the life of me see . . . However!"

"Will there be anything further, sir?" Alfred asked.

"What? No. No, thank you. Miss Cartell for luncheon, you remember. And Miss Maitland-Mayne."

"Certainly, sir. Arriving by the 10:20. Will there be anything required in the library, sir?"

"I can't think of anything. She's bringing her own typewriter." Mr. Period looked over the top of his paper and appeared to come to a decision. "Her grandfather," he said, "was General Maitland-Mayne. An old friend of mine."

"Indeed, sir?"

"Ah—yes. Yes. *And* her father. Killed at Dunkirk. Great loss."

A padded footfall was heard in the passage. A light tattoo sounded on the door, and a voice, male but pitched rather high, called out: "Bath's empty. For what it's worth." The steps receded.

Mr. Period repeated his sound of irritation.

"Have I or have I not," he muttered, "taken my bath in the evening for seven uncomfortable weeks?" He glanced at Alfred. "Well, well," he said. "Thank you."

"Thank you, sir," Alfred rejoined and withdrew. As he crossed the landing, he heard Mr. Cartell singing in his bedroom. It won't answer, Alfred thought, I never supposed it would—and descended to the kitchen. Here he found Mrs. Mitchell, the cook, a big and uninhibited woman. They exchanged routine observations, agreeing that spring really did seem to have come.

"All hotsy-totsy in the upper regions?" Mrs. Mitchell asked.

"As well as can be expected, Mrs. M."

A shrill yelp modulating into a long-drawn-out howl sounded outside. "That dog!" Mrs. Mitchell said.

Alfred went to the back door and opened it. An enormous half-bred boxer hurled itself against his legs and rushed past him to the kitchen. "Bitch!" Alfred said factually, but with feeling.

"Lay down! Get out of my kitchen! Shoo!" Mrs. Mitchell cried confusedly.

"Here—Pixie!"

The boxer slavered, ogled and threshed its tail.

"Upstairs! Pixie! Up to your master."

Alfred seized the bitch's collar and lugged it into the hall. A whistle sounded above. The animal barked joyously, flung itself up the stairs, skating and floundering as it went. Alfred sent a very raw observation after it and returned to the kitchen.

"It's too much," he said. "We never bargained for it. Never."

"I don't mind a nice cat."

"Exactly. And the damage it does!"

"Shocking. Your breakfast's ready, Mr. Belt. New-laid egg."

"Very nice," Alfred said.

He sat down to it, a neat dark man with quite an air about him, Mrs. Mitchell considered. She watched him make an incisive stab at the egg. The empty shell splintered and collapsed. Mrs. Mitchell, in a trembling voice, said: "First of April, Mr. B.," and threw her apron over her face. He was so completely silent that for a moment she thought he must be annoyed. However, when she peeped round her apron, he shook his eggspoon at her.

"You wait," he threatened. "You just wait, my lady. That's all."

"To think of you falling for an old wheeze like that."

"And I changed the calendar, too."

"Never mind. There's the genuine article, look. Under your serviette."

"Napkin," Alfred said. He had been in Mr. Period's service for ten years. "I don't know if you're aware of the fact," he added, taking the top off his egg, "but April Fool's Day goes back to pagan times, Mrs. Mitchell."

"Fancy! With your attainments, I often wonder you don't look elsewhere for employment."

"You might say I lack ambition." Alfred paused, his spoon halfway to his mouth. "The truth of the matter is," he added, "I like service. Given favourable circumstances, it suits me. And the circumstances here are—or were—very nice."

A telephone rang distantly. "I'll answer it," Mrs. Mitchell offered. "You take your breakfast in peace."

She went out. Alfred opened his second egg and his *Daily Mail* and was immersed in both when she returned.

"Miss Cartell," she said.

"Oh?"

"Asking for her brother. 'Oh,' she says. 'Mrs. Mitchell!' she says. 'Just the person I wanted to have a word with!' You know her way. Bluff, but doing the gracious."

Alfred nodded slightly.

"And she says, 'I want you,' she says, 'before I say anything to my brother, to tell me, *absolutely* frankly,' she says, 'between you and me and the larder shelf, if you think the kweezeen would stand two more for lunch.' Well!"

"To whom was she referring?"

"To that Miss Moppett and a friend. A gentleman friend, you may depend upon it. Well! Asking me! As far as the kweezeen is concerned, a nice curry can be stretched, as you know yourself, Mr. Belt, to ridiculous lengths."

"What did you say?"

" 'I'm sure, Miss,' I says—just like that! Straight out! 'My kitchen,' I says, 'has never been found wanting in a crisis,' I says. And with that I switched her up to his room."

"Mr. Period," Alfred said, "will not be pleased."

"You're telling me! Can't stand the young lady, to give her the benefit of the title, and I'm sure I don't blame him. Mr. Cartell feels the same, you can tell. Well, I mean to say! She's no relation. Picked up nobody knows where and educated by a spinster sister to act like his niece, which call her, as you may have remarked, Mr. Belt, he will not. A bad girl, if ever I see one, and Miss Cartell will find it out one of these days, you mark my words."

Alfred laid aside his paper and continued with his breakfast. "It's the Arrangement," he said, following out his own thought, "and you can't get away from it: Separate rooms, with the joint use of the bathroom, and meals to be shared—with the right of either party to invite guests." He finished his tea. "It doesn't answer," he said. "I never thought it would. We've been under our own steam too long for sharing. We're getting fussed. Looking forward to a nice day, with a letter of condolence to be written—Lady Bantling's brother, for your information, Mrs. M., with whom she has not been on speaking terms these ten years or more—and young lady coming in to help with the book; and now this has to happen. Pity."

She went to the door and opened it slightly. "Mr. C.," she said with a jerk of her head. "Coming down."

"His breakfast's in the dining-room," said Alfred.

That light tattoo sounded on the door. It opened and Mr. Cartell's face appeared: thin, anxious and tightly smiling. The dog, Pixie, was at his heels. Alfred and Mrs. Mitchell stood up.

"Oh—ah—good morning, Mrs. Mitchell. 'Morning, Alfred. Just to say that my sister telephoned to ask if we can manage two more. I hope it won't be too difficult, Mrs. Mitchell, at such short notice."

"I daresay we'll manage quite nicely, sir."

"Shall we? Oh, excellent. Ah—I'll let Mr. Period know. Good," said Mr. Cartell. He withdrew his head, shut the door and retired, whistling uncertainly, to the dining-room.

For the second time in half an hour Alfred repeated his leit-motif. "It won't answer," he said. "I never thought it would."

" 2 "

"Sawn-lee," a hollow voice on the loudspeaker announced. *"Sawn-lee. The four carriages in the front portion of the train now arrived at No. 1 platform will proceed to Rimble, Bornlee Green and Little Codling. The rear portion will proceed to Forthamstead and Ribblethorpe. Please make sure you are in the correct part of the train. Sawn-lee. The four carriages . . ."*

Nicola Maitland-Mayne heard this pronouncement with dismay. "But I don't know," she cried to her fellow passengers, "which portion I'm in! *Is* this one of the first four carriages?"

"It's the fifth," said the man in the corner. "Next stop Forthamstead."

"Oh, damn!" Nicola said cheerfully and hauled her typewriter and overcoat down from the rack. Someone opened the doors for her. She plunged out, staggered along the platform, and climbed into another carriage as the voice was saying: *"All seats, please, for Rimble, Bornlee Green and Little Codling."*

The first compartment was full and so was the second. She moved along the corridor, looked in at the third, and gave it up.

A tall man, further along the corridor, said: "There's plenty of room up at the end."

"I'm Second Class."

"I should risk it if I were you. You can always pay up if the guard comes along but he never does on this stretch, I promise you."

"Oh, well," Nicola said, "I believe I will. Thank you."

He opened the door of the First Class compartment. She went in and found nobody there. A bowler, an umbrella, and *The Times,* belonging, she supposed, to the young man himself, lay on one seat. She sat on the other. He shut the door and stood in the corridor, his back to her, smoking.

Nicola looked out of the window for a minute or two. Presently she remembered her unfinished crossword, and took her own copy of *The Times* out of her overcoat pocket.

Eight across: Vehicle to be sick on or just get a ringing in the ears? (8)

The train had roared through a cutting and was slowing down for Cabstock when she ejaculated: "Oh, good Lord! *Carillon,* of course, how stupid!" She looked up to find the young man smiling at her from the opposite seat.

"I stuck over that one, too," he said.

"How far did you get?"

"All but five. Maddening."

"So did I," Nicola said.

"I wonder if they're the same ones. Shall I look?"

He picked up his paper. She noticed that under the nail of the first finger of his right hand there was a smear of scarlet.

Between them they continued the crossword. It is a matter of conjecture how many complete strangers have been brought into communication by this means. Rimble and Bornlee Green were passed before they filled in the last word.

"I should say," the young man remarked as he folded up his *Times,* "that we're in much the same class."

"That may be true of crosswords, but it certainly isn't of railway carriages," Nicola rejoined. "Heavens, where are we?"

"Coming in to Codling. My station, what a bore!"

"It's mine too," Nicola exclaimed, standing up.

"No! Is it really? *Jolly* good," said the young man. "I'll be able to bluff you past the gate. Here we go. Are you putting your coat on? Give me that thing. What is it, a typewriter? Sorry about my unsuitable bowler, but I'm going to a cocktail party this evening. Where's me brolly? Come on."

They were the only passengers to leave the train at Little Codling. The sun was shining and the smell of a country lane mingled with the disinfectant-cardboard-and-paste atmosphere of the station. Nicola was only mildly surprised to see her companion produce a Second Class ticket.

"Joy-riding as usual, I suppose, Mr. Bantling," said the man at the gates.

Nicola gave up her ticket and they passed into the lane. Birds were fussing in the hedgerows, and the air ran freshly. A dilapidated car waited outside, with a mild-looking driver standing beside it.

"Hullo," the young man said. "There's the Bloodbath. It must be for you."

"Do you think so? And why 'Bloodbath'?"

"Well, they won't have sent it for me. Good morning, Mr. Copper."

"Good morning, sir. Would it be Miss Maitland-Mayne?" asked the driver, touching his cap.

Nicola said it would, and he opened the door.

"You'll take a lift too, sir, I daresay. Mr. Cartell asked me to look out for you."

"What!" the young man exclaimed, staring at Nicola. "Are *you*, too, bound for Ye Olde Bachelor's Lay-by?"

"I'm going to Mr. Pyke Period's house. Could there be some mistake?"

"Not a bit of it. In we get."

"Well, if you say so," Nicola said and they got into the back of the car. It was started up with a good deal of commotion and they set off down the lane. "What did you mean by 'Bloodbath'?" Nicola repeated.

"You'll see. I'm going," the young man shouted, "to visit my stepfather, who is called Mr. Harold Cartell. He shares Mr. Pyke Period's house."

"I'm going to type for Mr. Pyke Period."

"You cast a ray of hope over an otherwise unpropitious venture. Hold very nice and tight, please," said the young man, imitating a bus conductor. They swung out of the lane, brought up short under the bonnet of a gigantic truck loaded with a crane and drainpipes, and lost their engine. The truck driver blasted his horn. His mate leaned out of the cab. "You got the death-wish, Jack?" he asked the driver.

The driver looked straight ahead of him and restarted his engine. Nicola saw that they had turned into the main street of a village and were headed for the Green.

"Trembling in every limb, are you?" the young man asked her. "Never mind; *now* you see what I meant by 'Bloodbath.' " He leant towards her. "There is another rather grand taxi in the village," he confided, "but Pyke Period likes to stick to Mr. Copper, because he's come down in the world."

He raised his voice. "That was a damn' close-run thing, Mr. Copper," he shouted.

"Think they own the place, those chaps," the driver rejoined. "Putting the sewer up the side lane by Mr. Period's house, and what for? Nobody wants it."

He turned left at the Green, pulled in at a short drive and stopped in front of a smallish Georgian house.

"Here we are," said the young man.

He got out, extricated Nicola's typewriter and his own umbrella, and felt in his pocket. Although largish and exceptionally tall, he was expeditious and quick in all his movements.

"Nothing to pay, Mr. Bantling," said the driver. "Mr. Period gave the order."

"Oh, well. . . . One for the road, anyway."

"Very kind of you, but no need, I'm sure. All right, Miss Maitland-Mayne?"

"Quite, thank you," said Nicola, who had alighted. The car lurched off uproariously. Looking to her right, Nicola could see the crane and the top of its truck over a quickset hedge. She heard the sound of male voices.

The front door had opened and a small dark man in an alpaca coat appeared.

"Good morning, Alfred," her companion said. "As you see, I've brought Miss Maitland-Mayne with me."

"The gentlemen," Alfred said, "are expecting you both, sir."

Pixie shot out of the house in a paroxysm of barking.

"Quiet," said Alfred, menacing her.

She whined, crouched and then precipitated herself upon Nicola. She stood on her hind legs, slavering and grimacing, and scraped at Nicola with her forepaws.

"Here, you!" said the young man indignantly. "Paws off!"

He cuffed Pixie away and she made loud ambiguous noises.

"I'm sure I'm very sorry, Miss," said Alfred. "It's said to be only its fun. This way, if you please, Miss."

Nicola found herself in a modest but elegantly proportioned hall. It looked like an advertisement from a glossy magazine: *Small Georgian residence of character*—and, apart from being Georgian, had no other character to speak of.

Alfred opened a door on the right. "In the library, if you please, Miss," he said. "Mr. Period will be down immediately."

Nicola walked in. The young man followed and put her typewriter on a table by a window.

"I can't help wondering," he said, "what you're going to do for P.P. After all, he'd never type his letters of condolence, would he?"

"What can you mean?"

"You'll see. Well, I suppose I'd better launch myself on my ill-fated mission. You might wish me luck."

Something in his voice caught her attention. She looked up at him. His mouth was screwed dubiously sideways.

"It never does," he said, "to set one's heart on something, does it? Furiously, I mean."

"Good heavens, what a thing to say! Of course, one must. Continuously. . . . Expectation," said Nicola grandly, "is the springboard of achievement."

"Rather a phony slogan, I'm afraid."

"I thought it neat."

"I should like to confide in you. What a pity we won't meet over your nice curry. I'm lunching with my mama, who lives in the offing with her third husband."

"How do you know it's going to be curry?"

"It often is."

"Well," Nicola said, "I wish you luck."

"Thank you very much." He smiled at her. "Good typing!"

"Good hunting! If you are hunting."

He laid his finger against his nose, pulled a mysterious grimace and left her.

Nicola opened up her typewriter and a box of quarto paper and surveyed the library.

It looked out on the drive and the rose garden and it was like the hall in that it had distinction without personality.

Over the fireplace hung a dismal little water colour. Elsewhere on the walls were two sporting prints, a painting of a bewhiskered ensign in the Brigade of Guards pointing his sword at some lightning, and a faded photograph of several Edwardian minor royalties grouped in baleful conviviality about a picnic luncheon. In the darkest corner was a framed genealogical tree, sprouting labels, arms and mantling. There were bookcases with uniform editions, novels, and a copy of *Handley Cross.* Standing apart from the others, a *corps d'élite,* were Debrett, Burke, Kelly's and *Who's Who.* The desk itself was rich with photographs, framed in silver. Each bore witness to the conservative technique of the studio and the well-bred restraint of the sitter.

Through the side window, Nicola looked across Mr. Period's rose garden to a quickset hedge and an iron gate leading into a lane. Beyond this gate was a trench, with planks laid across it, a heap of earth and her old friend the truck—from which, with the aid of its crane, the workmen were unloading drainpipes.

Distantly and overhead, she heard male voices. Her acquaintance of the train (what had the driver called him?) and his stepfather, Nicola supposed.

She was thinking of him with amusement when the door opened and Mr. Pyke Period came in.

" 3 "

He was a tall, elderly man with a marked stoop, silver hair, large brown eyes and a small mouth. He was beautifully dressed, with exactly the correct suggestion of well-worn, scrupulously tended tweed.

He advanced upon Nicola with curved arm held rather high and bent at the wrist. The Foreign Office, or at the very least Commonwealth Relations, were invoked.

"This is *really* kind of you," said Mr. Pyke Period, "and awfully lucky for me."

They shook hands.

"Now, do tell me," Mr. Period continued, "because I'm the most inquisitive old party, and I'm dying to know—you *are* Basil's daughter, *aren't* you?"

Nicola, astounded, said that she was.

"Basil Maitland-Mayne?" he gently insisted.

"Yes, but I don't make much of a to-do about the 'Maitland,' " said Nicola.

"Now, that's naughty of you. A splended old family. These things matter."

"It's such a mouthful."

"Never *mind!* So you're dear old Basil's gel! I was sure of it. Such fun for me because, do you know, your grandfather was one of my very dear friends. A bit my senior, but he was one of those soldiers of the old school who never let you *feel* the gap in ages."

Nicola, who remembered her grandfather as an arrogant, declamatory old egoist, managed to make a suitable rejoinder. Mr. Period looked at her with his head on one side.

"Now," he said gaily, "I'm going to confess. Shall we sit down? Do you know, when I called on those perfectly splendid people to ask about typewriting and they gave me some names from their books, I positively leapt at yours. And do you know why?"

Nicola had her suspicions and they made her feel uncomfortable. But there was something about Mr. Period—what was it?—something vulnerable and foolish, that aroused her compassion. She knew she was meant to smile and shake her head and she did both.

Mr. Period said, sitting youthfully on the arm of a leather chair: "It was because I felt that we would be working together on—dear me, too difficult!—on a common ground. Talking the same language." He waited for a moment and then said cozily: "And now you know *all* about me. I'm the most dreadful old anachronism—a Period piece, in fact."

As Nicola responded to this joke she couldn't help wondering how often Mr. Period had made it.

He laughed delightedly with her. "So, speaking as one snob to another," he ended, "I couldn't be more enchanted that you are *you*. Well, never mind! One's meant not to say such things in these egalitarian days."

He had a conspiratorial way of biting his underlip and lifting his shoulders: it was indescribably arch. "But we mustn't be naughty," said Mr. Pyke Period.

Nicola said: "They didn't really explain at the agency exactly what my job is to be."

"Ah! Because they didn't exactly know. I was coming to that."

It took him some time to come to it, though, because he would dodge about among innumerable parentheses. Finally, however, it emerged that he was writing a book. He had been approached by the head of a publishing firm.

"Wonderful," Nicola said, "actually to be *asked* by a publisher to write."

He laughed. "My dear child, I promise you it would never have come from *me*. Indeed, I thought he must be pulling my leg. But not at all. So in the end I madly consented and—and there we are, you know."

"Your memoirs, perhaps?" Nicola ventured.

"No. No, although I must say—but no. You'll never guess!"

She felt that she never would, and waited.

"It's—how can I explain? Don't laugh! It's just that in these extraordinary times there are all sorts of people popping up in places where one would least expect to find them: clever, successful people, we must admit, but *not*—as we old fogies used to say—'not quite-quite.' And there they find themselves in a *milieu* where they really are, poor darlings, at a grievous loss."

And there it was: Mr. Pyke Period had been commissioned to write a book on etiquette. Nicola suspected that his publisher had displayed a remarkably shrewd judgment. The only book on etiquette she had ever read, a Victorian work unearthed in an attic by her brother, had been a favourite source for ribald quotation. " 'It is a mark of ill-breeding in a lady,' " Nicola's brother would remind her, " 'to look over her shoulder, still more behind her, when walking abroad.' "

" 'There should be no diminution of courteous observance,' " she would counter, " 'in the family circle. A brother will always rise when his sister enters the drawing-room and open the door to her when she shows her intention of quitting it.' "

" 'While on the sister's part some slight acknowledgment of his action will be made: a smile or a quiet "Thank you" will indicate her awareness of the little attention.' "

Almost as if he had read her thoughts, Mr. Period was saying: "Of course, one knows all about these delicious Victorian offerings—quite wonderful. And there *have* been contemporaries: poor Félicité Sankie-

Bond, after their crash, don't you know, and one mustn't overlap with dear Nancy. Very diffy. In the meantime . . ."

In the meantime, it at last transpired, Nicola was to make a typewritten draft of his notes and assemble them under their appropriate headings. These were: "The Ball-Dance," "Trifles That Matter," "The Small Dinner," "The Partie Carré," "Addressing Our Letters & Betters," "Awkwiddities," "The Debutante— Lunching and Launching," "Tips on Tipping."

And, bulkily, in a separate compartment, "The Compleat Letter-Writer."

She was soon to learn that letter-writing was a great matter with Mr. Pyke Period. He was, in fact, famous for his letters of condolence.

" 4 "

They settled to work: Nicola at her table near the front French windows, Mr. Period at his desk in the side one.

Her job was an exacting one. Mr. Period evidently jotted down his thoughts piecemeal, as they had come to him, and it was often difficult to know where a passage precisely belonged. "Never *fold* the napkin (there is no need, I feel sure, to put the unspeakable 'serviette' in its place), but drop it lightly on the table." Nicola listed this under "Table Manners," and wondered if Mr. Period would find the phrase "refeened," a word he often used with humorous intent.

She looked up to find him in a trance, his pen suspended, his gaze rapt, a sheet of headed letter-paper under his hand. He caught her glance, and said: "A few lines to my dear Désirée Bantling. *Soi-disante.* The Dowager, as the *Telegraph* would call her. You saw Ormsbury had gone, I daresay?"

Nicola, who had no idea whether the Dowager Lady

Bantling had been deserted or bereaved, said: "No, I didn't see it."

"Letters of condolence!" Mr. Period sighed with a faint hint of complacency. "How difficult they are!" He began to write again, quite rapidly, with sidelong references to his note-pad.

Upstairs a voice, clearly recognizable, shouted angrily: ". . . and all I can say, you horrible little man, is I'm bloody sorry I ever asked you." Someone came rapidly downstairs and crossed the hall. The front door slammed. Through her window, Nicola saw her travelling companion, scarlet in the face, stride down the drive, angrily swinging his bowler.

He's forgotten his umbrella, she thought.

"Oh, *dear!*" Mr. Period murmured. "An awkwiddity, I fear me. Andrew in one of his rages. You know him, of course."

"Not till this morning."

"Andrew Bantling? My dear, he's the son of the very Lady Bantling we were talking about. Désirée, you know. Ormsbury's sister. Bobo Bantling—Andrew's papa—was the first of her three husbands. The senior branch. Seventh Baron. Succeeded to the peerage . . ." Here followed inevitably one of Mr. Period's classy genealogical digressions. "My dear Nicola—" he went on, "I hope, by the way, I *may* so far take advantage of a family friendship?"

"Please do."

"Sweet of you. Well, my dear Nicola, you will have gathered that I don't vegetate all by myself. in this house. No. I share. With an old friend who is called Harold Cartell. It's a new arrangement and I hope it's going to suit us both. Harold is Andrew's stepfather and guardian. He is, by the way, a retired solicitor. I don't need to tell you about Andrew's *mum,*" Mr. Period added, strangely adopting the current slang. "She, poor darling, is almost *too* famous."

"And she's called Désirée, Lady Bantling?"

"She naughtily sticks to the title in the teeth of the most surprising remarriage."

"Then she's really Mrs. Harold Cartell?"

"Not now. That hardly lasted any time. No. She's now Mrs. Bimbo Dodds. Bantling . . . Cartell . . . Dodds. In that order."

"Yes, of course," Nicola said, remembering at last the singular fame of this lady.

"Yes. 'Nuff said," Mr. Period observed, wanly arch, "under that heading. But Hal Cartell was Lord Bantling's solicitor and executor and is the trustee for Andrew's inheritance. I, by the way, am the other trustee, and I do hope *that's* not going to be diffy. Well, now," Mr. Period went cozily on, "on Bantling's death, Hal Cartell was also appointed Andrew's guardian. Désirée, at that time, was going through a rather *farouche* phase, and Andrew narrowly escaped being made a Ward-in-Chancery. Thus it was that Hal Cartell was thrown in the widow's path. She rather wolfed him up, don't you know? Black always suited her. But they were too dismally incompatible. However . . . Harold remained, nevertheless, Andrew's guardian and trustee for the estate. Andrew doesn't come into it until he's twenty-five—in six months' time, by the way. He's in the Brigade of Guards, as you'll have seen, but I gather he wants to leave in order to paint, which is so unexpected. Indeed, that *may* be this morning's problem. A *great* pity. *All* the Bantlings have been in the Brigade. And if he must paint, poor dear, why not as a hobby? What his father would have said . . . !" Mr. Period waved his hands.

"But why isn't *he* Lord Bantling?"

"His father was a widower with one son when he married Désirée. That son, of course, succeeded."

"Oh, I see," Nicola said politely. "Of course."

"You wonder why I go into all these begatteries, as I

call them. Partly because they amuse me and partly because you will, I hope, be seeing quite a lot of my stodgy little household and, in so far as Hal Cartell is one of us, we—ah—we overlap. In fact," Mr. Period went on, looking vexed, "we overlap at luncheon. Harold's sister, Connie Cartell, who is our neighbour, joins us. With—ah—with a *protégée,* a—*soi-disante* 'niece,' adopted from goodness knows where. Her name is Mary Ralston and her nickname, an inappropriate one, is 'Moppett.' I understand that she brings a friend with her. However! To return to Désirée. Désirée and her Bimbo spend a lot of time at the dower house, Baynesholme, which is only a mile or two away from us. I believe Andrew lunches there today. His mother was to pick him up here, and I do hope he hasn't gone flouncing back to London: it would be too awkward and tiresome of him, poor boy."

"Then Mrs. Dodds—I mean Lady Bantling—and Mr. Cartell still . . . ?"

"Oh, Lord, yes! They hob-nob occasionally. Désirée never bears grudges. She's a remarkable person. I dote on her, but she *is* rather a law unto herself. For instance, one doesn't know in the very least how she'll react to the death of Ormsbury. Brother though he is. Better, I think, not to mention it when she comes, but simply to write. But there, I really mustn't bore you with all my dim little bits of gossip. To work, my child! To work!"

They returned to their respective tasks. Nicola had made some headway with the notes when she came upon one which was evidently a rough draft for a letter. "My dear—" it began—"What can I say? Only that you have lost a wonderful . . . ."—here Mr. Period had left a blank space—"and a most valued and very dear old friend." It continued in this vein with many erasures. Should she file it under "The Compleat Letter-Writer"? Was it in fact intended as an exemplar?

She laid it before Mr. Period.

"I'm not quite sure if this belongs."

He looked at it and turned pink. "No, no. Stupid of me. Thank you."

He pushed it under his pad, and folded the letter he had written, whistling under his breath. "That's that," he said, with rather forced airiness. "Perhaps you will be kind enough to post it in the village."

Nicola made a note of it and returned to her task. She became aware of suppressed nervousness in her employer. They went through the absurd pantomime of catching each other's eyes and pretending they had done nothing of the sort. This had occurred two or three times when Nicola said: "I'm so sorry. I've got the awful trick of staring at people when I'm trying to concentrate."

"My *dear* child! No! It is I who am at fault. In point of fact," Mr. Period went on with a faint simper, "I've been asking myself if I dare confide a little problem."

Not knowing what to say, Nicola said nothing. Mr. Period, with an air of hardihood, continued. He waved his hand.

"It's nothing. Rather a bore, really. Just that the—ah—the publishers are going to do something quite handsome in the way of illustrations and they—don't laugh—they want my old mug for their frontispiece. A portrait rather than a photograph is thought to be appropriate and, I can't *imagine* why, they took it for granted one had been done, do you know? And one hasn't."

"What a pity," Nicola sympathized. "So it will have to be a photograph."

"Ah! Yes. That was my first thought. But then, you see—They made such a point of it—and I did just wonder—My friends, silly creatures, urge me to it. Just a line drawing. One doesn't know what to think."

It was clear to Nicola that Mr. Period was dying to have his portrait done and was prepared to pay highly for it. He mentioned several extremely fashionable artists and then said suddenly: "It's naughty of dear Agatha Troy to be so diffy about who she does. She said something about not wanting to abandon bone for bacon, I think, when she refused—she actually *refused* to paint . . ."

Here Mr. Period whispered an extremely potent name and stared with a sort of dismal triumph at Nicola. "So she wouldn't dream of poor old me," he cried. " 'Nuff said!"

Nicola began to say, "I wonder, though. She often—" and hurriedly checked herself. She had been about to commit an indiscretion. Fortunately, Mr. Period's attention was diverted by the return of Andrew Bantling. He had reappeared in the drive, still walking fast and swinging his bowler, and with a fixed expression on his pleasantly bony face.

"He has come back," Nicola said.

"Andrew? Oh, good. I wonder what for."

In a moment they found out. The door opened and Andrew looked in.

"I'm sorry to interrupt," he said loudly, "but if it's not too troublesome, I wonder if I could have a word with you, P.P.?"

"My dear boy! But, of course."

"It's not private from Nicola," Andrew said. "On the contrary. At the same time, I don't want to bore anybody."

Mr. Period said playfully: "I myself have done nothing but bore poor Nicola. Shall we 'withdraw to the withdrawing-room' and leave her in peace?"

"Oh. All right. Thank you. Sorry." Andrew threw a distracted look at Nicola and opened the door.

Mr. Period made her a little bow. "You will excuse us, my dear?" he said, and they went out.

Nicola worked on steadily and was only once interrupted. The door opened to admit a small, thin, querulous-looking gentleman who ejaculated: "I beg your pardon. Damn!" and went out again. Mr. Cartell, no doubt.

At eleven o'clock Alfred came in with sherry and biscuits and Mr. Period's compliments. If she was in any difficulty would she be good enough to ring and Alfred would convey the message. Nicola was not in any difficulty, but while she enjoyed her sherry she found herself scribbling absent-mindedly.

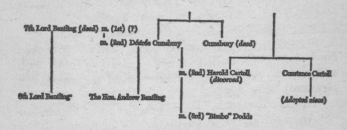

Good Lord! she thought. Why did I do that? A bit longer on this job and I'll be turning into a Pyke Period myself.

Two hours went by. The house was very quiet. She was half-aware of small local activities: distant voices and movement, the rattle and throb of machinery in the lane. She thought from time to time of her employer. To which brand of snobbery, that overworked but always enthralling subject, did Mr. Pyke Period belong? Was he simply a snob of the traditional school who dearly loves a lord? Was he himself a scion of incredibly ancient lineage—one of those old, uncelebrated families whose sole claim to distinction rests in their refusal to accept a title? No. That didn't quite fit Mr. Period. It wasn't easy to imagine him refusing a title, and yet . . .

Her attention was again diverted to the drive. Three persons approached the house, barked at and harassed by Pixie. A large, tweedy middle-aged woman, with a red face, a squashed hat and a walking stick, was followed by a pale girl with a fashionable coiffure and a young man who looked, Nicola thought, quite awful. These two lagged behind their elder, who shouted and pointed with her stick in the direction of the excavations. Nicola could hear her voice, which sounded arrogant, and her gusts of boisterous laughter. While her back was turned, the girl quickly planted an extremely uninhibited kiss on the young man's mouth.

That, thought Nicola, is a full-treatment job.

Pixie floundered against the young man and he kicked her rapidly in the ribs. She emitted a howl and retired. The large woman looked round in concern, but the young man was smiling damply. They moved round the corner of the house. Through the side window Nicola could see them inspecting the excavations. They returned to the drive.

Footsteps crossed the hall. Doors were opened. Mr. Cartell appeared in the drive and was greeted by the lady—who, Nicola saw, resembled him in a robust fashion. The sister, Nicola thought. Connie. And the adopted niece, Moppett, and the niece's frightful friend. I don't wonder Mr. Period was put out.

They moved out of sight. There was a burst of conversation in the hall, in which Mr. Period's voice could be heard, and a withdrawal (into the "withdrawing-room," no doubt). Presently Andrew Bantling came into the library.

"Hullo," he said. "I'm to bid you to drinks. I don't mind telling you it's a bum party. My bloody-minded stepfather, to whom I'm not speaking, his bully of a sister, her ghastly adopted what-not, and an unspeakable chum. Come on."

"Do you think I might be excused and just creep in to lunch?"

"Not a hope. P.P. would be as cross as two sticks. He's telling them all about you and how lucky he is to have you."

"I don't want a drink. I've been built up with sherry."

"There's tomato juice. Do come. You'd better."

"In that case . . ." Nicola said, and put the cover on her typewriter.

"That's right," he said, and took her arm. "I've had such a stinker of a morning—you can't think. How have you got on?"

"I hope, all right."

"Is he writing a book?"

"I'm a confidential typist."

"My face can't get any redder than it's been already," Andrew said and ushered her into the hall. "Are you at all interested in painting?"

"Yes. You paint, don't you?"

"How the hell did you know?"

"Your first fingernail. And anyway Mr. Period told me."

"Talk, talk, talk!" Andrew said, but he smiled at her. "And what a sharp girl you are, to be sure. Oh, calamity, look who's here!"

Alfred was at the front door, showing in a startling lady with tangerine hair, enormous eyes, pale orange lips and a general air of good-humoured raffishness. She was followed by an unremarkable, cagey-looking man, very much her junior.

"Hullo, Mum!" Andrew said. "Hullo, Bimbo."

"Darling!" said Désirée Dodds or Lady Bantling. "How lovely!"

"Hi," said her husband, Bimbo.

Nicola was introduced and they all went into the drawing-room.

Here Nicola encountered the group of persons with whom, on one hand disastrously and on the other to her greatest joy, she was about to become inextricably involved.

CHAPTER TWO

Luncheon

Mr. Pyke Period made much of Nicola. He took her round, introducing her to Mr. Cartell and all over again to "Lady Bantling" and Mr. Dodds; to Miss Connie Cartell; and, with a certain lack of enthusiasm, to the adopted niece, Mary or Moppett, and her friend, Mr. Leonard Leiss.

Miss Cartell shouted: "Been hearing all about you, ha, ha!"

Mr. Cartell said: "Afraid I disturbed you just now. Looking for P.P. So sorry."

Moppett said: "Hullo. I suppose you do shorthand? I tried but my squiggles looked like rude drawings. So I gave up." Young Mr. Leiss stared damply at Nicola and then shook hands—also damply. He was pallid and had large eyes, a full mouth and small chin. The sleeves of his violently checked jacket displayed an exotic amount of shirt-cuff and link. He smelt very strongly of hair oil. Apart from these features it would have been hard to say why he seemed untrustworthy.

Mr. Cartell was probably by nature a dry and pedantic man. At the moment he was evidently much put out. Not surprising, Nicola thought, when one looked at the company: his stepson with whom, presumably, he had just had a flaring row; his divorced wife and her husband; his noisy sister; her "niece," whom he obviously disliked; and Mr. Leiss. He dodged about, fussily attending to drinks.

"May Leonard fix mine, Uncle Hal?" Moppett asked. "He knows my kind of wallop."

Mr. Period, overhearing her, momentarily closed his eyes, and Mr. Cartell saw him do it.

Miss Cartell shouted uneasily: "The things these girls say, nowadays! Honestly!" and burst into her braying laugh. Nicola could see that she adored Moppett.

Leonard adroitly mixed two treble martinis.

Andrew had brought Nicola her tomato juice. He stayed beside her. They didn't say very much but she found herself glad of his company.

Meanwhile, Mr. Period, who, it appeared, had recently had a birthday, was given a present by Lady Bantling. It was a large brass paperweight in the form of a fish rampant. He seemed to Nicola to be disproportionately enchanted with this trophy, and presently she discovered why.

"Dearest Désirée," he exclaimed. "How wonderfully clever of you: my crest, you know! The form, the attitude, everything! Connie! Look! Hal, do look."

The paperweight was passed from hand to hand and Andrew was finally sent to put it on Mr. Period's desk.

When he returned Moppett bore down upon him. "Andrew!" she said. "You must tell Leonard about your painting. He knows quantities of potent dealers. Actually, he might be jolly useful to you. Come and talk to him."

"I'm afraid I wouldn't know what to say, Moppett."

"I'll tell you. Hi, Leonard! We want to talk to you."

Leonard advanced with drinks. "All right, all right," he said. "What about?"

"Which train are you going back by?" Andrew asked Nicola.

"I don't know."

"When do you stop typing?"

"Four o'clock, I think."

"There's a good train at twenty past. I'll pick you up. May I?"

His mother had joined them. "We really ought to be going," she said, smiling amiably at Nicola. "Lunch is early today, Andrew, on account we're having a grand party tonight. You're staying for it, by the way?"

"I don't think I can."

"I'm sure you can if you set your mind to it. We need you badly. I'd have warned you, but we only decided last night. It's an April Fool party: that makes the excuse. Bimbo's scarcely left the telephone since dawn."

"We ought to go, darling," said Bimbo over her shoulder.

"I know. Let's. Good-bye." She held out her hand to Nicola. "Are you coming lots of times to type for P.P.?"

"I think, fairly often."

"Make him bring you to Baynesholme. We're off, Harold. Thank you for our nice drinks. Good-bye, P.P. Don't forget you're dining, will you?"

"How could I?"

"Not possibly."

"It was—I wondered, dearest Désirée, if you'd perhaps rather . . . ? Still—I suppose . . ."

"My poorest sweet, what *are* you talking about?" said Lady Bantling and kissed him. She looked vaguely at Moppett and Leonard. "Good-bye. Come along, boys."

Andrew muttered to Nicola: "I'll ring you up about the train." He said good-bye cordially to Mr. Period and very coldly to his stepfather.

Moppett said: "I had something fairly important to ask you, you gorgeous Guardee, you."

"How awful never to know what it was," Andrew replied and, with Bimbo, followed his mother out of the room.

Watching Désirée go, Nicola thought: "Moppett would probably like to acquire that manner, but she never will. She hasn't got the style."

Mr. Period, in a fluster, extended his hands. "Désirée can't know!" he exclaimed. "Neither can he or Andrew! How extraordinary!"

"Know what?" asked Miss Cartell.

"About Ormsbury. Her brother. It was in the *Telegraph*."

"If Désirée is giving one of her parties," said Mr. Cartell, "she is not likely to put it off for her brother's demise. She hasn't heard of him since he went out to the Antipodes, where I understand he'd been drinking like a fish for the last twenty years."

"Really, Hal!" Mr. Period exclaimed.

Moppett and Leonard Leiss giggled and retired into a corner with their drinks.

Miss Cartell was launched on an account of some local activity. ". . . So I said to the Rector: 'We all know damn well what *that* means,' and he said like *lightning:* 'We may know but we don't let on.' He's got quite a respectable sense of humour, that man."

"Pause for laugh," Moppett said very offensively.

Miss Cartell, who had in fact thrown back her head to laugh, blushed painfully and looked at her ward with such an air of baffled vulnerability that Nicola, who had been thinking how patronizing and arrogant she was, felt sorry for her and furious with Moppett.

So, evidently, did Mr. Period. "My dear Mary," he said. "That was *not* the prettiest of remarks."

"Quite so. Precisely," Mr. Cartell agreed. "You should exercise more discipline, Connie."

Leonard said: "The only way with Moppett is to beat her like a carpet."

"Care to try?" she asked him.

Alfred announced luncheon.

It was the most uncomfortable meal Nicola had ever eaten. The entire party was at cross purposes. Everybody appeared to be up to something indefinable.

Miss Cartell had bought a new car. Leonard spoke of it with languid approval. Moppett said they had seen a Scorpion for sale in George Copper's garage. Leonard spoke incomprehensibly of its merits.

"Matter of fact," he said, "I'd quite like to buy it. Trade in my own heap with him, of course." He leant back in his chair and whistled quietly through his teeth.

"Shall we look at it again?" Moppett suggested, grandly.

"No harm in looking, is there?"

Nicola suddenly thought: That was a pre-planned bit of dialogue. Alfred returned with an envelope which he placed before Mr. Period.

"What's this?" Mr. Period asked pettishly. He peered through his eyeglass.

"From the Rectory, sir. The person suggested it was immediate."

"I do so dislike interruptions at luncheon," Mr. Period complained. " 'Scuse, everybody?" he added playfully.

His guests made acquiescent noises. He read what appeared to be a very short letter and changed colour.

"No answer," he said to Alfred. "Or rather—say I'll call personally upon the Rector."

Alfred withdrew. Mr. Period, after a fidgety interval and many glances at Mr. Cartell, said: "I'm very sorry, Hal, but I'm afraid your Pixie has created a parochial *crise.*"

Mr. Cartell said: "Oh, dear. What?"

"At the moment she, with some half-dozen other—ah—boon companions, is rioting in the Vicar's seed beds. There is a Mothers' Union luncheon in progress, but none of them has succeeded in catching her. It couldn't be more awkward."

Nicola had an uproarious vision of mothers thundering fruitlessly among rectorial flower beds. Miss Cartell broke into one of her formidable gusts of laughter.

"You always were hopeless with dogs, Boysie," she shouted. "Why you keep that ghastly bitch!"

"She's extremely well bred, Connie. I've been advised to enter her for the parish dog show."

"My God, who by? The Rector?" Miss Cartell asked with a bellow of laughter.

"I have been advised," Mr. Cartell repeated stuffily.

"We'll have to have a freak class."

"Are you entering your Pekingese?"

"They're very keen I should, so I might as well, I suppose. Hardly fair to the others, but she'd be a draw, of course."

"For people that like lapdogs, no doubt."

Mr. Period intervened: "I'm afraid you'll have to do something about it, Hal," he said. "Nobody else can control her."

"Alfred can."

"Alfred is otherwise engaged."

"She's on heat, of course."

"Really, Connie!"

Mr. Cartell, pink in the face, rose disconsolately, but at that moment there appeared in the garden a disheveled clergyman dragging the overexcited Pixie by her collar. They were watched sardonically by a group of workmen.

Mr. Cartell hurried from the room and reappeared beyond the windows with Alfred.

"It's too much," Mr. Period said. "Forgive me!"

He, too, left the room and joined the group in the garden.

Leonard and Moppett, making extremely uninhibited conversation, went to the window and stood there, clinging to each other in an ecstasy of enjoyment. They were observed by Mr. Period and Mr. Cartell. There followed a brief scene in which the Rector, his Christian forbearance clearly exercised to its limit, received the apologies of both gentlemen, patted Mr. Period, but not Mr. Cartell, on the shoulder, and took his leave. Alfred lugged Pixie, who squatted back on her haunches in protest, out of sight, and the two gentlemen returned—very evidently in high dudgeon with each other. Leonard and Moppett made little or no attempt to control their amusement.

"Well!" Mr. Period said with desperate savoir faire. "What were we talking about?"

Moppett spluttered noisily. Connie Cartell said: "You'll have to get rid of that mongrel, you know, Hal." Her brother glared at her. "You can't," Connie added, "make a silk purse out of a sow's ear."

"I entirely agree," Mr. Cartell said, very nastily indeed, "and have often said so much, I believe, to you."

There was a quite dreadful silence, broken at last by Mr. Period.

"Strange," he observed, "how, even in the animal kingdom, breeding makes itself felt." And he was off, in a very big way, on his favourite topic. Inspired, perhaps, by what he would have called Pixie's lack of form, he went to immoderate lengths in praising this quality. He said, more than once, that he knew the barriers had been down for twenty years but nevertheless . . . On and on he went, all through the curry and well into the apple flan. He became, Nicola had regretfully to admit, more than a little ridiculous.

It was clear that Mr. Cartell thought so. He himself grew more and more restive. Nicola guessed that he was fretted by divided loyalties and even more by the behaviour of Leonard Leiss, who, having finished his lunch, continued to lean back in his chair and whistle softly through his teeth. Moppett asked him, sardonically, how the chorus went. He raised his eyebrows and said, "Oh, pardon me—I just can't seem to get that little number out of my system," and smiled generally upon the table.

"Evidently," said Mr. Cartell.

Mr. Period said he felt sure that he himself made far too much of the niceties of civilized behaviour and told them how his father had once caused him to leave the dining-room for using his fishknife.

Mr. Cartell listened with mounting distaste. Presently he wiped his lips, leant back in his chair and said: "My dear P.P., that sort of thing is no doubt very well in its way, but surely one can make a little too much of it?"

"I happen to feel rather strongly about such matters," Mr. Period said, with a small deprecating smile at Nicola.

Miss Cartell, who had been watching her adopted niece with anxious devotion, suddenly shouted: "I always say that when people start fussing about family and all that, it's because they're a bit hairy round the heels themselves, ha ha!"

She seemed to be completely unaware of the implications of her remark or its effect upon Mr. Period.

"Well, really, Connie!" he said. "I must say!"

"What's wrong?"

Mr. Cartell gave a dry little laugh. "After all," he said. *"When Adam delved,* you know."

" 'Dolve,' I fancy, *not* 'delved,' " Mr. Period corrected rather smugly. "Oh, yes. The much-quoted Mr. Ball, who was afterwards hanged for his pains, wasn't he? *Who was then the gentleman?* The answer is, of course, 'Nobody.' It takes several generations to evolve the genuine article, don't you agree?"

"I've known it to be effected in less than no time," Mr. Cartell said dryly. "It's quite extraordinary to what lengths some people will go. I heard on unimpeachable authority of a man who forged his name in a parish register in order to establish descent from some ancient family or another."

Miss Cartell laughed uproariously.

Mr. Period dropped his fork into his pudding.

Leonard asked with interest: "Was there any money in it?"

Moppett said: "How was he found out? Tell us more."

Mr. Cartell said, "There has never been a public exposure. And there's really no more to tell."

Conversation then became desultory. Leonard muttered something to Moppett, who said: "Would anybody mind if we were excused? Leonard's car is having something done to its guts and the chap in the garage seemed to be quite madly moronic. We were to see him again at two o'clock."

"If you mean Copper," Mr. Period observed, "I've always understood him to be a thoroughly dependable fellow."

"He's a sort of half-pie, broken-down gent or something, isn't he?" Leonard asked casually.

"Jolly good man, George Copper," Miss Cartell said.

"Certainly," Mr. Period faintly agreed. He was exceedingly pale.

"Oh," Leonard said, stretching his arms easily, "I think I can manage Mr. George Copper quite successfully." He glanced round the table. "Smoking allowed?" he asked.

Miss Cartell swallowed her last fragment of cheese and her brother looked furious. Mr. Period murmured: "Since you are leaving us, why not?"

Leonard groped in his pockets. "I've left mine in the car," he said to Moppett. "Hand over, Sexy, will you?"

Mr. Period said: "Please," and offered his gold case. "These are Turks," he said. "I'm so sorry if you don't like them. Old-fogyishly, I can't get used to the others."

"Makes a change," Leonard said, obligingly. He took a cigarette, looked at the case and remarked: "That's nice." It was extraordinary how off-key his lightest observations could sound.

"Do let me see," Moppett asked, and took the case.

"It was left me," Mr. Period said, "by dear old Lady Barsington. An eighteenth-century cardcase. The jewelled clasp is said to be unique. There's an inscription, but it's very faint. If you take it to the light. . . ."

Moppett took it to the window, and Leonard joined her there. He began to hum and then to sketch in the words of his little number: *If you mean what I think you mean, O.K. by me. Things aren't always what they seem. O.K. by me.* Moppett gaily joined in.

Alfred came in to say that Mr. Period was wanted on the telephone, and he bustled out, after a pointedly formal apology.

Leonard strolled back to the table. He had evidently decided that some conventional apology was called for. "*So* sorry to break up the party," he said winningly. "But if it's all the same, I think we'd better toddle."

"By all means. Please," said Mr. Cartell.

"What P.P. and Uncle Hal will think of your manners, you two!" Miss Cartell said, and laughed uneasily.

They got up. Moppett said good-bye to Mr. Cartell quite civilly and was suddenly effusive in her thanks. Leonard followed her lead, but with an air of finding it only just worth while to do so.

"Be seeing you, ducks," Moppett said in Cockney to Miss Cartell, and they went out.

There followed a rather deadly little silence.

Mr. Cartell addressed himself to his sister. "My dear Connie," he said, "I should be failing in my duty if I didn't tell you I consider that young man to be an unspeakable bounder."

Mr. Period returned.

"Shall we have our coffee in the drawing-room?" he asked in the doorway.

Nicola would have dearly liked to excuse herself and go back to the study, but Mr. Period took her gently by the arm and led her to the drawing-room. His fingers, she noticed, were trembling. "I want," he said, "to show you a newly acquired treasure."

Piloting her into a far corner, he unfolded a brown-paper parcel. It turned out to be a landscape in water colour: the distant view of a manor house.

"It's charming," Nicola said.

"Thought to be an unsigned Cotman, but the real interest for me is that it's my great-grandfather's house at Ribblethorpe. Destroyed, alas, by fire. I came across it in a secondhand shop. Wasn't that fun for me?"

Alfred took round the coffee tray. Nicola pretended she couldn't hear Mr. Cartell and his sister arguing. As soon as Alfred had gone, Miss Cartell tackled her brother.

"I think you're jolly prejudiced, Boysie," she said. "It's the way they all talk nowadays. Moppett tells me he's brilliantly clever. Something in the City."

"Too clever by half if you ask me. And what in the City?"

"I don't know exactly *what*. He's got rather a tragic sort of background, Moppett says. The father was killed in Bangkok and the mother's artistic."

"You're a donkey, Connie. If I were you I should put a stop to the friendship. None of my business, of course. I am *not,*" Mr. Cartell continued with some emphasis, "Mary's uncle, despite the courtesy title she is good enough to bestow upon me."

"You don't understand her."

"I make no attempt to do so," he replied in a fluster.

Nicola murmured: "I think I ought to get back to my job." She said good-bye to Miss Cartell.

"Typin', are you?" asked Miss Cartell. "P.P. tells me you're Basil Maitland-Mayne's gel. Used to know your father. Hunted with him."

"We all knew Basil," Mr. Period said with an attempt at geniality.

"I didn't," Mr. Cartell said, crossly.

They glared at each other.

"You're very smart all of a sudden, P.P.," Miss Cartell remarked. "Private secretary! You'll be telling us next that you're going to write a book." She laughed uproariously.

Nicola returned to the study.

" 2 "

Nicola had a ridiculously overdeveloped capacity for feeling sorry. She was sorry now for Mr. Period, because he had been upset and had made a silly of himself; and for Miss Cartell, because she was boisterous and vulnerable and besotted with her terrible Moppett who treated her like dirt. She was sorry for Mr. Cartell, because he had been balanced on a sort of tightrope of irritability. He had been angry with his guests when they let him down, and angry with Mr. Period out of loyalty to his own sister.

Even Nicola was unable to feel sorry for either Moppett or Leonard.

She ordered herself back to work and was soon immersed in the niceties of polite behaviour. Every now and then she remembered Andrew Bantling and wondered what the row with his stepfather had been about. She hoped she would meet him on the train, though she supposed Lady Bantling would insist on his staying for the party.

She had worked solidly for about half an hour when her employer came in. He was still pale, but he smiled at her, and tiptoed with playful caution to his desk.

"Pay no attention to me," he whispered. "I'm going to write another little note."

He sat at his desk and applied himself to this task. Presently he began dismally to hum an erratic version of Leonard Leiss's song: *If you mean what I think you mean, O.K. by me.* He made a petulant little sound. "Now, why in the world," he cried, "should that distressingly vulgar catch come into my head? Nicola, my dear, what a perfectly dreadful young man! That you should be let in for that sort of party! Really!"

Nicola reassured him. By-and-by he sighed, so heavily that she couldn't help glancing at him. He had folded his letter and addressed an envelope and now sat with his head on his hand. "Better wait a bit," he muttered. "Cool down."

Nicola stopped typing and looked out of the window. Riding up the drive on a bicycle was a large policeman.

He dismounted, propped his machine against a tree trunk and removed his trouser clips. He then approached the house.

"There's a policeman outside."

"What? Oh, really? Noakes, I suppose. Splendid fellow, old Noakes. I wonder what he wants. Tickets for a concert, I misdoubt me."

Alfred came in. "Sergeant Noakes, sir, would like to see you."

"What's it all about, Alfred?"

"I don't know, I'm sure, sir. He says it's important."

"All right. Show him in, if I must."

"Thank you, sir."

The impressive things about Sergeant Noakes were his size and his mildness. He was big, even for a policeman, and he was mild beyond belief. When Mr. Period made him known to Nicola, he said: "Good afternoon, Miss," in a loud but paddy voice and added that he hoped she would excuse them for a few minutes. Nicola took this as a polite dismissal and was about to conform, when Mr. Period said that he wouldn't dream of it. She must go on typing and not let them bore her. Please. He insisted.

Poor Nicola, fully aware of Sergeant Noakes's wishes to the contrary, sat down again and banged away at her machine. She couldn't help hearing Mr. Period's airy and inaccurate assurance that she was entirely in his confidence.

"Well," Sergeant Noakes said, "sir . . . in that case . . ."

"Sit down, Noakes."

"Thank you, sir. I've dropped in to ask if you can help me in a small matter that has cropped up."

"Ah, yes? More social activities, Noakes?"

"Not exactly, this time, sir. More of a routine item, really. I wonder if you'd mind telling me if a certain name is known to you." He lowered his voice.

"Leiss!" Mr. Period shrilly ejaculated. "Did you say *Leonard Leiss?*"

"That was the name, yes."

"I encountered him for the first time this morning."

"Ah," said Sergeant Noakes warmly. "That makes everything much easier, sir. Thank you. For the first time . . . So you are not at all familiar with Mr. Leiss?"

"Familiar!"

"Quite so, sir. And Mr. Cartell?"

"Nor is Mr. Cartell. Until this morning Mr. Leiss was a complete stranger to both of us. He may be said to be one still."

"Perhaps I could see Mr. Cartell?"

"Look here, Noakes, what the deuce are you talking about?" Nicola, my dear, pray stop typing, will you be so good? But don't go."

Nicola stopped.

"Well, sir," Sergeant Noakes said. "The facts are as follows. George Copper happened to mention to me, about half an hour ago, that he's selling a Scorpion sports model to a young gentleman called Leonard Leiss and he stated, further, that the customer had given your name and Mr. Cartell's and Miss Cartell's as references."

"Good God!"

"Now, sir, in the Service there's a regular system by which all stations are kept informed about the activities of persons known to be operating in a manner contrary to the law, or if not contrary within the meaning of the Act, yet in a suspicious and questionable manner. You might describe them," Sergeant Noakes said with a flash of imagery, "as ripening fruit. Just about ready for the picking."

"Noakes, what in heaven's name—Well. Go on."

"The name of Leonard Sydney Leiss appears on the most recent list. Two previous convictions. Obtaining goods under false pretenses. The portry-parly coincides. It's a confidential matter, Mr. Period, but seeing that the young man gave your name with such assurance and seeing he was very warmly backed up by the young lady, who is Miss Constance Cartell's adopted niece, I thought I would come and mention it quietly. Particularly, sir, as there's a complication."

Mr. Period stared dismally at him. "Complication?" he said.

"Well, sir, yes. You see, for some time Leiss has been working in collusion with a young female who— I'm very sorry, I'm sure, sir—but the description of this young female does tally rather closely with the general appearance of Miss Cartell's aforesaid adopted niece."

There was a long silence. Then Mr. Period said: "This is all rather dreadful."

"I take it, sir, you gave the young man no authority to use your name?"

"Merciful Heavens—NO."

"Then perhaps we may just have a little chat with Mr. Cartell?"

Mr. Period rang the bell.

Mr. Cartell behaved quite differently from Mr. Period. He contracted into the shell of what Nicola supposed to be his professional manner as a solicitor. He looked pinched. Two isolated spots of colour appeared on his cheekbones. Nicola thought he was very angry indeed.

"I am much obliged to you, Sergeant," he said at last, "for bringing this affair to my attention. You have acted very properly."

"Thank you, sir."

"Very properly. If I may suggest a course of action it will be this. I shall inform my sister of the undesirability of having any further communication with this person, and she will see that his acquaintance with Miss Mary Ralston is terminated. Copper, of course, must be advised at once and he may then, if he thinks it proper, decline any further negotiations."

Sergeant Noakes opened his mouth, but Mr. Cartell raised a finger and he shut it again.

"I need not add," Mr. Cartell said crisply, "that no undertaking of any kind whatever was given by Mr. Period or by myself. Permission was not asked, and would certainly have been declined, for the use of our names. It might be as well, might it not, if I were to telephone Copper at once and suggest that he rids himself of Leiss and the other car, which he left, I understand, to be repaired at the garage. I shall then insist that Miss Ralston, who I imagine is there, returns at once. . . . What's the *matter*, Noakes?"

"The matter," Sergeant Noakes said warmly, "is this, sir. George Copper can't be told not to make the sale and Miss Ralston can't be brought back to be warned."

"My dear Noakes, why not?"

"Because George Copper has been fool enough to let young Leiss get away with it. And he *has* got away with it. With the sports car, sir, and the young lady inside it. And where they've gone, sir, is, to use the expression, nobody's business."

" 3 "

Who can form an objective view of events with which, however lightly, he has been personally involved? Not Nicola. When, after the climax, she tried to sort out her impressions of these events she found that in every detail they were coloured by her own preferences and sympathies.

At the moment, for instance, she was concerned to notice that, while Mr. Period had suffered a shrewd blow to his passionate snobbery, Mr. Cartell's reaction was more disingenuous and resourceful. And while Mr. Period was fretful, Mr. Cartell, she thought, was nipped with bitter anger.

He made a complicated noise in his throat and then said sharply: "They must be traced, of course. Has Copper actually transacted the sale? Change of ownership and so on?"

"He's accepted Mr. Leiss's car, which is a souped-up old bag of a job, George reckons, in part payment. He's let Mr. Leiss try out the Scorpion on the understanding that, if he likes it, the deal's on."

"Then they will return to the garage?"

"They *ought* to," Sergeant Noakes said with some emphasis. "The point is, sir, *will* they? Likely enough, he'll drive straight back to London. He may sell the car before he's paid for it and trust to his connection here to get him out of the red if things become awkward. He's played that caper before, and he may play it again."

Mr. Cartell said: "May I, P.P.?" and reached for the telephone.

"If it's all the same with you, gentlemen, I think I'll make the call," Sergeant Noakes said unexpectedly.

Mr. Cartell said: "As you wish," and moved away from the desk.

Mr. Period began feeling, in an agitated way, in his pockets. He said fretfully: "What have I done with my cigarettes?"

Nicola said: "I think the case was left in the dining-room. I'll fetch it."

As she hurried out she heard the telephone ring.

The dining-room table was cleared and the window opened. The cigarette case was nowhere to be seen. She was about to go in search of Alfred, when he came in. He had not seen the case, he said. Nicola remembered very clearly that, as she stood back at the door for Miss Cartell, she had noticed it on the window sill, and she said as much to Alfred.

A shutter came down over Alfred's face.

"It wasn't there when I cleared, Miss."

Nicola said: "Oh well! I expect, after all, Mr. Period—" And then remembered that Mr. Period had left the dining-room to answer the telephone and had certainly not collected the cigarette case when he briefly returned.

Alfred said: "The window was on the latch, as it is now, when I cleared, Miss. I'd left it shut, as usual."

Nicola looked at it. It was a casement window and was hooked open to the extent of some eight inches. Beyond it were the rose garden, the side gate and the excavations in the lane. As she stared out of it a shovelful of earth was thrown up; derisively, she might almost have thought, by one of the workmen, invisible in the trench.

"Never mind," she said. "We'll find it. Don't worry."

"I hope so, I'm sure, Miss. It's a valuable object."

"I know."

They were staring doubtfully at each other when Mr. Period came in looking exceedingly rattled.

"Nicola, my dear: Andrew Bantling on the telephone, for you. *Would* you mind taking it in the hall? We are *un peu occupé,* in the study. I'm so sorry."

"Oh dear!" Nicola said. "So am I—that you've been bothered. Mr. Period, your cigarette case isn't in here, I'm afraid."

"But I distinctly remember—" Mr. Period began. "Well, never mind. Your telephone call, child."

Nicola went into the hall.

Andrew Bantling said: "Oh, there you are at last! What goes on in the Lay-by? P.P. sounded most peculiar."

"He's awfully busy."

"You're being discreet and trustworthy. Never mind, I shall gimlet it out of you in the train. You couldn't make the 3:30, I suppose?"

"Not possibly."

"Then I shall simply have to lurk in the lane like a follower. There's nowhere for me to be in this district. Baynesholme has become uninhabitable on account—" He lowered his voice and evidently put his mouth very close to the receiver, so that consonants popped and sibilants hissed in Nicola's eardrum.

"What did you say?"

"I said *the Moppett* and her *Leonard* have arrived in a smashing Scorpion under pretense of wanting to see the family portraits. What's the matter?"

"I've got to go. Sorry. Good-bye," Nicola said, and rushed to the library.

Mr. Cartell and Mr. Period broke off their conversation as she entered. Sergeant Noakes was dialling a number.

She said: "I thought I should tell you at once. They're at Baynesholme. They've driven there in the Scorpion."

Mr. Cartell went into action. "Noakes," he said, "tell Copper I want him here immediately in the car."

"Which car, sir?" Noakes asked, startled, the receiver at his ear.

"The Bloodbath," Mr. Period said impatiently. "What else? Really, Noakes!"

"He's to drive me to Baynesholme as fast as the thing will go. At once, Noakes."

Sergeant Noakes began talking into the telephone.

"Be quick," Mr. Cartell said, "and you'd better come too."

"Yes, George," said Sergeant Noakes into the telephone. "That's correct. Now."

"Come along, Noakes. My hat and coat!" Mr. Cartell went out. "*Alfred!* My topcoat."

"And you might ask them, Harold, while you're about it," Mr. Period quite shouted after him, "what they did with my cigarette case."

"What?" the retreating voice asked.

"Lady Barsington's cardcase. Cigarettes."

There was a shocked pause. Mr. Cartell returned, half in and half out of an overcoat, a tweed hat cocked over one eye.

"What do you mean, P.P.? Surely you don't suggest . . . ?"

"God knows! But ask them. *Ask!*"

" 4 "

Désirée, Lady Bantling (ex-Cartell, factually Dodds), sat smiling to herself in her drawing-room.

She smoked incessantly and listened to Moppett Ralston and Leonard Leiss, and it would have been impossible for anyone to say what she thought of them. Her ravaged face, with its extravagant make-up, and her mop of orange hair made a flagrant statement against the green background of her chair. She was possibly not unamused.

Moppett was explaining how interested Leonard was in art and what a lot he knew about the great portrait painters.

"So I do hope," Moppett was saying, "you don't think it too boring and bold of us to ask if we may look. Leonard said you would, but I said we'd risk it and if we might just see the pictures and creep away again . . . ?"

"Yes, do," Désirée said. "They're all Bantling ancestors. Gentlemen in skin-tight breeches, and ladies with high foreheads and smashing bosoms. Andrew could tell you all about them, but he seems to have disappeared. I'm afraid I've got to help poor Bimbo make up pieces of poetry for a treasure hunt and in any case

I don't know anything about them. I want my pictures to be modern and gay and, if possible, rude."

"And, of course, you're *so* right, Lady Bantling," Leonard said eagerly. He leant forward with his head on one side sending little waves of hair oil towards her. Désirée watched him and accepted everything he said without comment. When he had talked himself to an ingratiating standstill, she remarked that, after all, she didn't think she was all that interested in painting.

"Andrew has done a portrait of me which I do quite fancy," she said. "I look like the third witch in Macbeth before she gave up trying to make the best of herself. Hullo, my darling, how's your muse?"

Bimbo had come in. He threw an extremely cold glance at Leonard.

"My muse," he said, "is bitching on me. You must help me, Désirée; there ought to be at least seven clues and it's more amusing if they rhyme."

"Can we help?" Moppett suggested. "Leonard's quite good at *really* improper ones. What are they for?"

"A treasure hunt," he said, without looking at her.

"Treasure hunts are my vintage," Désirée said. "I thought it might be fun to revive them. So we've having one tonight."

Moppett and Leonard cried excitedly. "But I'm *utterly* sold on them," Moppett said. "They're quite the gayest way of having parties. How exactly are you working it?" she asked Bimbo. He said shortly that they were doing it the usual way.

Désirée stood up. "Bimbo's planting a bottle of champagne somewhere and the leading-up clues will be dotted about the landscape. If you don't mind just going on your picture crawl under your own steam we'd better begin racking our brains for rhymes. Please do look wherever you like." She held out her hand to Moppett. "I'm sorry not to be more hospitable, but we are, as you see, in a taking-on. Good-bye." She looked at Leonard. "Good-bye."

"My God!" Bimbo suddenly ejaculated. "The food from Magnums! It'll be at the station."

Moppett and Leonard stopped short and looked passionately concerned.

"Can't you pick it up," Désirée asked, "when you lay your trail of clues?"

"I can't start before we've done the clues, can I?"

"They're too busy to send anyone from the kitchen and they want the stuff. Madly. We'd better get the Bloodbath to collect it."

"Look!" Moppett and Leonard said together and then gaily laughed at each other. " 'Two minds with *butter . . .*' " Moppett quipped. "But please—please do let us collect the things from Magnums. We'd *adore* to."

Désirée said: "Jolly kind, but the Bloodbath will do it."

Bimbo much more emphatically added: "Thank you, but we wouldn't dream of it."

"But why not?" Moppett protested. "Leonard's longing to drive that thing out there, aren't you, sweetie?"

"Of course. And, as a matter of fact," Leonard said, "I happen to know the Bloodbath—if that's George Copper's crate—is out of commission. It won't take us any time."

"Do let us, or we'll think," Moppett urged engagingly, "that we really *are* being hideously in the way. Please."

"Well—" Désirée said, not looking at her husband, "if you really don't mind it would, I must say, be the very thing."

"Andrew!" Bimbo ejaculated. "He'll do it. Where is he?"

"He's gone. Do you know, darling, I'm afraid we'd better accept the kind offer."

"Of *course!*" Moppett cried. "Come on, Face! Is there anything else to be picked up, while we're about it?"

Désirée said, with a faint twist in her voice: "You think of everything, don't you? I'll talk to the kitchen."

When she had gone, Bimbo said: "Isn't that the Scorpion Copper had in his garage?"

"The identical job," Leonard agreed, man-to-man. "Not a bad little heap by and large, and the price is O.K. Like to have a look at her, Mr. Dodds? I'd appreciate your opinion."

Bimbo, with an air of mingled distaste and curiosity, intimated that he would, and the two men left Moppett in the drawing-room. Standing well back from the French window, she watched them at the car: Leonard talking, Bimbo with his hands in his pockets. Trying, thought Moppett, not to be interested, but he *is* interested. He's a car man. He's married her for his Bentley and his drinks and the grandeur and fun. She's old. She can't have all that much of what it takes. Or, by any chance, can she?

A kind of contempt possessed her: a contempt for Désirée and Bimbo and anybody who was not like herself and Leonard. *Living dangerously,* she thought, that's us. She wondered if it would be advisable to ask Leonard not to say "appreciate," "O.K.," "Pardon me," and "appro." She herself didn't mind how he talked, she even enjoyed their rows when he would turn foul-mouthed, adderlike, and brutal. Still, if they *were* to crash the County—They'll *have* to ask us, she thought, after this. They can't not. We've been clever as clever.

She continued to peer slantways through the window.

When Désirée returned, Moppett was looking with respect at a picture above the fireplace.

Désirée said there would be a parcel at the grocer's in Little Codling. "Your quickest way to the station is to turn right, outside the gates," she said. "We couldn't be more obliged to you."

She went out with Moppett to the car, and when it had shot out of sight down the avenue, linked her arm in her husband's.

"Shockers," she said, "aren't they?"

"Honestly, darling, I can't think what you're about."

"Can't you?"

"None of my business, of course," he muttered. She looked at him with amusement.

"Don't you like them?" she asked.

"Like them!"

"I find myself quite amused by them," she said, and added indifferently, "They do know what they want, at least."

"It was perfectly obvious from the moment they crashed their way in that they were hell-bent on getting asked for tonight."

"I know."

"Are you going to pretend not to notice their hints?"

"Oh," she said with a faint chuckle, "I don't think so. I expect I'll ask them."

Bimbo said: "Of course I never interfere—"

"Of course," she agreed. "And how wise of you, isn't it?" He drew away from her. "You don't usually sulk either."

"You let people impose on you."

"Not," she said gently, "without realizing it," and he reddened.

"That young man," he said, "is a monster. Did you *smell* him?"

"In point of fact, he's got quite a share of what it takes."

"You can't mean it!"

"Yes, I do. I never tell lies about sex, as such. I should think he's probably a bad hat, wouldn't you?"

"I would. As shifty as they make them."

"P'raps he's a gangster and Moppett's his moll."

"Highly probable," he said angrily.

"I can't wait to hear Leonard being the life and soul of my party."

"I promise you, if you do ask them, you'll regret it."

"Should we hire a detective to keep an eye on the spoons?"

"At least you can come in and help me with the bloody poetry."

"I think I shall ask them," she said, in her rather hoarse voice. "Don't you think it could be fun? Would you really not want it?"

"You know damn' well what I want," he muttered, staring at her.

She raised her eyebrows. "I forgot to tell you," she said. "Ormsbury's dead."

"Your brother?"

"That's right. In Australia."

"Ought you to—"

"I haven't seen him for thirty years, and I never liked him. A horrid, dreary fellow."

Bimbo said: "Good God, who's this?"

"The Bloodbath," Désirée said calmly. "So it isn't out of commission. Bad luck for Leonard."

It came slowly roaring and boiling up the long drive with George Copper at the wheel and Noakes beside him.

"Do you *see* who's in the back seat?" Désirée asked her husband. "It's Harold."

"It can't be."

"But it is. His first visit since we had our final row and he shook my dust from his boots forever. Perhaps he's going to claim me back from you after all these years."

"What the hell *can* he want?"

"Actually I'm livid with him. He's being beastly to Andrew about that money. I shall pitch into him."

"Why's he got Noakes? I'll never get my clues done," Bimbo complained.

"You bolt indoors. I'll cope."

Bimbo said: "Fair enough," and did so.

The car drew up with a jerk. Sergeant Noakes got out and opened the rear door for Mr. Cartell, who was clearly flustered.

"Harold!" Désirée said with amusement. "How are you? I recognized your hat. Good afternoon, Mr. Copper. Good afternoon, Mr. Noakes."

"I wonder," Mr. Cartell began as he removed his hat, "if you could spare me a moment."

"Why not? Come in."

Bareheaded, baldish and perturbed, he followed her distrustfully into the house.

"What do *we* do?" Mr. Copper asked Noakes.

"Wait. What else? The Scorpion's not here, George."

"You don't say," Mr. Copper bitterly rejoined, looking round the open expanse of drive.

Noakes walked to the front of the Bloodbath and looked at the surface of the drive. He laid his hand pontifically on the bonnet and snatched it away with an oath.

"She's boiling," Mr. Copper observed.

"Ta for the information."

"You would insist on the hurry. She can't take it."

"All right. All right. I said I ought to come on the bike. Stay where you are, George."

Mr. Copper watched him with resentment. Doubled forward, he cast about the drive.

"The Scorpion," he said, "drips her grease rather heavy, doesn't she?"

"That's right."

"And she's shod on three feet with Griprich and on the off hind with Startread. Correct?"

"Yes."

"She's came," Sergeant Noakes said, "and went. Look for yourself."

Mr. Copper said: "So what do we do? Roar after her with the siren screaming? If we had a siren."

"We'll follow it up for you through the usual channels. Don't worry."

"What'll I say to the owner? Tell me that. I'm selling her on commission, mind! I'm responsible!"

"No need to panic. They might come back."

"More likely to be halfway to London with changed number plates. Who started the panic, anyway? You, with your police records. *Come back?* Them!"

The front door opened and Mr. Cartell appeared, white-faced, in the entrance.

"Oh—Noakes," he said. "I've a little further business to discuss indoors, but will join you in a moment. Will you stay where you are and deal with the car situation when they return?"

"Sir?"

"Yes," said Mr. Cartell. "There's no immediate need for alarm. They are coming back."

With a sharp look at both of them he returned indoors.

"There you are," Sergeant Noakes said. "What did I tell you? You leave this one to me."

" 5 "

"What I can't see," Désirée said, turning her enormous lacklustre eyes upon her former husband, "is why you've got yourself into such a state. Poor Mr. Copper's been told that you and P.P. and Connie won't guarantee the sale. All he's got to do is take the car away from them."

"*If* they return it," Mr. Cartell amended.

"I hope, Harold darling, you're not suggesting that they'll make a break for Epping Forest and go native on Magnums' smoked salmon! That really would be too tiresome. But I'm sure they won't. They're much too anxious to worm their way into my party."

"You can't," Mr. Cartell said in a hurry, "possibly allow that, of course."

"So everybody keeps telling me."

"My dear Désirée—"

"Harold, I want to tackle you about Andrew."

Mr. Cartell gave her one sharp glance and froze. "Indeed," he said.

"He tells me you won't let him have his money."

"He will assume control of his inheritance at the appointed time, which is on the sixth of October next."

"He did explain, didn't he, why he needs it now? About the Grantham Gallery for sale and wanting to buy it?"

"He did. He also explained that he wishes to leave the Brigade in order to manage the Gallery."

"And go on with his own painting."

"Precisely. I cannot agree to anticipating his inheritance for these purposes."

"He's gone into it very carefully and he's not a baby or a fool. He's twenty-four and extremely level-headed."

"In this matter I cannot agree with you."

"Bimbo's been into it, too. He's prepared to put up some of the cash and go in as a partner."

"Indeed. I am surprised to learn he is in a position to do so."

She actually changed colour at this. There was a short silence, and then she said: "Harold, I ask you very seriously to let Andrew have his inheritance."

"I'm sorry."

"You may remember," she said, with no change of manner, "that when I do fight, it's no holds barred."

"In common with most—"

"Don't say 'with most of my delightful sex,' Harold."

"One can always omit the adjective," said Mr. Cartell.

"Ah, well," Désirée said pleasantly and stood up. "I can see there's no future in sweet reasonableness. Are you enjoying life in P.P.'s stately cottage?"

Mr. Cartell also rose. "It's a satisfactory arrangement," he said stiffly, "for me. I trust, for him."

"He won't enjoy the Moppett-Leonard *crise,* will he? Poor P.P., such a darling as he is and such a Godalmighty snob. Does he know?"

"Know what?" Mr. Cartell asked unguardedly.

"About your niece and her burglar boyfriend?"

Mr. Cartell turned scarlet and closed his eyes. "She is NOT," he said in the trembling voice of extreme exasperation, "my niece."

"How do you know? I've always thought Connie might have popped her away to simmer, and then adopted her back, as you might say."

"That is a preposterous and possibly an actionable statement, Désirée. The girl—Mary Ralston—came from an extremely reputable adoption centre."

"Connie might have put her there."

"If you will forgive me, I'll have a word with

Noakes. I regret very much that I have troubled you."

"P.P. is dining with us. He and I are going to have a cozy old chum's gossip before my treasure hunt party arrives."

Mr. Cartell said: "I am not susceptible to moral blackmail, Désirée. I shall not reconsider my decision about Andrew."

"Look," Désirée said. "I fancy you know me well enough to realize that I'm not a sentimental woman."

"That," said Mr. Cartell, "I fully concede. A woman who gives a large party on the day her brother's death is announced—"

"My dear Hal, you know you looked upon Ormsbury as a social scourge and so did I. By and large, I'm not madly fond of other people. But I am fond of Andrew. He's my son and I like him very much indeed. You watch out for yourself, Harold. I'm on the warpath."

A motor horn sounded distantly. They both turned to the windows.

"And here," Désirée said, "are your friends. I expect you want to go to meet them. Good-bye."

When Mr. Cartell had left her, she moved into the French window and, unlike Moppett, very openly watched the scene outside.

The Scorpion came up the drive at a great pace, but checked abruptly. Then it moved on at a more decorous speed and pulled up. Leonard and Moppett got out simultaneously. Sergeant Noakes advanced and so did they, all smiles and readiness, but with the faintest suggestion of self-consciousness, Désirée considered, in their joints. It's people's elbows, she reflected, that give them away.

They approached the group of three. Moppett, with

girlish insouciance, linked her arm through Mr. Cartell's, causing him to become rigid with distaste.

First blood to Moppett, thought Désirée with relish.

Leonard listened to Sergeant Noakes with an expression that progressed from bonhomie through concern towards righteous astonishment. He bowed ironically and indicated the Scorpion. Catching sight of Désirée, he shook his head slowly from side to side as if inviting her to share his bewilderment. He then removed two large packages from the Scorpion.

Désirée opened the French window and strolled down the steps towards them. Mr. Cartell furiously disengaged himself from Moppett.

"I think," he said, "that we should get back, Noakes. If Copper drives the other car, you, I suppose—"

Sergeant Noakes glanced at Moppett and muttered something.

"Don't let *us* keep you," Leonard said quickly and with excessive politeness. "Please."

They touched their hats to Désirée and mounted their respective cars. They drove away, inexplicably at a disadvantage.

"Well," Désirée asked cheerfully, "did you find my tiresome food?"

Moppett and Leonard, all smiles, began to chatter and give way to each other.

Finally Moppett said: "Dear Lady Bantling—yes. We've got it all, but, as you see, we ran into a muddle of sorts. Mr. Copper's made a nonsense about the Scorpion, and we've missed buying it."

"Inefficient," Leonard said. "It appears somebody else had first refusal."

"How very disappointing."

"Isn't it!" Moppett agreed. "Too sickening." She

gave a little scream and put her hand to her mouth. "Leonard!" she cried. "Fools that we are!"

"What, darling?"

"We ought to have gone back with them. Look at us! *Now* what do we do?"

Leonard allowed the slightest possible gap to occur before he said: "I'm afraid Mr. George Copper will have to make a return trip in my car. Too bad!"

"What *will* you think of us?" Moppett asked Désirée.

"Oh," she said lightly, "the worst," and they laughed with possibly a shade less conviction.

"At least," Moppett said, "we can bring the food in, can't we? And if we *might* ring up for *some* sort of transport . . ."

Bimbo came out of the house and fetched up short when he saw them. Désirée grinned at him.

"Why not stay?" she said very distinctly to Moppett. "After fetching all our food, the least we can do is to ask you to eat it. Do stay."

CHAPTER THREE

Aftermath to a Party

Andrew put Nicola's overcoat on the seat and sat opposite to her.

"The best thing about this train," he said, "is that it's nearly always empty. So you're returning to the fold tomorrow, are you?"

Nicola said Mr. Period had asked her to do so, and that was why she had left her typewriter behind.

"But you're *not* returning to Little Codling tomorrow," Andrew said, with the air of taking a plunge, "you're returning tonight. At least I hope so. Don't say another word. I've got an invitation for you."

He produced it and gave it to her with an anxious smile.

It was from his mother and it said: *Do come to my dotty party tonight. Andrew will bring you and we'll put you up. He'll explain all about it, but do come.*

Nicola stared at him in amazement.

"My mum," he said, "has taken a fancy to you. So, as is no doubt abundantly obvious, have I. Now don't go into a *brouhaha* and say you can't. Just say: 'Thank you, Andrew. How sweet of your mum, I'd love to.' "

"But *how* can I?"

"How?" Andrew said grandly. "Anyhow. Why not?"

"I tell you what," Nicola said. "You've nagged at your mum to ask me."

"I swear I haven't. She nagged at me and I said I would if you would."

"There you are, you see."

"No, I don't. And anyway, do stop carping and come. It's definitely not one of my mama's more rococo parties. I wouldn't dream of taking you to one of them, of course."

Nicola, who remembered hearing rumours of some of Lady Bantling's parties, felt relieved.

"What I thought," Andrew continued, "I'll drop you wherever you live and you can nip into your Number One ceremonials and then I'll pick up my dinner jacket. I have a car of sorts and we'll dine somewhere and then we'll drive down to Baynesholme."

"What about the cocktail party you're all dressed up for?"

"Forget it, completely. Do come, Nicola. Will you?"

"Thank you, Andrew. How sweet of your mum to ask me. I'd love to."

"Thank you, Nicola."

For the rest of the journey Andrew talked to Nicola about himself. He said he wanted to paint more than anything else in life and that he'd been having lessons and was "meant to be not too bad," but bad or not he had to go on with it. He said that if he could take the Grantham Gallery over, there was a studio at the back where he could paint and manage the Gallery at the same time. Then he described his unproductive and bad-tempered meeting that morning with his guardian and stepfather, Mr. Cartell.

"It was a snorter," Andrew said thoughtfully. "He treated the whole thing as if it were a sort of adolescent whim. I'd brought down all the figures of the turnover and he wouldn't look at them, damn him. I gave him the names of jolly good people who would supply an expert opinion, and he wouldn't listen. All he would say was that my father wouldn't have wanted me to resign my commission. What the hell," Andrew shouted and then pulled himself up. "It's not so much the practical side that infuriates me—I could, after all, I imagine, borrow the money and insure my life or whatever one does. It's his bloody pontificating philistinism. What I believe I most resented," he said, "was having to talk about my painting. I said things that are private to me and he came back at me with the sort of remarks that made them sound phony. Can you understand that?"

"I think I can. And I suppose in the end you began to wonder if, after all, you were any good."

"You do understand, don't you? Does everybody off-load their difficulties on you, or . . . No," Andrew said, "I'd better not say that—yet. Thank you, anyway, for listening."

"Do you admire Agatha Troy's painting?"

He stared at her. "Well, of course. Why?"

"I know her. She's married to Roderick Alleyn in the C.I.D. I go there quite often. As a matter of fact, I'm paying them a visit tomorrow evening."

"What's she like? I know what she looks like. Lovely bone. Kind of gallant. Is she alarming?"

"Not at all. She's rather shy. She's jolly good about being interested in younger people's work," Nicola added. She hesitated and then said: "You may not care for the idea at all, but if you liked I could show her one of your things."

He turned very red and Nicola wondered if she had offended him.

He said at last, "Do you know, I don't think I'd dare."

"So Mr. Cartell really has downed you, I see."

"No, he hasn't, you low-cunning girl."

"If you'd rather not I shan't take umbrage. On the other hand I'll be delighted if you say: 'Thank you, Nicola. How sweet of you to ask me. I'd love to.' "

Andrew grinned and for an appreciable interval was silent.

"You win," he said at last. "I'll say that same small thing."

The rest of the journey passed quickly for both of them, and in London they followed the plan proposed by Andrew.

At half past eight they were in his car on their way back into Kent. The night was warm for early April, the lights sailed past and there was a young moon in the sky. Nicola knew that she was beginning to fall in love.

" 2 "

"I tell you what, Mrs. M.," Alfred said as he prepared to set the dinner table. "The weather in this household has deteriorated and the forecast is for atmospheric disturbances followed by severe storms."

"Go on!" Mrs. Mitchell said eagerly. "How?"

"How, I don't know. If you ask me *why,* I can give a pretty good guess. For ten years, Mrs. M., We've organized ourselves quietly and comfortably in the way that suits Us. Everything very nice and going by clockwork. Nothing unexpected. Settled. No upsets of any kind whatsoever. Suits Us and, incidentally, I may say, suits you and me. *Now* what? What's the present situation? Look at today! We've had more upsets in this one day, Mrs. M., than We've had to put up with in the total length of my service."

Mrs. Mitchell executed the toss of the head and upward turn of the eyes that had only one connotation.

"Him?" she suggested.

"Exactly. Him," Alfred said. "Mr. Harold Cartell."

"Good God, Mr. Belt!" Mrs. Mitchell ejaculated. "What ever's the matter?"

"The matter, Mrs. M.?"

"The way you looked! Coo! Only for a sec. But my word! Talk about old-fashioned."

"You'd look old-fashioned yourself," Alfred countered, "if suggestions of the same nature were made to you."

"By 'im?" she prompted unguardedly.

"Correct. In reference to Our cigarette case. Which, as I mentioned earlier, was left by those two on the window ledge and has disappeared. Well. As we noticed this afternoon, Mr. Cartell went off in the Bloodbath with George Copper and Bert Noakes."

"Very peculiar, yes."

"Yes. All right. It now appears they went to Baynesholme."

"To the Big House?"

"Exactly."

"Well! To see her ladyship?"

"To see *them*. Those two. They'd gone there, if you please. Unasked, by all accounts."

"Sauce!"

"What it was all about I have not yet gathered, but will from George Copper. The point is that when I take drinks to the library just now, they're at it hammer-and-tongs."

"Our two gentlemen?"

"Who else? And so hot they don't stop when they see me. At least *he* doesn't—Mr. C. He was saying he'd forgotten in the heat of the moment at Baynesholme to ask young Leiss and that Moppett about where they'd left the cigarette case, and Mr. Period was saying the young lady, Miss Maitland-Mayne, saw it on the sill. And I was asked to say if it was there when I cleared and I said no. And I added that someone had opened the window."

"Who?"

"Ah! You may well ask. So Mr. Cartell says, in a great taking-on, that the chaps doing the sewage in Green Lane must have taken it and my gentleman says they're very decent chaps and he can't believe it. 'Very well, then,' says Mr. C., very sharp and quite the lawyer, 'perhaps Alfred would care to reconsider his statement.' And the way he said it was sufficient! After that suggestion, Mrs. M., I don't mind telling you it's him or me. Both of us this residence will not accommodate."

"What did our gentleman say?"

"Ah! What would you expect? Came out very quiet and firm on my behalf. 'I think,' he said, 'that Alfred has given us a perfectly clear picture and that there is no need to ask him to repeat it. Thank you, Alfred. I'm sorry to have troubled you.' So, of course, I said: 'Thank you, sir,' with what I trust was the proper emphasis, and withdrew. But you can take it from me, there's serious trouble and deep feeling in more than one direction. Something was said at luncheon that was very ill-received by our gentleman. Said by Mr. C. Speculation," added Alfred, who had grown calmer and reverted to his normal habit of speech, "speculation is unprofitable. Events will clarify."

"Why Noakes, though?" she pondered.

"Ah! And I happened to ascertain from the chaps in the lane that Noakes brought Mr. C. back in George Copper's Bloodbath and George himself turned up in that Scorpion he's got in his garage. And what's more, the rural mail van gave those two a lift back. They've been invited to the Big House party tonight. They're dining and staying with Miss Cartell. They were very pleased with themselves, the mail van said, but cagey in their manner."

The kitchen door was ajar and Mr. Cartell's voice sounded clearly from the hall.

"Very well," he was saying. "If that should prove to be the case I shall know how to act and I can assure you, P.P., that I shall act with the utmost rigour. I trust that you are satisfied."

The front door slammed.

"Mercy on us!" Mrs. Mitchell apostrophized. "Now what?" And added precipitately: "My bedroom window!"

She bolted from the kitchen and Alfred heard her thundering up the back stairs.

Presently she returned, flushed and fully informed.

"Across the Green," she reported, "to Miss Cartell's."

"And you may depend upon it, Mrs. M.," Alfred said, "that the objective is Miss Moppett."

" 3 "

Moppett had changed into the evening dress she kept in her bedroom at Miss Cartell's house. It was geranium red, very décolleté and flagrantly becoming to her. She lay back in her chair, admiring her arms and glancing up from under her eyebrows at Mr. Cartell.

"Auntie Con's at a Hunt Club committee do of sorts," she said. "She'll be in presently. Leonard's collecting his dinner jacket off the bus."

"I am glad," Mr. Cartell said, giving her one look and thereafter keeping his gaze on his own folded hands, "of the opportunity to speak to you in private. I will be obliged if, as far as my sister is concerned, you treat our conversation as confidential. There is no need, at this juncture, to cause her unnecessary distress."

"Dear me," she murmured, "you terrify me, Uncle Hal."

"I will also be obliged if the assumption of a relationship which does not exist is discontinued."

"Anything you say," she agreed after a pause, "Mr. Cartell."

"I have two matters to put before you. The first is this. The young man, Leonard Leiss, with whom you appear to have formed a close friendship, is known to the police. If he persists in his present habits it will only be a matter of time before he is in serious trouble, and, if you continue in your association with him, you will undoubtedly become involved. To a criminal extent. I would prefer, naturally, to think you were unaware of his proclivities, but I must say that I am unable to do so."

"I certainly am unaware of anything of the sort and I don't believe a word of it."

"That," Mr. Cartell said, "is nonsense."

"I'm very sorry, but I'm afraid it's you that's talking nonsense. All this to-do because poor Leonard wants to buy a car and I simply mention to Copper that Auntie Con—I hope you don't mind if I go on calling her that—knows him and that you and P.P. might give him the O.K. It was only a matter of form, anyway. Of course, if we'd thought you wouldn't like it we wouldn't have dreamt of doing it. I'm jolly sorry we did, and Leonard is, too."

Mr. Cartell raised his eyes and looked at her. For a moment she boggled, but only for a moment. "And I must say," she said boldly, "we both take a pretty poor view of your coming to Baynesholme and creating a scene. Not that it made any difference with Lady Bantling. She's asked us both for tonight in spite of whatever nonsense she may have been told about us," Moppett announced and laughed rather shrilly.

He waited for a moment and then said: "It would be

idle to discuss this matter any further. I shall turn to my second point and put it very bluntly. What did you do with Mr. Period's cigarette case?"

Moppett recrossed her legs and waited much too long before she said: "I don't know what you mean."

"Precisely what I have said. You and Leiss examined it after luncheon. What did you do with it?"

"How dare you—" Moppett began. "How *dare* you—" and Leonard came into the room.

When he saw Mr. Cartell he fetched up short. "Pardon me," he said elegantly. "Am I interrupting something?"

Moppett extended her arm towards him. "Darling," she said. "I'm being badgered. Can you cope?"

He took her hand and sat on the arm of her chair. "What goes on?" he asked. He was normally a white-faced young man—this characteristic at the moment was particularly noticeable.

"To be perfectly honest," Moppett began, "I haven't a clue. But it appears that we're meant to know where poor old P.P. puts his museum pieces."

"Mr. Period's cigarette case has disappeared," Mr. Cartell said, addressing Leonard exclusively. "You and Miss Ralston were the last persons known to handle it. You may care to make a statement as to what you did with it."

Leonard said: *"Disappeared!* By Jove, that's too bad, isn't it?" His pale fingers closed tightly over Moppett's. "Of *course* we must help, if we can. Yes, now— Yes. I do remember. I left it on the window ledge in the dining-room. You remember, sweetie, don't you?"

"Perfectly."

"Was the window open or shut?"

"Oh," Leonard said easily, "open. Yes. Open."

"Did you open it, Mr. Leiss?"

"Me? What would I do that for? It *was* open."

"It was shut," Mr. Cartell said, "during luncheon."

"Then I suppose the butler-chap—what's-'is-name—must have opened it."

"No."

"That," Leonard remarked, smiling, "is what *he* says."

"It is what I say."

"Then I'm afraid I don't much fancy the way you say it." Leonard produced a silver case from his pocket, offered it to Moppett, helped himself, and with great deliberation lit both cigarettes. He snapped the case shut, smiled at Mr. Cartell and returned it to his pocket. He inhaled deeply, breathed out the vapour and fanned it with his hand. He wore an emerald ring on his signet finger. "How about the sewer men in the lane?" he asked. "Anything in that?"

"They could not open the window from outside."

"Perhaps it was opened for them."

Mr. Cartell stood up. "Mr. Leiss," he said, "I consider myself responsible to Mr. Period for any visitors who, however unwelcome, come to his house under my aegis. Unless his case is returned within the next twelve hours, I shall call in the police."

"You're quite an expert at that, aren't you?" Leonard remarked. He looked at the tip of his cigarette. "One other thing," he said. "I resent the way you're handling this, Mr. Cartell, and I know exactly what I can do about it."

Mr. Cartell observed him with a sort of astonished disgust. He addressed himself to Moppett. "There's no point," he said, "in pursuing this conversation."

A door banged, footsteps were heard in the hall together with an outbreak of yapping and long-drawn-out whines. A loud, uninhibited voice shouted: "Geddown! *Geddown,* you brute." There followed a canine yelp and a renewed outbreak of yapping.

"Quiet, Li. Quiet, sweetie. Who the hell let this blasted mongrel in! *Trudi!"*

"I have changed my mind," Mr. Cartell said. "I shall speak to my sister."

He went out and found her, clasping a frenzied Pekingese to her bosom, kicking Pixie and shouting at her Austrian house-parlourmaid.

"My God, Boysie," she said when she saw her brother, "are you dotty, bringing that thing in here? Take it out. Take it *out!"*

The Pekingese turned in her arms and bit her thumb.

Mr. Cartell said, with dignity: "Come along, old girl, you're not wanted." He withdrew Pixie to the garden, tied her to the gatepost, and returned to the hall, where he found his sister stanching her wound. The Pekingese had been removed.

"I am sorry, Constance. I apologize. Had I imagined—"

"Oh, come off it," Miss Cartell rejoined. "You're hopeless with animals. Let's leave it at that. If you want to see me, come in here while I get some stuff on my thumb."

He followed her into her "den": a small room, crowded with photographs that she had long ago ceased to look at, with the possible exception of those that recorded the progress of Moppett from infancy to her present dubious effulgence.

Miss Cartell rummaged in a drawer and found some cotton wool, which she applied to her thumb with stamp paper and a heavy coating of some black and evil-smelling unguent.

"What is that revolting stuff?" asked her brother, taking out his handkerchief.

"I use it on my mare for girth-gall."

"Really, Connie!"

"Really what? Now then, Boysie," she said, "what's up? I can see you're in one of your moods. Let's have a drink and hear all about it."

"I don't want a drink, Connie."

"Why not? I do," she shouted, with her inevitable gust of laughter, and opened a little cupboard. "I've been having a go at the Hunt Club," she added and embarked on a vigorous exposé of a kennel maid. Mr. Cartell suffered her to thrust a whisky-and-soda into his hand and listened to her with something like despair.

In the end he managed to get her to attend to him. He saw the expected and familiar look of obstinacy come into her face.

"I can't put it too strongly, Connie," he said. "The fellow's a bad lot, and, unless you put your foot down, the girl's going to be involved in serious trouble."

But it was no use. She said, readily enough, that she would tackle Moppett, but almost at once she began to defend her—and before long they had both lost their tempers and had become a middle-aged brother and sister furiously at odds.

"The trouble with you, Boysie, is that you've grown so damned selfish. I don't wonder Désirée got rid of you. All you think of is your own comfort. You've worked yourself up into a stink because you're dead-scared P.P. will turn you out."

"That's an insufferable construction to put on it. Naturally, I don't relish the thought—"

"There you are, you see."

"Nonsense, Constance! *Will* you realize that you are entertaining a young man with a criminal record?"

"Moppett has told me all about him. She's taken him in hand, and he's going as straight as a die."

"You've made yourself responsible for Mary, you

appear to be quite besotted on her—and yet you can allow her to form a criminal association—"

"There's nothing like that about it. She's sorry for him."

"She'll be sorry for herself before long."

"Why?"

"This cigarette case—"

"P.P.'ll find it somewhere. You've no right—"

"I have every right," Mr. Cartell cried, now quite beside himself with chagrin. "And I tell you this, Connie. The girl is a bad girl. If you've any authority over her, you'd better use it. But in my opinion your sensible course would be to let her be brought to book and pay the consequences. She's got a record, Connie. You'll be well rid of her. And I promise you that unless this wretched cigarette case is returned before tomorrow, I shall call in the police."

"You wouldn't!"

"I shall. And the upshot, no doubt, will be jail for the pair of them."

"You miserable little pipsqueak, Boysie!"

"Very well," Mr. Cartell said and rose. "That's my final word, Connie. Good evening to you."

He strode from the hall into the garden, where he fell over his dog. With some commotion they effected an exit—and returned, presumably, to Mr. Period's house across the Green.

" 4 "

Désirée wore black for her April Fool's party. On any other woman of her age it would have been a disastrous dress, but, by virtue of a sort of inward effrontery, she got away with it. Her neck, her bosom and that dismal little region known, unprettily, as the armpit were all so many statements of betrayal, but she triumphed over them and not so much took them in her own stride as she obliged other people to take them in theirs. With her incredible hair brushed up into a kind of bonfire, her carefree makeup, her eyeglass, and her general air of raffishness, she belonged, as Mr. Period mildly reflected, to Toulouse-Lautrec rather than to any contemporary background.

They had dined. The party had assembled, made a great deal of noise and gone off in pairs by car to follow up the clues. Bimbo was driving round the terrain to keep observation, rescue any couple that had become unintentionally lost and whip in the deliberate stragglers.

Everyone was to be in by midnight. Supper was set out in the ballroom, and in the meantime Désirée and Mr. Period sat over a fire in her boudoir enjoying coffee and brandy. It was, Mr. Period noticed, Désirée's third brandy, but she carried her drink with astonishing bravura. He nursed his own modest potion and cozily lamented his fate.

"Désirée, my dear," he was saying, "I really don't know what it is about you, but you have *so* got the gift of drawing one out. Here am I letting my back hair down in the naughtiest way, and about poor old Hal, which is not at all the done thing, considering."

"Why not?" she said, propping her feet in their preposterously high heels above the fireplace. Mr. Period, as she noticed with amusement, gazed tactfully at the flames. "Why not? I found Harold plain hell to live with, and I don't know why you should fare any better. Except that you're nicer than me and have probably got more patience."

"It's the *little* things. *Every* morning to tap on one's door and say, 'Bath's empty. For what it's worth.' *Every* day to clear his throat before he opens his *Telegraph,* and say he may as well know the worst. And his *dog,* Désirée! The noise," Mr. Period exclaimed, unconsciously plagiarizing, "and the smell! And the destruction!"

"One of those mixed-up dogs that try to marry one's foot, I've noticed."

Mr. Period gave a little cough and murmured, "Exactly. Moreover, every night, at one o'clock precisely, he takes it out of doors and it sets up the most hideous barking until, and indeed for some time after, he shuts it up. There have been complaints from all over the village. And now," he added, throwing up his hands, "this afternoon! This afternoon was *too* much."

"But do tell me, P.P., what happened? With Moppett and her flash friend and the car? I've heard Harold's version, of course, but I'm having my own private war with him and was too angry to pay all that much attention."

Mr. Period told her the whole story.

"And I do feel, darling Désirée, that you should be warned. It's plain to be seen that this frightful person, the Leiss, is an out-and-out bad 'un. And indeed, for your ear alone, we most strongly suspect—" Mr. Period looked about him as if the boudoir concealed microphones and began to whisper the story of the cigarette case.

"Oh, no!" Désirée said with relish. "Actually a burglar! And is Moppett his con-girl, do you suppose?"

"I fear, only too probably. And, my dear, here you are, in the kindness of your heart, asking them to your wonderful party."

"It wasn't kindness. It was to spite Harold. He won't give Andy his money. I can't tell you how livid it makes me."

She looked rather fixedly at Mr. Period. "You're a trustee, P.P. Have you discussed it with Hal, or with Andrew?"

Mr. Period said uncomfortably: "Not really *discussed* it, my dear."

"Don't tell me you disapprove, too!"

"No, no, no!" he said in a hurry. "Not *disapprove* exactly. It's just—leaving the Brigade and so on. For that *rather* outré world. Art . . . the Chelsea set . . . Not that Andrew . . . But there! 'Nuff said."

"We're not going to quarrel over it, I hope?"

"My *dear*. Quarrel!"

"Well," she said, suddenly giving Mr. Period a kiss. "Let's talk about something more amusing."

They embarked on a long gossip and Mr. Period eased up. He was enjoying himself immensely, but he did not wish to stay until the return of the treasure hunters. He looked at his watch, found it was eleven o'clock, and asked if he might telephone for the Bloodbath.

"No need," Désirée said, "my car's outside. I'd love to take you. Don't fuss, P.P., I'd really like to. I can have a cast around the village and see how the hunt's going. By the way, one of Bimbo's clues leads to your sewage excavation. It says: *All your trouble and all your pain will only land you down the drain.* He's not very good at poetry, poor sweet, but I thought that one of his neater efforts. Come on, darling. I can see you're in a fever lest Slick Len and his moll should get back with the first prize before you make your getaway."

They went out to her car. Mr. Period was a little apprehensive because of the amount of liqueur brandy Désirée had consumed, but she drove with perfect *expertise* and all the way to Little Codling they talked about Mr. Cartell. Presently they turned into Green Lane. A red lantern marked the end of the open ditch. They passed an elderly sports car, parked in the rough grass on the opposite side.

"Andy," said his mother, giving a long hoot on her horn. "He's going to fall in love with your secretary, I can see."

"Already!" ejaculated Mr. Period.

"Going to. Heavily, I fancy. I took to the girl rather."

"Charming! A *really* nice gel. I'm delighted with her."

"P.P.," Désirée said, as they drew near the house, "there's something extra Harold's done to inflame you, isn't there?"

There was a silence.

"Don't tell me if you'd rather not, of course."

"It's very painful to me. Something he said. One shouldn't," Mr. Period added in a constrained and unnatural voice, "let such things upset one, but——No, dearest Désirée, I shan't bore you with it. It was nothing. I prefer to forget it."

"Fair enough," she said and pulled up.

Mr. Period did not immediately get out of the car. He made another little speech of thanks for his entertainment and then, with many hesitations and apologetic noises, hinted obscurely at bereavement.

"I haven't said anything, my dear," he murmured, "because I felt you preferred *not*. But I wouldn't like you to think——But never mind, I only wanted you to know . . ." He waved his hands and was silent.

"Do you mean about Ormsbury?" she said in her direct way. Mr. Period made a small confirmatory sound. "You didn't say anything," he added. "So, of course——"

"There are some sorrows," Désirée said and it was impossible to catch any overtones in her voice, "that go too deep for words."

Mr. Period gave a little groan of sympathy, kissed her hand, and left her.

He went in by the side gate. She watched him, by the light of her headlamps, pick his way in a gingerly fashion over the planks that had been laid across the ditch. He was safely inside his house and Désirée was about to drive away when she caught sight of a figure

in an upper window. She stopped her engine and got
out of the car.

" 5 "

By midnight the winning pair had presented themselves with their prize, a magnum of champagne. They
were, inevitably, Moppett and Leonard, all smiles, but
with a curious tendency to avoid looking at each other.
Leonard was effulgent in the matter of cuff links and
lapels and his tie was large and plum-coloured. Bimbo
looked upon him with loathing, gave them both drinks
and put a jazz record on the machine. Leonard with
ineffable grace extended his hands towards Désirée.
"May we?" he said and in a moment was dancing with
her. He was a superb dancer. "Much too good," she
said afterwards. "Like the really expensive gigolos used
to be. He smells like them too: it quite took me back. I
adored it."

Bimbo, sulking, was then obliged to dance with
Moppett, who made businesslike passes at him. These
exercises were interrupted by the arrival in straggling
pairs of the rest of the treasure hunters, Nicola and
Andrew being the last to come in—both looking radi-
antly pleased with themselves.

Désirée had a talent for parties. Sometimes they
began presentably and ended outrageously, sometimes
they were presentable almost all the time and sometimes they began, continued and ended outrageously. It was for the last sort that she had gained her
notoriety. This one was, at the moment, both gay and
decorous, possibly because Andrew had unexpectedly
said he hoped it would be.

They were all dancing, and the time was a quarter
past one, when a rumpus broke out on the drive.
Bimbo was changing records, so the noise established
itself readily: it was that of a multiple dogfight.

Growls, yaps, full-blooded barking and strangulated cries of anguish mounted in a ragged crescendo.

Désirée said: "A rival show, it seems"—and then: "Bimbo! Ours! They must have got out!"

Bimbo swore, pulled back curtains and went through French windows to the terrace, followed by Andrew, Désirée and most of the men.

Nicola found herself on the terrace in a group composed of all the other ladies and Leonard.

The combat was joined among parked cars at the head of the drive and was illuminated by lights from the house. All was confusion. Some six or seven contestants bit at each other in a central engagement, others rolled together under cars. One very large, isolated dog sat on its haunches howling dispassionately, and one could be discerned bolting down the drive screaming its classic cry of "pen-and-ink."

Bimbo, Andrew and an advance guard went down into the arena and at first added greatly to the confusion. They shouted, swore, grabbed and kicked. Désirée suddenly joined them, was momentarily hidden, but emerged carrying an outraged poodle by the scruff of its neck. Servants ran out, offering hunting crops and umbrellas. Expressions of human as well as canine anguish were now perceptible. Andrew detached himself, dragging two frenzied Aberdeens by their collars. They were Baynesholme dogs and were thrust with the poodle into a cloakroom, where they got up a half-hearted row on their own account.

Bimbo now appeared carrying an air-gun. He waved the other men aside and presented his weapon at the central mêlée. There was a mild explosion, followed by cries of distress, and suddenly the arena had emptied and the night was plangent with the laments of rapidly retreating dogs.

Only one remained. Exhausted, gratified, infamous and complacent, her tongue lolling out of one side of her mouth, and her lead trailing from her collar, sat a boxer bitch: Mr. Cartell's Pixie, the Helen of the engagement. Whem Bimbo approached her she gathered herself together and bit him.

" 6 "

The next morning Connie Cartell woke slowly from a heavy sleep. She experienced that not unusual sensation, during half-consciousness, in which the threat of something unpleasant anticipates the recollection of the thing itself. She lay, blinking and yawning for a second or two. She heard her Austrian maid stump along the passage and knock on a door.

Damn! Connie thought. I forgot to tell her not to disturb either of them.

Then the full realization of all the horrors of the preceding evening came upon her.

She was not an imaginative woman, but it hadn't taken much imagination, after her brother's visit, to envisage what would happen to Moppett if Mr. Period's cigarette case was not discovered. Connie had tried to tackle Moppett, and, as usual, had got nowhere at all. Moppett had merely remarked that P.P. and Mr. Cartell had dirty minds. Whcn Connie had broached the topic of Leonard Leiss and his reputation, Moppett had reminded her of Leonard's unhappy background and of how she, Moppett, was pledged to redeem him. She had assured Connie, with tears in her eyes and a great many caresses, that Leonard was indeed on the upward path.

If Connie herself had had any experience at all of the Leiss milieu and any real inclination to cope with it, she might possibly have been able to bring a salutary point of view to bear on the situation. She might, it is not too preposterous to suppose, have been able to direct Moppett towards a different pattern of behaviour. But she had no experience and no real inclination. She only doted upon Moppett with the whole force of her unimaginative and uninformed being. She was in a foreign country, and, like many another woman of her class and kind, behaved stupidly, as a foreigner.

So she bathed and dressed and went down to breakfast in a sort of fog, and ate large quantities of eggs, bacon and kidneys indifferently presented by her Austrian maid. She was still at her breakfast when she saw Alfred, in his alpaca jacket and the cloth cap he assumed for such occasions, crossing the Green with an envelope in his hand.

In a moment he appeared before her.

"I beg pardon, Miss," Alfred said, laying the envelope on the table, "for disturbing you, but Mr. Period asked me to deliver this. No answer is required, I understand."

She thanked him and, when he had withdrawn, opened the letter.

Silent minutes passed. Connie read and reread the letter. Incredulity followed bewilderment, and was replaced in turn by alarm. A feeling of horrid unreality possessed her and again she read the letter.

My Dear:

What can I say? Only that you have lost a devoted brother and I a very dear friend. I know so well, believe me so *very* well, what a grievous shock this has been to you and how bravely you will have taken it. If it is not an impertinence in an old fogy to do so, may I offer you these very simple lines written by my dear and *so Victorian* Duchess of Rampton? They are none the worse, I hope, for their unblushing sentimentality.

So must it be, dear heart, I'll not repine,
For while I live the Memory is Mine.

I should like to think that we know each other well enough for you to believe me when I say that I hope you won't dream of answering this all-too-inadequate attempt to tell you how sorry I am.

Yours sincerely,

PERCIVAL PYKE Period

The Austrian maid came in and found Connie still gazing at this letter.

"Trudi," she said with an effort, "I've had a shock."

"*Bitte?*"

"It doesn't matter. I'm going out. I won't be long."

And she went out. She crossed the Green and tramped up Mr. Pyke Period's drive to his front door.

The workmen were assembled in Green Lane.

Alfred opened the front door to her.

"Alfred," she said, "what's happened?"

"Happened, Miss?"

"My brother. Is he——?"

"Mr. Cartell is not up yet, Miss."

She looked at him as if he had addressed her in an incomprehensible jargon.

"He's later than usual, Miss," Alfred said. "Did you wish to speak to him?"

"Hull—Oh, Connie! Good morning to you."

It was Mr. Pyke Period, as fresh as paint, but perhaps not quite as rubicund as usual. His manner was overeffusive.

Connie said: "P.P., for God's sake what is all this? Your letter?"

Mr. Period glanced at Alfred, who withdrew. He then, after a moment's hesitation, took Connie's hand into both of his.

"Now, now!" he said. "You mustn't let this upset you, my dear."

"Are you mad?"

"Connie!" he faintly ejaculated. "What do you mean? Do you—do you *know?*"

"I must sit down. I don't feel well."

She did so. Mr. Period, his fingers to his lips, eyed her with dismay. He was about to speak when a shrill female ejaculation broke out in the direction of the servants' quarters. It was followed by the rumble of men's voices. Alfred reappeared, very white in the face.

"Good God!" Mr. Period said. "What now?"

Alfred, standing behind Connie Cartell, looked his employer in the eyes and said: "May I speak to you, sir?" He made a slight warning gesture and opened the library door.

"Forgive me, Connie. I won't be a moment."

Mr. Period went into the library followed by Alfred, who shut the door.

"Merciful heavens, Alfred, what's the matter with you? Why do you look at me like that?"

"Mr. Cartell, sir." Alfred moistened his lips. "I, really, I scarcely know how to put it, sir. He's—he's—"

"What are you trying to tell me? What's happened?"

"There's been an accident, sir. The men have found him. He's—"

Alfred turned towards the library window. Through the open gate in the quickset hedge, the workmen could be seen, grouped together, stooping.

"They found him—" Alfred said—"not to put too fine a point on it, sir—in the ditch. I'm very sorry I'm sure, sir, but I'm afraid he's dead."

CHAPTER FOUR

Alleyn

"There you are," said Superintendent Williams. "That's the whole story and those are the local people involved. Or not involved, of course, as the case may be. Now, the way I looked at it was this. It was odds-on we'd have to call you people in anyway, so why muck about ourselves and let the case go cold on you? I don't say we wouldn't have liked to go it alone, but we're too damned busy and a damn' side too understaffed. So I rang the Yard as soon as it broke."

"The procedure," Alleyn said dryly, "is as welcome as it's unusual. We couldn't be more obliged, could we, Fox?"

"Very helpful and clearsighted, Super," Inspector Fox agreed with great heartiness.

They were driving from the Little Codling constabulary to Green Lane. The time was ten o'clock. The village looked decorous and rather pretty in the spring sunshine. Miss Cartell's Austrian maid was shaking mats in the garden. The postman was going his rounds. Mr. Period's house, as far as it could be seen from the road, showed no signs of disturbance. At first sight, the only hint of there being anything unusual might have been given by a group of three labourers who stood near a crane truck at the corner, staring at their boots and talking to the driver. There was something guarded and uneasy in their manner. One of them looked angry.

A close observer might have noticed that, in several houses round the Green, people who stood back from their windows were watching the car as it approached the lane. The postman checked his bicycle and, with one foot on the ground, also watched. George Copper stood in the path outside his corner garage and was joined by two women, a youth and three small boys. They, too, were watching. The women's hands moved furtively across their mouths.

"The village has got on to it," Superintendent Williams observed. "Here we are, Alleyn."

They turned into the lane. It had been cordoned off with a rope slung between iron stakes and a DETOUR sign in front. The ditch began at some distance from the corner, and was defined on its inner border by neatly heaped-up soil and on its outer by a row of heavy drainpipes laid end to end. There was a gap in this row opposite Mr. Period's gate, and a single drainpipe on the far side of the ditch.

One of the workmen made an opening for the car and it pulled up beyond the truck.

Two hundred yards away, by the side gate into Mr. Period's garden, Sergeant Noakes waited self-consciously by a disorderly collection of planks, tools, a twelve-foot steel ladder, and an all-too-eloquent shape covered by a tarpaulin. Nearby, on the far side of the lane, was another car. Its occupant got out and advanced: a middle-aged, formally dressed man with well-kept hands.

"Dr. Elkington, our divisional surgeon," Superintendent Williams said, and completed the introductions.

"Unpleasant business, this," Dr. Elkington said. "Very unpleasant. I don't know what you're going to think."

"Shall we have a look?"

"Yes, of course."

"Bear a hand, Sergeant," said Williams. "Keep it screened from the Green, we'd better."

"I'll move my car across," Dr. Elkington said.

He did so. Noakes and Williams released the tarpaulin and presently raised it. Alleyn being particular in such details, he and Fox took their hats off and so, after a surprised glance at them, did Dr. Elkington.

The body of Mr. Cartell lay on its back, not tidily. It was wet with mud and water, and marked about the head with blood. The face, shrouded in a dark and glistening mask, was unrecognizable, the thin hair clotted and dirty. It was clothed in a dressing gown, shirt and trousers, all of them stained and disordered. On the feet were black socks and red leather slippers. One hand was clenched about a clod of earth. Thin trickles of muddy water had oozed between the fingers.

Alleyn knelt beside it without touching it. He looked incongruous. Not his hands, his head, nor, for that matter, his clothes, suggested his occupation. If Mr. Cartell had been a rare edition of any subject other than death, his body would have seemed a more appropriate object for Alleyn's fastidious consideration.

After a pause he replaced the tarpaulin, rose, and, keeping on the hard surface of the lane, stared down into the drain.

"Well," he said. "And he was found below, there?" His very deep, clear voice struck loudly across the silence.

"Straight down from where they've put him. On his face. With the drainpipe on top of him."

"Yes. I see."

"They thought he might be alive. So they got him out of it. They had a job," said Superintendent Williams. "Had to use the gear on the truck."

"He was like this when you saw him, Dr. Elkington?"

"Yes. There are multiple injuries to the skull. I haven't made an extensive examination. My guess would be it's just about held together by the scalp."

"Can we have a word with the men?"

Noakes motioned them to come forward and they did so with every sign of reluctance. One, the tallest, carried a piece of rag and he wiped his hands on it continually, as if he had been doing so, unconsciously, for some time.

"Good morning," Alleyn said. "You've had an unpleasant job on your hands."

The tall man nodded. One of his mates said: "Terrible."

"I want you, if you will, to tell me exactly what happened. When did you find him?"

Fox unobtrusively took out his notebook.

"When we come on the job. Eight o'clock or near after."

"You saw him at once?"

"Not to say there and then, sir," the tall man said. He was evidently the foreman. "We had a word or two. Nutting out the day's work, like. Took off our coats. Further along, back there, we was. You can see where the truck's parked. There."

"Ah, yes. And then?"

"Then we moved up. And I see the planks are missing that we laid across the drain for a bridge. And one of the pipes gone. So I says: 'What the hell's all this? Who's been mucking round with them planks and the pipe?' That's correct, isn't it?" He appealed to the others.

"That's right," they said.

"It's like I told you, Mr. Noakes. We all told you."

"All right, Bill," Williams said easily. "The Superintendent just wants to hear for himself."

"If you don't mind," said Alleyn. "To get a clear idea, you know . . . It's better at first hand."

The foreman said: "It's not all that pleasant, though, is it? And us chaps have got our responsibility to think of. We left the job like we ought to: everything in order. Planks set. Lamps lit. Everything safe. Now look!"

"Lamps? I saw some at the ends of the working. Was there one here?"

"A-course there was. To show the planks. That's the next thing we notice. It's gone. Matter of fact they're all laying in the drain now."

"So they are," Alleyn said. "It's a thumping great drain you're digging here, by the way. What is it, a relief outfall sewer or something?"

This evidently made an impression. The foreman said that was exactly what it was and went into a professional exposition.

"She's deep," he said. "She's as deep as you'll come across anywhere. Fourteen-be-three she lays, and very nasty spoil to work, being wet and heavy. One in a thou'-fall. All right. Leaving an open job you take precautions. Lamp. Planks. Notice given. The lot. Which is what we done, and done careful and according. . . . And this is what we find. All right; we see something's wrong. All right; so I says, 'And where's the bloody lamp?' and I walk up to the edge and look down. And then I seen."

"Exactly what?"

The foreman ground the rag between his hands.

"First go off," he said, "I notice the pipe, laying down there with a lot of the spoil, and then I notice an electric torch—it's there now."

"It's the deceased's," Williams said. "His man recognized it. I thought best to leave it there."

"Good. And then?" Alleyn asked the foreman.

"Well, I noticed all this, like, and—it's funny when you come to think of it—I'm just going to blow my top about this pipe, when I kind of realize I've been looking at something else. Sticking out, they was, at the end, half sunk in mud. His legs. It didn't seem real. Like I said to the chaps: 'Look, what's that?' Daft! Because I seen clear enough what it was."

"I know."

"So we get the truck and go down and clear the pipe and planks out of it. Had to use the crane. The planks are laying there now, where we left them. We slung the pipe up and off him and across to the far bank like. Then we seen more—all there was to see. Sunk, he was. Rammed down, you might say, be the weight. I knew, first go off, he was a goner. Well—the back of his head was enough. But—" The foreman glared resentfully at Noakes. "I don't give a b—— what anyone tells me, you can't leave a thing like that. You got to see if there's anything to be done."

Noakes made a noncommittal noise and looked at Alleyn. "I think you do, you know, Sergeant," Alleyn said, and the foreman, gratified, continued.

"So we got 'im out like you said, sir. It was a very nasty job, what with the depth and the wet and the state he was in. And once out—finish! Gone. No mistake about it. So we give the alarm in the house there and they take a fit of the horrors and fetch the doctor."

"Good," Alleyn said, "couldn't be clearer. Now look here. You can see pretty well where he was lying although, of course, the impression has been trodden out a bit. Unavoidably. Now, the head was about there, I take it, so that he was not directly under the place where the planks had been laid, but at an angle to it. The feet beneath, the head out to the left. The left hand, now. Was it stretched out ahead of him? Like that? With the arm bent? Was the right arm extended—so?"

The foreman and his mates received this with grudging approval. One of the mates said: "Dead right, innit?" and the other: "Near enough." The foreman blew a faint appreciative whistle.

"Well," Alleyn said, "he's clutching a clod of mud and you can see where the fingers dragged down the side of the ditch, can't you? All right. Was one plank—how? Half under him or what?"

"That's right, sir."

Superintendent Williams said: "You can see where the planks were placed all right, before they fell. Clear as mud, and mud's the word in this outfit. The ends near the gate were only just balanced on the edge. Look at the marks where they scraped down the side. Bound to give way as soon as he put his weight on them."

The men broke into an angry expostulation. They'd never left them like that. They'd left them safe: overlapping the bank by a good six inches at each side; a firm bridge.

"Yes," Alleyn said, "you can see that, Williams. There are the old marks. Trodden down but there, undoubtedly."

"Thank you, sir," said the foreman pointedly.

"Now then, let's have a look at this lamp," Alleyn suggested. Using their ladder, they retrieved it from its bed in the ditch, about two feet above the place where the body had lain. It was smothered in mud, but unbroken. The men pointed out an iron stanchion from which it had been suspended. This was uprooted and lying near the edge of the drain.

"The lamp was lit when you knocked off yesterday, was it?"

"Same as the others, and they was still burning, see, when we come on the job this morning."

Alleyn murmured: "Look at this, Fox." He turned the lamp towards Fox, who peered into it.

"Been turned right down," he said under his breath. "Hard down."

"Take charge of it, will you?"

Alleyn rejoined the men. "One more point," he said. "How did you leave the drainpipe yesterday evening? Was it laid out in that gap, end to end with the others?"

"That's right," they said.

"Immediately above the place where the body was found?"

"That's correct, sir."

The foreman looked at his mates and then burst out again with some violence. "And if anyone tries to tell you it could be moved be accident you can tell him he ought to get his head read. Them pipes is main sewer pipes. It takes a crane to shift them, the way we've left them, and only a lever will roll them in. Now! Try it out on one of the others if you don't believe me. Try it. That's all."

"I believe you very readily," Alleyn said. "And I think that's all we need bother you about at the moment. We'll get out a written record of everything you've told us and ask you to call at the Station and look it over. If it's in order, we'll want you to sign it. If it's not, you'll no doubt help us by putting it right. You've acted very properly throughout, as I'm sure Mr. Williams and Sergeant Noakes will be the first to agree."

"There you are," Williams said. "No complaints."

Huffily reassured, the men retired.

"The first thing I'd like to know, Bob," Alleyn said, "is what the devil's been going on round this dump? Look at it. You'd think the whole village had been holding Mayday revels over it. Women in evening shoes, women in brogues. Men in heavy shoes, men in light shoes, and the whole damn' mess overtrodden, of course, by working boots. Most of it went on before the event, *all* of it except the boots, I fancy, but what the hell was it about?"

"Some sort of daft party," Williams said. "Cavorting through the village, they were. We've had complaints. It was up at the Big House: Baynesholme Manor."

"One of Lady Bantling's little frolics," Dr. Elkington observed dryly. "It seems to have ended in a dogfight. I was called out at two-thirty to bandage her husband's hand. They'd broken up by then."

"Can you be talking about Désirée, Lady Bantling?"

"That's the lady. The main object of the party was a treasure hunt, I understand."

"A hideous curse on it," Alleyn said heartily. "We've about as much hope of disentangling anything useful in the way of footprints as you'd get in a wine press. How long did it go on?"

"The noise abated before I went to bed," Dr. Elkington said, "which was at twelve. As I've mentioned, I was dragged out again."

"Well, at least we'll be able to find out if the planks and lantern were untouched until then. In the meantime we'd better go through the hilarious farce of keeping our own boots off the area under investigation. . . . What's this? . . . Wait a jiffy."

He was standing near the end of one of the drainpipes. It lay across a slight depression that looked as if it had been scooped out. From this he drew a piece of blue letter paper. Williams looked over his shoulder.

"Poytry," Williams said disgustedly.

The two lines had been amateurishly typed. Alleyn read them aloud.

If you don't know what to do
Think it over in the loo.

"Elegant, I must say!" Dr. Elkington ejaculated.

"That'll be a clue, no doubt," Fox said and Alleyn gave it to him.

"I wish the rest of the job were as explicit," he remarked.

"What," Williams asked, "do you make of it, Alleyn? Any chance of accident?"

"What do you think yourself?"

"I'd say, none."

"And so would I. Take a look at it. The planks had been dragged forward until the ends were only just supported by the lip of the bank. There's one print, the deceased's by the look of it, on the original traces of the planks before they were moved. It suggests that he came through the gate, where the path is hard and hasn't taken an impression. I think he had his torch in his left hand. He stepped on the trace and then on the planks, which gave under him. I should say he pitched forward as he fell, dropping his torch, and one of the planks pitched back, striking him in the face. That's guesswork, but I think, Elkington, that when he's cleaned up you'll find the nose is broken. As he was face down in the mud, the plank seems a possible explanation. All right. The lantern was suspended from an iron stanchion. The stanchion had been driven into the earth at an angle and overhung the edge between the displaced drainpipe and its neighbour. And, by the way, it seems to have beem jammed in twice: there's a second hole nearby. The lantern would be out of reach for him and he couldn't have grabbed at it. How big is the dog?"

"What's that?" Williams asked, startled.

"Prints that have escaped the boots of the drainlayers suggest a large dog."

"Pixie," said Sergeant Noakes, who had been silent for a considerable time.

"Oh!" said Superintendent Williams disgustedly. "Her."

"It's a dirty great mongrel of a thing, Mr. Alleyn," Noakes offered. "The deceased gentleman called it a boxer. He was in the habit of bringing it out here before he went to bed, which was at one o'clock, regular as clockwork. It's a noisy brute. There have been," Noakes added, sounding a *leitmotif,* "complaints about Pixie."

"Pixie," Alleyn said, "must be an athletic girl. She jumped the ditch. There *are* prints if you can sort them out. But have a look at Cartell's right hand, Elkington, would you?"

Dr. Elkington did so. "There's a certain amount of contusion," he said, "with ridges. And at the edges of the palm, well-defined grooves."

"How about a leather leash, jerked tight?"

"It might well be."

"Now the stanchion, Fox."

Fox leant over from his position on the hard surface of the lane. He carefully lifted and removed the stanchion. Handling it as if it were some fragile *objet d'art,* he said: "There are traces, Mr. Alleyn. Lateral rubbings. Something dragged tight and then pulled away might be the answer."

"So it's at least possible that as Cartell dropped, Pixie jumped the drain. The lead jerked. Pixie entangled herself with the stanchion, pulled it loose, freed herself from it and from the hand that had led her, and made off. The lantern fell in the drain. Might be. Where *is* Pixie, does anyone know?"

"Shall I inquire at the house?" Noakes asked.

"It can wait. All this is the most shameless conjecture, really."

"To me," Williams said, considering it, "it seems likely enough."

"It'll do to go on with. But it doesn't explain," Alleyn said, "why the wick in the lantern's been turned hard off, does it?"

"Is that a fact!" Noakes remarked, primly.

"This stanchion . . ." said Williams, who had been looking at it. "Have you noticed the lower point? You'd expect it to come out of the soil clean, or else dirty all round. But it's dirty on one side and sort of scraped clean on the other."

"You'll go far in the glorious profession of your choice."

"Come off it!" said Williams, who had done part of his training with Alleyn.

"Look at the ground where that great walloping pipe was laid out. That at least is not entirely obliterated by boots. See the scars in the earth on this side? Slanting holes with a scooped depression on the near side."

"What of them?"

"Try it, Fox."

Fox, who was holding the stanchion by its top, laid the pointed end delicately in one of the scars. "Fits," he said. "There's your lever, I reckon."

"If so, the mud on one side was scraped off on the pipe. Wrap it up and lay it by. The flash-and-dabs boys will be here any moment now. We'll have to take casts, Br'er Fox."

Dr. Elkington said: "What's all this about the stanchion?"

"We're wondering if it was used as a lever for the drainpipe. We're not very likely to find anything on the pipe itself, after the rough handling it's been given, but it's worth trying."

He walked to the end of the drain, returned on the far side to the solitary pipe and squatted beside it. Presently he said: "There *are* marks—scrapings—same distance apart, at a guess. I think we'll find they fill the bill."

When he had rejoined the others, he stood for a

moment and surveyed the scene. A capful of wind blew down Green Lane, snatched at a corner of the tarpaulin and caused it to ripple very slightly, as if Mr. Cartell had stirred. Fox attended to it, tucking it under, with a macabre suggestion of coziness.

Alleyn said: "If ever it behooved us to keep open minds about a case it behooves us to do so over this one. My reading, so far, may be worth damn'-all, but such as it is I'll make you a present of it. . . .

"On the surface appearance it looks to me as though this was a premeditated job and was carried out with the minimum of fancywork. Some time before Cartell tried to cross it, the plank bridge was pulled towards the road side of the drain until the further ends rested on the extreme edge. The person who did this then put out the light in the lantern, and hid: very likely by lying down on the hard surface alongside one of the pipes. The victim came out with his dog on a leash. He stepped on the bridge, which collapsed. He was struck in the face by a plank and stunned. The leash bit into his right hand before it was jerked free. The dog jumped the drain, possibly got itself mixed up with the iron stanchion and, if so, probably dislodged the lantern, which fell into the drain. The concealed person came back, used the stanchion as a lever and rolled the drainpipe into the drain. It fell fourteen feet on his victim and killed him. He—Hullo! What's that?"

He leant forward, peering into the ditch: "This looks like something," he sighed. "Down, I fear, into the depths I go."

"I will, sir." Fox offered.

"You keep your great boots out of this," Alleyn rejoined cheerfully.

He placed the foot of the steel ladder near the place where the body was found and climbed down it. The drain sweated dank water and smelt sour and disgusting. From where he stood, on the bottom rung, he pulled out his flashlight.

From above they saw him stoop and reach under the plank that rested against the wall.

When he came up he carried something wrapped in his handkerchief. He knelt and laid his improvised parcel on the ground.

"Look at this," he said and they gathered about him. He unfolded his handkerchief.

On it lay a gold case, very beautifully worked. It had a jewelled clasp and was smeared with slime.

"His?" Williams said.

"Or somebody else's? . . . I wonder."

They stared at it in silence. Alleyn was about to wrap it again when they were startled by a loud, shocking and long-drawn-out howl.

About fifty yards away, sitting in the middle of the lane in an extremely dishevelled condition, with a leash dangling from her collar, was a half-bred boxer bitch, howling lamentably.

"Pixie," said Noakes.

" 2 "

They met with difficulty trying to catch Pixie. If addressed she writhed subserviently, threshed her tail, and whined. If approached she sprang aside, ran a short distance in a craven manner, sat down again, and began alternately to bark and howl.

The five men whistled, stalked, ran and cursed, all to no avail. "She'll rouse the whole bloody village at this rate," Superintendent Williams lamented, and indeed several persons had collected beyond the cars at the road barrier.

Alleyn and Dr. Elkington tried a scissors movement, Noakes and Williams an ill-conceived form of indirect strategy. Fox made himself hot and cross in a laughable attempt to jump upon Pixie's lead and all had come to nothing before they were aware of the presence of a small, exceedingly pale man in an alpaca jacket on the far side of Mr. Period's gate. It was Alfred Belt.

How long he had been there it was impossible to say. He was standing quite still with his well-kept hands on the top of the gate and his gaze directed respectfully at Alleyn.

"If you will allow me, sir," he said. "I think I may be able to secure the dog."

"For God's sake do," Alleyn rejoined.

Alfred whistled. Pixie, with a travesty of canine archness, cocked her head on one side. "Here, girl," Alfred said disgustedly. "Meat." She loped round the top end of the drain and ran along the fence towards him. "You bitch," he said dispassionately as she fawned upon him.

Superintendent Williams, red with his exertions, formally introduced Alfred across the drain. Alfred said: "Good morning, sir. Mr. Period has asked me to present his compliments and to say that if there is anything you require he hopes you will call upon him."

"Thank you," Alleyn rejoined. "I was going to. In about five minutes. Will you tell him?"

"Certainly, sir," Alfred said and withdrew.

Alleyn said to Williams: "When the flash-and-dabs lot turn up, ask them to cover the whole job, will you, Bob? Everything. I'll be in the house if I'm wanted. You know the story and can handle this end of it better than I. I'd be glad if you'd stay in."

It was by virtue of such gestures as these that Alleyn maintained what are known as "good relations" with the county forces. Williams said: "Be pleased to," and filled out his jacket.

Dr. Elkington said: "What about the body?"

"Could you arrange for it to be taken to the nearest

mortuary? Sir James Curtis will do the P.M. and will be hoping to see you. He'll be here by midday."

"I've laid on the ambulance. The mortuary's at Rimble."

"Good. Either Fox or I will look you up at the Station at noon. There's one other thing. What do you make of that?" He walked a few paces up the lane and pointed to a large damp patch on the surface. "There was no rain last night and it's nothing to do with the digging. Looks rather as if a car with a leaky radiator had stood there. Might even have been filled up and overflowed. Damn this hard surface. Yes, look. There's a bit of oil there, too, where the sump might well have dripped. Ah, well, it may not amount to a row of beans. Ready, Fox? Let's go in through the side gate, shall we?"

They fetched a circuitous course round the drain and entered Mr. Period's garden by the side gate. Near the house, Alleyn noticed a standpipe with a detached hose coiled up beside it and a nearby watering can from which the rose had been removed.

"Take a look at this, Br'er Fox," he said and indicated a series of indentations about the size of sixpence leading to and from the standpipe.

"Yes," Fox said. "And the can's been moved and replaced."

"That's right. And who, in this predominantly male household, gardens in stiletto heels? Ah, well! Come on."

They walked round the house to the front door, where Alfred formally admitted them.

"Mr. Period is in the library, sir," he said. "May I take your coat?"

Fox, who, being an innocent snob, always enjoyed the treatment accorded to his senior officer on these occasions, placidly removed his own coat.

"What," Alleyn asked Alfred, "have you done with the dog?"

"Shut her up, sir, in the woodshed. She ought never to have been let loose."

"Quite so. Will you let me have her leash?"

"Sir?"

"The lead. Inspector Fox will pick it up. Will you, Fox? And join us in the library?"

Alfred inclined his head, straightened his arms, turned his closed hands outward from the wrists and preceded Alleyn to the library door.

"Mr. Roderick Alleyn, sir," he announced.

It was perhaps typical of him that he omitted the rank and inserted the Christian name. "Because, after all, Mrs. M," he expounded later on to his colleague, "whatever opinions you and I may form on the subject, class is class and to be treated as such. *In* the Force he may be, and with distinction. *Of* it, he is not."

Mrs. Mitchell put this detestable point of view rather more grossly. "The brother's a baronet," she said. "And childless, at that. I read it in the *News of the World*. 'The Handsome Super,' it was called. Fancy!"

Meanwhile Alleyn was closeted with Mr. Pyke Period, who, in a different key, piped the identical tune.

"My dear Alleyn," he said. "I can't tell you how relieved I am to see you. If anything could lessen the appalling nature of this calamity it would be the assurance that we are in your hands." There followed, inevitably, the news that Mr. Period was acquainted with Alleyn's brother and was also an ardent admirer of Alleyn's wife's paintings. "She won't remember an old backwater buster like me," he said, wanly arch, "but I have had the pleasure of meeting her."

All this was said hurriedly and with an air of great anxiety. Alleyn wondered if Mr. Period's hand was normally as tremulous as it was this morning or his speech as breathless and uneven. As soon as Alleyn decently could, he got the conversation on a more formal basis.

He asked Mr. Period how long Mr. Cartell had been sharing the house, and learned that it was seven weeks. Before that Mr. Cartell had lived in London, where he had been the senior partner of an extremely grand and vintage firm of solicitors, from which position he had retired upon his withdrawal into the country. The family, Mr. Period said, came originally from Gloucestershire—Bloodstone Parva, in the Cotswolds. Having got as far as this he pulled himself up short and, unaccountably, showed great uneasiness.

Alleyn asked him when he had last seen Mr. Cartell.

"Ah—yesterday evening. I dined out. At Baynesholme. Before the party."

"The treasure hunt?"

"You've heard about it? Yes. I saw them start and then I came home. He was in his room, then, walking about and talking to that—his dog. Great heavens!" Mr. Period suddenly exclaimed.

"What is it?"

"Désirée—his—Lady Bantling, you know! And Andrew! They must be told, I suppose. I wonder if Connie has thought of it—but no! No, she would hardly— My dear Alleyn, I beg your pardon, but it has only just struck me." He explained, confusedly, the connection between Baynesholme and Mr. Cartell, and looked distractedly at his watch. "They will be here at any moment. My secretary—a delightful gel—and Andrew, who is to drive her. I suggested an eleven o'clock start as it was to be such a very late party."

By dint of patient questioning, Alleyn got this sorted out. He noticed that Mr. Period kept feeling in his pockets. Then, apparently recollecting himself, he would look about the room. He opened a cigarette box, and when he found it empty ejaculated pettishly.

Alleyn said: "I wonder if you'll let me give you a cigarette and smoke one myself? It's all wrong, of course, for a policeman on duty—" He produced his case.

"My *dear* Alleyn! Thank you. Do. Do. So will I. But I should have offered you one long ago, only with all this upset Alfred hasn't filled the boxes and—it's too tiresome—I've mislaid my case."

"Really? Not lost, I hope."

"I—I hope not," he said hurriedly. "It's all very unfortunate, but never mind." And again he showed great uneasiness.

"It's infuriating to lose a good case," Alleyn remarked. "I did myself, not long ago. It was a rather special and very old one and I regret it."

"So is this," Mr. Period said abruptly. "A cardcase." He seemed to be in two minds whether to go on and then decided against it.

Alleyn said: "When you saw Mr. Cartell last evening was he his usual self? Nothing had happened to upset him at all?"

This question, also, produced a flurried reaction. "Upset? Well—it depends upon what one means by 'upset.' He was certainly rather put out, but it was nothing that could remotely be related . . ." Mr. Period fetched up short and appeared to summon all his resources. When he spoke again it was with very much more reserve and control. "You would not," he said, "ask me a question of that sort, I think, unless you felt that this dreadful affair was not to be resolved by—by a simple explanation."

"Oh," Alleyn said lightly, "we needn't put it as high as that, you know. If he was at all agitated or absent-minded, he might not be as careful as usual when he negotiated the bridge over the ditch. The dog—"

"Ah!" Mr. Period exclaimed. "The dog! Now, why on earth didn't one think of the dog before! It is—she—I assure you, Alleyn, a most powerful and undisciplined dog. At the moment, I am given to understand, particularly so. May she not have taken one of those great plunging leaps of hers, possibly across the drain, and dragged him into it? May she not have done that?"

"She seems, at least, to have taken a great plunging leap."

"There! You see?"

"She would also," Alleyn said, "have had to dislodge a walloping big drainpipe and precipitate it into the ditch."

Mr. Period put his hands over his eyes. "It's so horrible!" he said faintly. "It's so unspeakably horrible." And then, withdrawing his hands, "But may she not have done precisely that very thing?"

"It's—not very likely, I'm afraid."

Mr. Period stared at him. "You don't think it was an accident," he said. "Don't bother to say anything. I can see you don't."

"I'll be very glad if I find reason to change my opinion."

"But why? Why not accident? That dog, now: she *is* dangerous. I've told him so over and over again."

"There are certain appearances: things that don't quite tally. We must clear them up before we can come to any conclusion. There must, of course, be an inquest. And that is why," Alleyn said, cheerfully, "I shall have to ask you any number of questions all of which will sound ridiculous and most of which, I daresay, will turn out to be just that and no more."

It was at this juncture that Fox joined them, his excessively bland demeanour indicating, to Alleyn at least, that he had achieved his object and secured Pixie's leash. The interview continued. Fox, as usual, managed to settle himself behind the subject and to take notes quite openly and yet entirely unnoticed. He had a talent for this sort of thing.

Mr. Period's conversation continued to be jumpy and disjointed, but gradually a fairly comprehensive picture of his ménage emerged. Alleyn heard of Cartell's sister, who was, of course, deeply shocked. "One of those red women who don't normally seem to feel anything except the heat," Mr. Period said oddly. "Never wear gloves. And look, don't you know, as if they never sit on anything but their hats or a shooting-stick. But I assure you she's dreadfully cut up, poor Connie."

Alleyn felt that Mr. Period had invented this definition of Miss Cartell long ago and was so much in the habit of letting fly with it that it had escaped him involuntarily.

"I mustn't be naughty," Mr. Period said unhappily. "Poor Connie!" And looked exquisitely uncomfortable.

"Apart from Miss Cartell and Lady Bantling, who I suppose is in one sense a connection, or an ex-connection, are there any near relations?"

"None that one would call near. It's an old family," Mr. Period said with a pale glance at his ruling passion, "but going—going. Indeed, I fancy he and Connie are the last. Sad."

Alleyn said: "I'm afraid I shall have to ask you for an account of yesterday's activities. I really am very sorry to pester you like this when you've had such a shock, but there it is. *Duty, duty must be done.*"

Mr. Period brightened momentarily at this Gilbertian reference and even dismally hummed the tune, but the next second he was in the doldrums again. He worked backwards through the events of the previous day, starting with his own arrival in the lane, driven by Lady Bantling, at twenty past eleven. The plank bridge over the drain had supported him perfectly: the lamp was alight. As he approached the house he saw Mr.

Cartell at his bedroom window, which was wide open.
Mr. Cartell never, Mr. Period explained, went to bed
before one o'clock, when he took Pixie out, but he
often pottered about his room for hours before he
retired. Alleyn thought he detected a note of petulance
and also of extreme reticence.

"I think," Mr. Period said restlessly, "that Hal must
have heard me coming home. He was at his window.
He seemed—ah—he seemed to be perfectly well."

"Did you speak to him?"

"I—ah—I—ah—I did just call out something after I
came upstairs. He replied . . . I don't remember . . .
However!"

Mr. Period himself, it transpired, had gone to bed,
but not to sleep, as the arrival and departure of treasure hunters in the lane was disturbing. However, the
last couple had gone before midnight and he had dozed
off.

"Did you wake again?"

"That's what's so appalling to think of. I did. At one
o'clock, when he took Pixie out. She made the usual
disturbance, barking and whining. I heard it. I'm afraid
I cursed it. Then it stopped."

"And did you go to sleep again?"

"Yes. Yes, I did. Yes."

"Were you disturbed again?"

Mr. Period opened his mouth and remained agape
for some seconds and then said, "No."

"Sure?"

"Nobody disturbed me," Mr. Period said, and
looked perfectly wretched.

Alleyn took him back through the day. It was with
reluctance that he was brought to admit that Mr. Cartell had entertained his sister and two acquaintances at
luncheon. As an afterthought he remarked that Lady
Bantling and her son, Andrew Bantling, had been there
for drinks.

"Who," Alleyn asked, "were the acquaintances?" He was told, sketchily, about Mary Ralston, Miss Cartell's ward, and her friend, Leonard Leiss. At the Yard, Alleyn was often heard to lament the inadequacy of his memory, an affectation which was tolerantly indulged by his colleagues. His memory was in fact like any other senior detective officer's, very highly trained, and in this instance it at once recalled the paragraph in the *Police Gazette* of some months ago in which the name and *portrait-parlé* of Leonard Leiss had appeared, together with an account of his activities—which were varied and dubious. He had started life in Bermondsey, shown some promise, achieved grammar school status and come under the protection of a benevolent spinster whom he subsequently robbed and deserted. This episode was followed by an association with a flick-knife gang and an interval of luxury spent with a lady of greater wealth than discretion and employment as a chauffeur with forged references. There had been two convictions. *Passes himself off,* the *Police Gazette* had concluded, *as a person of superior social status.*

"Is Mr. Leiss," Alleyn asked, "a young man of about twenty-seven? Dark, of pale complexion, rather too smartly dressed, and wearing a green ring on the signet finger?"

"Oh, dear!" Mr. Period said helplessly. "I suppose Noakes has told you. Yes. Alas, he is!"

After that it was not hard to induce a general lament upon the regrettability of Leonard. Although Sergeant Noakes had in fact not yet reported the affair of the Scorpion sports car, Mr. Period either took it for granted that he had done so or recognized the inevitability of coming round to it before long. He said enough for Alleyn to get a fair idea of what had happened. Leonard, Mr. Period concluded, was a really rather dreadful young person whom it would be the greatest mistake to encourage.

"When I tell you, my dear fellow, that he leant back in his chair at luncheon and positively whistled! Sang even! I promise. And the girl joined in! A terrible fellow. Poor Connie should have sent him packing at the first glance."

"Mr. Cartell thought so too, I daresay?"

"Oh, yes!" said Mr. Period, waving it away. "Yes, indeed. Oh, rather!"

"To your knowledge, had he any enemies? That sounds melodramatic, but had he? Or, to put it another way, do you know of anyone to whom he might have done any damage if he had lived?"

There was a long pause. From the lane came the sound of a car in low gear. Alleyn could see through the window that a canvas screen had been erected. His colleagues, evidently, had arrived.

"I'm just trying to think," said Mr. Period. He turned sheet-white. "Not in the sense you mean. No. Unless—but, no."

"Unless?"

"You see, Alleyn, one does follow you. One does realize the implication."

"Naturally," Alleyn said. "It's perfectly obvious, I'm sure. If a trap was laid for Mr. Cartell last night, I should like to know if there's anyone who might have had some motive in laying it."

"A *booby*-trap, for instance?" He stared at Alleyn, his rather prominent front teeth closed over his under-lip. "Of course I don't know what you've found. I—I—had to go out there and—and identify him; but frankly, it distressed me very much and I didn't notice . . . But—had, for instance, the planks over the ditch—had they been interfered with?"

"Yes," said Alleyn.

"Oh, my God! I see. Well, then: might it not all have been meant for a joke? A very silly, dangerous one, but still no more than a booby-trap? Um? Some of those young people in the treasure hunt. Yes!" Mr. Period ejaculated. "Now, isn't that a possibility? Someone had moved the planks and poor Harold fell, you know, and perhaps he knocked himself out and then, while he was lying unconscious, may not a couple—they hunted in couples—have come along and—and inadvertently dislodged the drainpipe?"

"You try dislodging one of those pipes," Alleyn said. "It could scarcely be done inadvertently, I think."

"Then—then: even done deliberately out of sheer exuberance and not knowing he was there. A prank! One of those silly pranks. They were a high-spirited lot."

"I wonder if you can give me their names?"

As most of them had come from the County, Mr. Period was able to do this. He got up to twenty-four, said he thought that was all, and then boggled.

"Was there somebody else?"

"In point of fact—yes. By a piece of what I can only describe, I'm afraid, as sheer effrontery, the wretched Leiss and that tiresome gel, Mary Ralston, got themselves asked. Désirée is quite too hopelessly good-natured. Now *he*," Mr. Period said quickly, "in my opinion, would certainly be capable of going too far—*capable de tout*. But I shouldn't say that. No. All the same, Alleyn, an accident resulting from some piece of comparatively innocent horseplay would not be as appalling as—as—"

"As murder?"

Mr. Period flung up his hands. "Alas!'" he said. "Yes. Of course, I've no real knowledge of how you go to work, but you've examined the ground, no doubt. One reads of such astonishing deductions. Perhaps I shouldn't ask."

"Why not?" Alleyn said amiably. "The answer's regrettably simple. At the moment, there are no deductions, only circumstances. And in point of fact there's nothing, as far as we've gone, to contradict your theory of a sort of double-barrelled piece of hooliganism. Somebody gets the enchanting idea of rearranging the planks. Somebody else gets the even more amusing idea of dislodging a main sewer pipe. The victim of the earlier *jeu d'esprit,* by an unfortunate coincidence, becomes the victim of the second."

"Of course, if you put it like that . . ."

"Coincidences do happen with unbelievable frequency. I sometimes think they're the occupational hazards of policework. So far, for all we've seen, there's no reason to suppose that Mr. Cartell has not been the victim of one of them. Unless," Alleyn said, "you count this."

He had a very quick, dexterous way of using his hands. With the least possible amount of fuss he had produced, laid upon Mr. Period's writing desk and lightly unfolded from his handkerchief, the gold case with a jewelled clasp. "I'm afraid," he said, "I shall have to keep it for the time being. But can you identify it?"

Mr. Period gave a stifled ejaculation and got to his feet.

At the same moment there was a tap on the door, which at once opened to admit a girl and a tall young man.

"I'm so sorry," Nicola said, "the front door was open and we thought—I'm awfully sorry." She stopped short, catching sight of the gold case lying on the handkerchief. "Oh," she exclaimed. "I *am* glad. Your lovely cigarette case! You've found it!"

"Ah—yes," Mr. Period said with a little gasp. "Yes. It—it would appear so." He pulled himself together. "Nicola, my dear," he said, "may I introduce—"

"But we've met!" Nicola cried. "Often. Haven't we? I was talking about you only yesterday. Bless my soul," she added gaily. "Who, to coin a phrase, would have thought of meeting you?"

"To coin another," Alleyn said mildly, "it's quite coincidence, isn't it? Hullo, Nicola."

" 3 "

"Put it like this," Alleyn said. "I don't say you'll ever have to, but suppose you were asked to swear on oath that the window was shut during the luncheon-Pixie episode, would you do it?"

Nicola said: "I'd have to, wouldn't I? Because it was."

"Not a shadow of doubt?"

"Not onc. Alfred will say the same."

"I dare say."

"I wish I knew what you were up to," Nicola said, staring out into the garden.

"I? I'm on my job."

"Yes, but are you peering into petty larceny or mucking into a—I'm sure I don't know why I'm trying to be facetious—into a murder? Or do they tie in together? Or what?"

"I don't know. No more than you do."

"I suppose," Nicola said with some penetration, "you're not very pleased to find me here."

"Not as enchanted as I would be to find you elsewhere."

"It's funny. Because, before this blew up, I was thinking of Troy. I'm coming in tomorrow evening and I wondered if I could bring a young man with me."

"My dear child, she'll be delighted. Do I detect—"

"No!" Nicola said in a hurry. "You don't detect anything. He paints."

"Ah. Mr. Andrew Bantling?"

"I suppose you spotted the paint under his finger-nail."

"So I did. It reminded me of my wife."

"That sounds human, anyway."

Alleyn said: "Look here, Nicola, we'll have to keep all this on an aseptically impersonal basis, you know. I've got to look into a case that may well involve something that is generally called a serious charge. You, unfortunately, may be a relevant witness. I wish it wasn't like that, but it is. O.K.?"

"Do I have to call you Superintendent?"

"You needn't call me anything. Now, let's press on, shall we? I'm bringing Mr. Fox in to take notes."

"Lor!" Nicola looked at him for a moment and then said: "Yes, O.K. I won't be tiresome. I do see."

"Of course you do."

Fox came in and was introduced.

In great detail Alleyn led her through the events of the past twenty-four hours, and as he did so it seemed to Nicola that she grew physically colder. Her relationship with the Alleyns was something that she had taken for granted. Without realizing that she did so, she had depended upon them, as the young do with established friends, for a sort of anchorage. They were old enough to give her a feeling of security and young enough, she felt, to "understand." She had been free to turn up at their London house when she felt like it and was one of the few people that Alleyn's wife could endure in the studio when she was working. With Alleyn himself, Nicola had progressed by way of a schoolgirl crush, from which she had soon managed to recover, into solid affection. She called him "Le Cid," shortened it into "Cid," and by this time had forgotten the origin of the pun.

Now, here he was, C.I.D. in action, being friendly enough: considerate and impersonal, but she had to face it, quietly panic-striking. She began to see him in headline terms. "Superintendent Alleyn interviews Society Secretary."

"Don't," Alleyn's voice said, "go fussing yourself with unnecessary complications. Be as objective as you can and it'll all pass off very quietly. Where had we got to? Ah, yes. You've arrived. You've started on your job. You're assisting at the pre-luncheon-drinks party. This consists of Mr. Cartell; his sister, Miss Constance Cartell; his former wife, the *soi-disante* Lady Bantling; her present husband, Mr. Bimbo Dodds; her son by her first marriage, Mr. Andrew Bantling; Miss Cartell's adopted niece or what-not, what's she called—Miss Mary or Moppett—what?"

"Ralston, I think."

"That's right. And the Moppett's boyfriend, Mr. Leonard Leiss. And of course, Mr. Period. So we have the piquant situation of a lady with two husbands, a young man with two stepfathers, and a brother and sister with a courtesy niece. How did the party go?"

"Not with a swing," Nicola said.

"Because of the muddled relationships, would you say?"

"No. They seem to take those in their stride."

"Because of what, then?"

"Well—Moppett and Leonard, principally. Leonard really is a monster."

"What sort? Beatnik? Smart-alec? Bounder? Straight-out cad? Or just plain nasty?"

"All except the beatnik. He's as clean as a whistle and smells dreadfully of lilies."

"Not Period's cup of tea. Or, I should have thought, Cartell's."

"Indeed not. He and Moppett were self-invited. Or rather, I think Moppett had bludgeoned poor Miss Cartell into getting them there."

"Why 'poor'?"

"Did I say 'poor'?" Nicola exclaimed, surprised at herself. "I suppose because I sort of felt she was vulnerable."

"Go on."

"Well—she's one of those clumsy women who sound arrogant but probably hoot and roar their way through life to cover up their shyness. I expect she's tried to compensate for her loneliness by pouring all her affection into Moppett. What a hope, poor darling!"

"O wise young judge," Alleyn murmured and Nicola wondered how much he was laughing at her.

"Can you remember," he asked, "any of the conversation?"

"At lunch it was about Pixie and Miss Cartell saying she was a mongrel and Mr. Cartell turning huffy and about a car Leonard had seen in the local garage—I don't remember—"

"We know about the car. What else?"

"Well: about poor Mr. Period's favourite thing: family grandeur and blue blood and *noblesse oblige.* I'm sure he didn't mean to have digs at Leonard and Moppett, but it came over like that. And then Mr. Cartell told a story about someone who cooked a baptismal record to pretend he was blue-blooded when he wasn't, and that didn't exactly ring out like a peal of joybells, although Leonard seemed quite interested. And then there was the Pixie episode and then the cigarette-case thing." She elaborated on these themes.

"Plenty of incident throughout. What about the pre-luncheon party? Young Bantling, for instance? How did he fit in? Did he seem to get on quite well with his senior stepfather?"

Nicola was aware of silence: the silence of Mr. Period's drawing-room, which had been given over to Alleyn. There was the alleged Cotman water colour in its brown paper wrappings. There were the unexceptionable chairs and curtains. Outside the windows was the drive, down which Andrew had walked so angrily, swinging his hat. And upstairs, somewhere, was dead

Mr. Cartell's room, where Andrew's voice had shouted yesterday morning.

"What's the matter?" Alleyn said.

"Nothing. He didn't stay for lunch. He lunched at Baynesholme."

"But he came here, with you, from the station, didn't he?"

"Yes."

"And stayed here until his mother and her husband called for him?"

"Yes. At least—"

"Yes?"

"He went out for a bit. I saw him go down the drive."

"What did he do while he was here?"

"I think he saw Mr. Cartell. Mr. Cartell's his guardian and a trustee for his inheritance as well as his stepfather. And Mr. Period's the other trustee."

"Did you gather that it was a business call?"

"Something of the sort. He talked to both of them."

"About what, do you know?"

Could Nicola hear or did she only feel, the thud of her heart?

"Do you know?" Alleyn repeated.

"Only roughly. He'd tell you himself."

"You think he would?"

"Why not?"

"He told you about it?"

"A bit. But it was—it was sort of confidential. In a way."

"Why are you frightened, Nicola?" Alleyn asked gently.

"I'm not. It's just that . . . well, the whole thing's rather a facer. What's happened. I suppose I've got a bit of a delayed shock or something."

"Yes," Alleyn said. "It might, of course, be that."

He rose and looked down at her from his immoderate height. "As my maiden aunt said to her cat: 'I can accept the urge and I can deal with the outcome: what I cannot endure are these pointless preliminaries!' She ought to have been in the C.I.D."

"What am I supposed to make of that?"

"Don't have kittens before they're hatched. And for pity's sake don't hedge or shuffle: that never did anybody any good. Least of all your young man."

"He is *not* my young man. I only met him yesterday."

"Even so quickly may one catch the plague. Did you stay here last night?"

"No. I was at Baynesholme for a party."

"Not Désirée Bantling's party!" Alleyn ejaculated.

"Yes, but it wasn't the sort you mean. It was a lovely party," said Nicola, looking mistily at him. She described it.

"Any unforeseen incidents?"

"Only Moppett and Leonard, who practically gatecrashed. And Pixie, of course."

"What? What about Pixie?"

Nicola told him. "Pixie," she added, "bit Bimbo. He had to go and have his hand bandaged."

"You wouldn't," Alleyn asked, "know what time it was when Pixie staged this show?"

"Yes, I would," Nicola said promptly and blushed. "It was a little after one o'clock."

"How do you know?"

"We got back at half-past twelve from the treasure hunt. It was not much more than half an hour after that."

"We?"

"Andrew and I. We hunted in pairs."

"I thought you said you all had to be in by midnight?"

"All right. Yes, we were meant to. But Andrew

thought the treasure hunt was pretty tiresome, so we talked instead. He told me about his painting and somehow we didn't notice."

Nicola looked squarely at Alleyn. "It couldn't matter less," she said, "but I would like to mention that I did *not* have a casual affair with Andrew. We talked—and talked . . ."

Her voice faded on an indeterminate note. She was back at the end of Mr. Period's lane, in Andrew's draughty car, tucked up in Andrew's old duffel coat that smelt of paint. The tips of their cigarettes glowed and waned. Every now and then a treasure hunter's car would go hooting past and they would see the occupants get out and poke about the drainpipes and heaps of spoil, flicking their torches and giggling. And Andrew talked—and didn't initiate any of the usual driver's seat techniques but was nevertheless very close to her. And the moon had gone down and the stars were bright and everything in the world seemed brand-new and shining. She gave Alleyn the factual details of this experience.

"Do you remember," he asked, "how many cars stopped by the drain or who any of the people were?"

"Not really. They were all new to me: lots of Nigels and Michaels and Sarahs and Davids and Gileses."

"You could see them fairly clearly?"

"Fairly. There was a hurricane lantern shining on two planks across the ditch and they all had torches."

"Any of them walk across the planks?"

"I think most of them. But the clue was under one of the drainpipes on the road side of the ditch. We'd see them find it and giggle over it and put it back and then go zooming off."

"Anyone touch the planks? Look under the ends for the clue?"

"I don't think so." Nicola hesitated and then said: "I

remember Leonard and Moppett. They were the last, and they hadn't got a torch. He crossed the plank and stooped over as if he was looking in the ditch. I got the impression that they stared at us. There was something, I don't know what, kind of furtive about him. I can see him now," Nicola said, surprised at the vivid memory. "I think he had his hand inside his overcoat. The lamplight was on him. He turned his back to us. He stooped and straightened up. Then he recrossed the bridge and found the clue. They looked at it by the light of the lantern and he put it back and they drove away."

"Was he wearing gloves?"

"Yes, he was. Light-coloured ones. Tight-fitting, wash leather, I should think: a bit too svelte—like everything else about Leonard."

"Anything more?"

"No. At least—well, they didn't sort of talk and laugh like the others. I don't suppose any of this matters."

"Don't you, indeed? And then, you good, observant child?"

"Well, Andrew said: 'Funny how ghastly they look even at this distance!' And I said: 'Like—' No, it doesn't matter."

"Like what?"

" 'Like Grand Opera assassins' was what I said, but it was a silly remark. Actually, they looked more like sneak thieves, but I can't tell you why. It's nothing."

"And then?"

"Well, they were the last couple. You see, Andrew kept count, vaguely, because he thought it would be all right to continue our conversation as long as there were still hunters to come. But, before them, Lady Bantling and Mr. Period came past. She was driving him home. She stopped the car by the planks and I fancy she called out to a hunting couple that were just leaving.

Mr. Period got out and said good night with his hat off, looking rather touching, poor sweet, and crossed the planks and went in by his side gate. And she turned the car." Nicola stopped.

"What is it?"

"Well, you see, I—I don't want—"

"All right. Don't bother to tell me. You're afraid of putting ideas into my head. How can I persuade you, Nicola, that it's only by a process of elimination that I can get anywhere with this case? Incidents that look as fishy as hell to you may well turn out to be the means of clearing the very character you're fussing about."

"May they?"

"Now, look here. An old boy of, as far as we know, exemplary character, has been brutally and cunningly murdered. You think you can't bring yourself to say anything that might lead to an arrest and its possible consequences. I understand and sympathize. But, my poor girl, will you consider for a moment the possible consequences of withholding information? They can be disastrous. They have led to terrible miscarriages of justice. You see, Nicola, the beastly truth is that if you are involved, however accidentally, in a crime of this sort, you can't avoid responsibility."

"I'm sorry. I suppose you're right. But in this instance—about Lady Bantling, I mean—it's nothing. It'll sound disproportionate."

"So will lots of other things that turn out to be of no consequence. Come on. What happened? What did she do?"

Nicola, it transpired, had a gift for reportage. She gave a clear account of what had happened. Alleyn could see the car turn in the lane and stop. After a pause the driver got out, her flaming hair haloed momentarily in the light of the lantern as she crossed the planks, walking carefully in her high heels. She had gone through Mr. Period's garden gate and disappeared. There had been a light in an upper window. Andrew Bantling had said: "Hullo, what's my incalculable mama up to?" They had heard quite distinctly the spatter of pebbles against the upper window. A figure in a dark gown had opened it, "Great grief!" Andrew had ejaculated. "That's Harold! She's doing a balcony scene in reverse! She must be tight."

And indeed, Lady Bantling had, surprisingly, quoted from the play. "What light," she had shouted, "from yonder window breaks?" and Mr. Cartell had replied irritably, "Good God, Désirée, what are you doing down there?"

Her next remark was in a lower tone and they had only caught the word "warpath," to which he had rejoined: "Utter nonsense!"

"And then," Nicola told Alleyn, "another light popped up and another window opened and Mr. Period looked out. It was like a Punch-and-Judy show. He said something rather plaintive that sounded like: 'Is anything the matter?' and Lady Bantling shouted: 'Not a thing, go to bed, darling,' and he said: 'Well, really! How odd!' and pulled down his blind. And then Mr. Cartell said something inaudible and Lady Bantling quite yelled: 'Ha! Ha! You jolly well watch your step!' And then *he* pulled *his* blind down and we saw her come out, cross the ditch, and get into the car. She drove past us and leant out of the driving window and said: 'That was a tuppeny one. Don't be too late, darlings!' and went on. And Andrew said he wished he knew what the hell she was up to and soon after that we went back to the party. Leonard and Moppett had arrived."

"Was Désirée Bantling, in fact, tight?"

"It's hard to say. She was perfectly in order afterwards and acted with the greatest expedition, I must say, in the Pixie affair. She's obviously," Nicola said, "a law unto herself."

"I believe you. You've drifted into rather exotic and dubious waters, haven't you?"

"It was all right," Nicola said quickly. "And Andrew's not a bit exotic or dubious. He's a quiet character. Honestly. You'll see."

"Yes," Alleyn said. "I'll see. Thank you, Nicola." Upon which the door of Mr. Period's drawing-room burst open and Andrew, scarlet in the face, stormed in.

"Look here!" he shouted. "What the hell goes on? Are you grilling my girl?"

" 4 "

Alleyn, with one eyebrow cocked at Nicola, was crisp with Andrew. Nicola herself, struggling between exasperation and a maddening tendency to giggle, invited Andrew not to be an ass and he calmed down and presently apologized.

"I'm inclined to be quick-tempered," he said with an air of self-discovery and an anxious glance at Nicola.

She cast her eyes up and, on Alleyn's suggestion, left Andrew with him and went to the study. There she found Mr. Period in a dreadful state of perturbation, writing a letter.

"About poor old Hal," he explained distractedly. "To his partner. One scarcely knows what to say."

He implored Nicola to stay, and as she still had a mass of unassembled notes to attend to, she set to work on them in a strange condition of emotional uncertainty.

Alleyn had little difficulty with Andrew Bantling. He readily outlined his own problems, telling Alleyn about the Grantham Gallery and how Mr. Cartell had refused to let him anticipate his inheritance. He also confirmed Nicola's account of their vigil in the car. "You don't," he said, "want to take any notice of my mama. She was probably a thought high. It would amuse her to bait Harold. She always does that sort of thing."

"She was annoyed with him, I take it?"

"Well, of course she was. Livid. We both were."

"Mr. Bantling," Alleyn said, "your stepfather has been murdered."

"So I feared," Andrew rejoined. "Beastly, isn't it? I can't get used to the idea at all."

"A trap was laid for him and when, literally, he fell into it, his murderer lowered an eight-hundred-pound drainpipe on him. It crushed his skull and drove him, face down, into the mud."

The colour drained out of Andrew's cheeks. "All right," he said. "You needn't go on. It's loathsome. It's too grotesque to think about."

"I'm afraid we have to think about it. That's all for the moment. Thank you."

"Well, yes. All right, I see. Thank you." Andrew fidgeted with his tie and then said: "Look: I daresay you think I'm being pretty callous about all this, but the fact is I just can't assimilate it. It's so unreal and beastly."

"Murder is beastly. Unfortunately, it's not unreal."

"So it seems. Is it in order for me to go up to London? I'm meant to be on guard tomorrow. As a matter of fact I had thought of going up on business."

"Important business?"

"Well—to me. I wanted to ask them to give me a few days' grace over the Gallery." He stared at Alleyn. "I suppose this will make a difference," he said. "I hadn't thought of that."

"And now you have thought of it . . . ?"

"I don't know," Andrew said slowly. "It seems a bit low to think of it at all. I'd like to talk it over with

Nicola. As a matter of fact—" He looked sideways at Alleyn. "I rather thought of coming back and then going up with her. After I've telephoned my mama, I suppose. I can't imagine what she'll make of all this, I must say."

"Where are you going to be on guard?"

"The Tower," Andrew said dismally.

"All right. We'll get in touch if we want you."

Leaving Andrew where he was, Alleyn had a discussion with Fox and Williams in Mr. Period's garden, and checked the story of the cigarette case with Alfred. Then he crossed the Green to interview Miss Cartell.

She received him in her den. He found it a depressing room. Everything seemed to be the colour of mud. . . . Faded snapshots of meets, of foxhounds and of other canines covered the walls. On the desk, which was a shambles, were several framed photographs of a cagey-looking girl whom he supposed to be Moppett. The room smelt of dog, damp tweed and raw liver, this last being explained by a dish labeled FIDO in which a Pekingese was noisily snuffling. It broke off to bare its needlelike teeth at Alleyn and make the noise of a toy kettledrum.

Miss Cartell sat with her hands on her knees, staring dolefully at him. Her left thumb was decorated with dirty, bloodstained cotton wool and stamp paper. She had evidently been crying.

"It's pretty ghastly," she said. "Poor old Boysie! I can't take it in. He was a bit of an old maid, but a brother's a brother. We didn't see eye-to-eye over a lot of things, but still . . ."

Alleyn was visited by the fleeting wish that he could run into somebody who at least pretended to have liked Mr. Cartell.

"When," he asked her, "did you last see him?"

"I don't know. Yes, I do. Last evening. He came over here with that ghastly bitch. It upset Li-chi.

They're very highly strung animals, Pekes. He's still nervous. Eat up, my poppet," said Miss Cartell to the Pekingese. "Lovely livvy!"

She poked her finger temptingly in the raw liver.

"Eat up," she said and wiped her finger on the Pekingese. Alleyn noticed that her hand was unsteady.

"Was it just a casual, friendly visit?" he asked.

Miss Cartell's rather prominent blue eyes, slightly bloodshot, seemed to film over.

"He was taking the bitch for a walk," she said, after a pause. "Brought it into the house, like a fool, and of course Li became hysterical and bit me, poor little chap. I've fixed it up with girth-gall stuff," she added, "it smells a bit, but it's good."

"Did Mr. Cartell meet anybody else during his call, do you remember?"

With a manner that was at once furtive and anxious she said: "Not that I know. I mean I didn't see anything." She might have been a great elderly schoolgirl caught on the hop. "He was here when I came in," she added. "I don't know *who* he'd seen."

"Miss Cartell," Alleyn said, "I'm anxious to find out if your brother had any enemies. I expect that sounds rather melodramatic, but I'm afraid it's unavoidable. Is there, do you know, anyone who had cause, for any reason, however trivial, to dislike or fear him?"

She waited much too long before she said: "No one in particular," and then after a pause: "He wasn't awfully popular, I suppose. I mean he didn't make friends with people all that easily." She reached down her blunt ill-kept hand to the Pekingese and fondled it. "He was a dry old stick," she said. "You know. Typical solicitor: I used to tell him he had ink instead of blood in his veins."

She broke into one of her ungainly laughs and blew her nose on a man's handkerchief.

"There was a luncheon party," Alleyn said, "wasn't there? Yesterday, at Mr. Pyke Period's house?"

Instead of answering him she suddenly blurted out: "But I thought it was an accident! The way they told me, it sounded like an accident."

"Who told you?"

"P.P." she said. "Alfred told him and he told me. He made it sound like an accident."

"The odds against," Alleyn said, "are considerable."

"Why?"

Everything about her was dull: her face, her manner, her voice. He wondered if she was really attending to him.

"Because," he said, "accident would imply at least two lots of people behaving independently like dangerous hoodlums at the same spot and with different objectives."

"I don't follow that," said Miss Cartell.

"Never mind. Just tell me about the luncheon party. There were you and your adopted niece and Miss Nicola Maitland-Mayne and Mr. Leonard Leiss. And of course, your brother and Mr. Period. Is that right?"

"That's right."

"What did you talk about?"

Nicola had given him a pretty full account of the luncheon party. Miss Cartell was much less explicit. She described the Pixie incident with one or two dismal hoots of retrospective laughter and she dwelt, disjointedly, upon Mr. Period's references to blue blood and polite behaviour. She was clearly very ill-at-ease.

"He's got a bee in his bonnet over that sort of thing," she said. "My brother ragged him about it, and he got jolly ratty. You could see. Can't take a joke."

"What sort of joke?" Alleyn ventured.

"Well—I dunno. Some story about a baptismal register in a vestry. I didn't listen."

Alleyn asked her about the cigarette case and she at once exhibited all the classic signs of a clumsy and unaccustomed liar. She changed colour, avoided his glance and again fondled the unenthusiastic Pekingese.

"I didn't notice anything about that," she said. "He'd *got* the case. I didn't know he'd lost it. He's an old fuss-pot anyway." The colour started out in blotches on her flattish cheeks. "He probably lost it himself," she said, "muddling about."

Alleyn said: "Miss Cartell, I'm sorry to badger you when you've had such a shock, but I'm sure you want to get this wretched business cleared up, don't you?"

"Don't know," she countered. "Not if it's going to lead to a lot of unpleasantness. Won't bring poor old Boysie back, will it?"

Alleyn disregarded this. "Your adopted niece and a friend of hers, called Mr. Leiss, were at the luncheon, weren't they?"

"Yes," she said, staring at him. She seemed to be in two minds whether to go on. Then she said: "You don't want to pay any attention to what P.P. says about them. He's out of touch with the young. Expects them to behave like his generation: and a lot of pie-faced little humbugs *they* were, if you like."

"Was there some talk of Mr. Leiss buying a car?"

She bent over the dog. "That's enough," she said to it. "You've had enough." And then to Alleyn: "It all petered out. He didn't buy it."

The door opened and her Austrian maid came in with a letter.

"From Mr. Period, please," she said. "The man left it."

Miss Cartell seemed unwilling to take the letter. The maid put it on the desk at her elbow.

"All right, Trudi," Miss Cartell mumbled. "Thank you," and the maid went out.

"Pay no attention to me," Alleyn said.

"It'll wait."

"Don't you think, perhaps, you should look at it?"

She opened the letter unhandily, and as she read it turned white to the lips.

"What is it?" he asked. "Miss Cartell, what's the matter?"

The letter was still quivering in her hands.

"He must be mad," she said. "Mad'!'

"May I see it?"

She seemed to consider this, but in an aimless sort of way as if she only gave him half her attention. When he took the sheet of paper from her fingers she suffered him to do so as if they were inanimate.

Alleyn read the letter.

MY DEAR CONNIE:

What can I say? Only that you have lost a devoted brother and I a very dear old friend. I know so well, believe me, so very well, what a shock this has been for you and how bravely you will be taking it. If it is not an impertinence in an old friend to do so, may I offer you these few simple lines written by my dear and so Victorian Duchess of Rampton? They are none the worse, I hope, for their unblushing sentimentality.

So must it be, dear heart, I'll not repine
For while I live the Memory is Mine.

I should like to think that we know each other well enough for you to believe me when I say that I hope you won't dream of answering this all-too-inadequate attempt to tell you how sorry I am.

Yours sincerely,

PERCIVAL PYKE PERIOD

Alleyn folded the paper and looked at Miss Cartell. "But why," he said, "do you say that? Why do you say he must be mad?"

She waited so long, gaping at him like a fish, that he thought she would never answer. Then she made a fumbling inelegant gesture towards the letter.

"Because he must be," she said. "Because it's all happening twice. Because he's written it before. The lot. Just the same."

"You mean—? But when?"

"This morning," Connie said and began rooting in the litter on her desk. "Before breakfast. Before I knew."

She drew in her breath with a whistling noise. "Before *everybody* knew," she said. *"Before they had found him."*

She stared at Alleyn, nodding her head and holding out a sheet of letter paper.

"See for yourself," she said miserably. "Before they had found him."

Alleyn looked at the two letters. Except in a few small details they were, indeed, exactly the same.

CHAPTER FIVE

Postscript to a Party

Connie raised no objections to Alleyn's keeping the letters, and with them both in his pocket he asked if he might see Miss Ralston and Mr. Leiss. She said that they were still asleep in their rooms and added with a slight hint of gratification that they had attended the Baynesholme festivities.

"One of Désirée Bantling's dotty parties," she said. "They go on till all hours. Moppett left a note asking not to be roused."

"It's now one o'clok," Alleyn said, "and I'm afraid I shall have to disturb Mr. Leiss."

He thought she was going to protest, but at that moment the Pekingese set up a petulant demonstration, scratching at the door and raising a crescendo of imperative yaps.

"Clever boy!" Connie said distractedly. "I'm coming!" She went to the door. "I'll have to see to this," she said, "in the garden."

"Of course," Alleyn agreed. He followed them into the hall and saw them out through the front door. Once in the garden the Pekingese bolted for a newly raked flower-bed.

"Oh, no!" Connie ejaculated. "After lunch," she shouted as she hastened in pursuit of her pet. "Come back later."

The Pekingese tore round a corner of the house and she followed it.

Alleyn re-entered the house and went quickly upstairs.

On the landing he encountered Trudi, the maid, who showed him the visitors' rooms. They were on two sides of a passage.

"Mr. Leiss?" Alleyn asked.

A glint of feminine awareness momentarily transfigured Trudi's not very expressive face.

"He is sleeping," she said. "I looked at him. He sleeps like a god."

"We'll see what he wakes like," Alleyn said, tipping her rather handsomely. "Thank you, Trudi."

He tapped smartly on the door and went in.

The room was masked from its entrance by an old-fashioned scrap screen. Behind this a languid, indefinably Cockney voice said: "Come in."

Mr. Leiss was awake but Alleyn thought he saw what Trudi meant.

The violet silk pajama jacket was open, the torso bronzed, smooth and rather shiny as well as hirsute. A platinum chain lay on the chest. The glistening hair was slightly disarranged and the large brown eyes were open. When they lighted upon Alleyn they narrowed. There was a slight convulsive movement under the bedclothes. The room smelt dreadfully of some indefinable unguent.

"Mr. Leiss?" Alleyn said. "I'm sorry to disturb you. I am a police officer."

A very old familiar look started up in Leonard's face: a look of impertinence, cageyness, conceit and fear. It was there as if it had been jerked up from within and in a moment it was gone.

"I don't quite follow you," Leonard said. Something had gone amiss with his voice. He cleared his throat and recovered. "Is anything wrong?" he asked.

He raised himself on his elbow, plumped up his pillows and lay back on them. He reached out languidly for a cigarette case and lighter on his bedside table. The ashtray was already overloaded.

"How can I help you?" he said and lit a cigarette. He inhaled deeply and blew out a thin vapour.

"You can help me," Alleyn said, "by answering one or two questions about your movements since you arrived at Little Codling yesterday morning."

Leonard raised his eyebrows and exhaled a drift of vapour. "And just why," he asked easily, "should I do that small thing?"

"For reasons," Alleyn said, "that will explain themselves in due course. First of all, there's the matter of an attempted car purchase. You gave Mr. Pyke Period and Mr. Cartell and Miss Cartell as references. They considered you had no authority to do so. I suggest," Alleyn went on, "that you don't offer the usual unconvincing explanations. They really won't do. Fortunately for the other persons involved, the deal collapsed; and, apart from adding to your record, the incident has only one point of interest: it made Mr. Cartell very angry." He stopped and looked hard at Leonard. "Didn't it?" he asked.

"Look," Leonard drawled, "do me a favour and get the hell out of this, will you?"

"Next," Alleyn went on, "there's the business of Mr. Period's cigarette case."

It was obvious that Leonard was prepared for this. He went at once into an elaborate pantomime of turning up his eyes, wagging his head and waving his fingers. "No, honestly," he ejaculated. "It's *too* much. Not again!"

"Oh?" Alleyn mildly remarked. "Again? Who's been tackling you about Mr. Period's cigarette case? Mr. Cartell?"

Leonard took his time. "I don't," he said at last,

"like your tone. I resent it, in fact." He looked at Alleyn through half-closed eyes and seemed to come to a decision. "Pardon me," he added, "if I appear abrupt. As a matter of fact, we had a latish party up at Baynesholme. Quite a show. Her ladyship certainly knows how to turn it on."

Alleyn caught himself wondering what on earth in charity and forbearance could be said for Leonard Leiss. It was an unprofessional attitude and he abandoned it.

"Mr. Cartell spoke to you about the cigarette case," he said, taking a sizable chance, "when he called here yesterday evening."

"Who—" Leonard began and pulled himself together. "Look," he said, "have you been talking to other people?"

"Oh, yes, several."

"To him?" Leonard demanded. "To Cartell?"

There was a long pause.

"No," Alleyn said. "Not to him."

"Then who—Here!" Leonard ejaculated. "There's something funny about all this. What is it?"

"I'll answer that one," Alleyn said, "when you tell me what you did with Mr. Period's cigarette case. Now don't," he went on, raising a finger, "say you don't know anything about it. I've seen the dining-room window. It can't be opened from the outside. It was shut during luncheon. You and Miss Ralston examined the case by the window and left it on the sill. No one else was near the window. When the man came in to clear, the window was open and the case had gone."

"So he says."

"So he says, and I believe him."

"Pardon me if I seem to be teaching you your job," Leonard said, "but if I was going to pinch this dreary old bit of tat, why would I open the window? Why not put it in my pocket there and then?"

"Because you would then quite obviously be the thief, Mr. Leiss. If you or Miss Ralston left it on the sill and returned by way of the garden path—"

"How the hell—" Leonard began and then changed his mind. "I don't accept that," he said. "I resent it, in fact."

"Did you smoke any of Mr. Period's cigarettes?"

"Only one, thank you very much. Turkish muck."

"Did Miss Ralston?"

"Same story. Now, look," Leonard began with a sort of spurious candour. "There's such a thing as collusion, isn't there? We left this morsel of antiquery on the sill. All right. This man—Alfred Whathaveyou—opens the window. The workmen in the lane get the office from him and it's all as sweet as kiss-your-hand."

"And would you suggest that we search the men in the lane?"

"Why not? Do no harm, would it?"

"We might even catch them handing the case round after elevenses?"

"That's right," Leonard said coolly. "You might at that. Or, they might have cached it on the spot. You can search this room, or me or my car or my girlfriend. Only too pleased. The innocent don't have anything to hide, do they?" asked Leonard.

"Nor do the guilty, when they've dumped the evidence."

Leonard ran the tip of his tongue over his lips. "Fair enough," he said. "So what?"

"Mr. Leiss," Alleyn said, "the cigarette case has been found."

A second flickered past before Leonard, in a tone of righteous astonishment said: "Found! Well, I ask you! Found! So why come at me? Where?"

"In my opinion, exactly where you dropped it. Down the drain."

The door was thrust open. On the far side of the

screen a feminine voice said: "Sorry, darling, but you'll have to rouse up." The door was shut. "We *are* in a spot of bother," the voice continued as its owner came round the screen. "Old Cartell, dead as a doornail and down the drain!"

" 2 "

When Moppett saw Alleyn she clapped her hands to her mouth and eyed him over the top.

"I'm terribly sorry," she said. "Auntie Con thought you'd gone."

She was a dishevelled figure, half saved by her youth and held together in a négligé that was as unfresh as it was elaborate. "Isn't it frightful?" she said. "Poor Uncle Hal! I can't believe it!"

Either she was less perturbed than Leonard or several times tougher. He had turned a very ill colour and had jerked cigarette ash across his chest.

"What the hell are you talking about?" he said.

"Didn't you *know?*" Moppett exclaimed, and then to Alleyn, "Haven't you *told* him?"

"Miss Ralston," Alleyn said, "you have saved me the trouble. It is Miss Ralston, isn't it?"

"That's right. Sorry," Moppett went on after a moment, "if I'm interupting something. I'll sweep myself out, shall I? See you, ducks," she added in Cockney to Leonard.

"Don't go, if you please," said Alleyn. "You may be able to help us. Can you tell me where you and Mr. Leiss lost Mr. Period's cigarette case?"

"No, she can't," Leonard intervened. "Because we didn't. We never had it. We don't know anything about it."

Moppett opened her eyes very wide and her mouth slightly. She turned in fairly convincing bewilderment from Leonard to Alleyn.

"I don't understand," she said. "P.P.'s cigarette case? Do you mean the old one he showed us when we lunched with him?"

"Yes," Alleyn agreed. "That's the one I mean."

"Lenny, darling, what did happen to it, do you remember? I know! We left it on the window sill. Didn't we? In the dining-room?"

"O.K., O.K., like I've been telling the Chief Godalmighty High Commissioner," Leonard said and behind his alarm, his fluctuating style and his near-Americanisms, there flashed up an unrepentant barrow-boy. "So now it's been found. So what?"

"It's been found," Alleyn said, "in the open drain a few inches from Mr. Cartell's body."

Leonard seemed to retreat into himself. It was as if he shortened and compressed his defenses.

"I don't know what you're talking about," he said. He shot a glance at Moppett. "That's a very nasty suggestion, isn't it? I don't get the picture."

"The picture will emerge in due course. A minute or two ago," Alleyn said, "you told me I was welcome to search this room. Do you hold to that?"

Leonard went through the pantomime of inspecting his fingernails but gave it up on finding his hands were unsteady.

"Naturally," he murmured. "Like I said. Nothing to hide."

"Good. Please don't go, Miss Ralston," Alleyn continued as Moppett showed some sign of doing so. "I shan't be long."

He had moved over to the wardrobe and opened the door when he felt a touch on his arm. He turned and there was Moppett, smelling of scent, hair and bed, gazing into his face, unmistakably palpitating.

"I won't go, of course," she said opening her eyes very wide, "if you don't want me to, but you *can* see, can't you, that I'm not actually dressed for the prevailing climate? It's a trifle chilly, this morning, isn't it?"

"I'm sure Mr. Leiss will lend you his dressing-gown."

It was a brocade and velvet affair and lay across the foot of the bed. She put it on.

"Give us a fag, ducks," she said to Leonard.

"Help yourself."

She reached for his case. "It's not one of those . . . ?" she began and then stopped short. "Fanks, ducks," she said and lit a cigarette, lounging across the bed.

The room grew redolent of Virginian tobacco.

The wardrobe doors were lined with looking-glass. In them Alleyn caught a momentary glimpse of Moppett leaning urgently towards Leonard and of Leonard baring his teeth at her. He mouthed something and closed his hand over her wrist. The cigarette quivered between her fingers. Leonard turned his head as Alleyn moved the door and their images swung out of sight.

Alleyn's fingers slid into the pockets of Leonard's checked suit, dinner suit and camel's-hair overcoat. They discovered three greasy combs, a pair of wash-leather gloves, a membership card from a Soho club called La Hacienda, a handkerchief, loose change, a pocketbook and finally, in the evening trousers and the overcoat, the object of their search: strands of cigarette tobacco. He withdrew a thread and sniffed at it. Turkish. The hinges of Mr. Period's case, he had noticed, were a bit loose.

He came out from behind the wardrobe door with the garments in question over his arm. Moppett, who now had her feet up, exclaimed with a fair show of gaitey: "Look, Face, he's going to valet you."

Alleyn said: "I'd like to borrow these things for the moment. I'll give you a receipt, of course."

"'Like hell you will," Leonard ejaculated.

"If you object, I can apply for a search warrant."

"Darling, don't be bloody-minded," Moppett said. "After all, what *does* it matter?"

"It's the principle of the thing," Leonard mumbled through bleached lips. "That's what I object to. People break in without a word of warning and start talking about bodies and—and—"

"And false pretenses. And attempted fraud. And theft," Alleyn put in. "As you say, it's the principal of the thing. May I borrow these garments?"

"O.K., O.K., O.K."

"Thank you."

Alleyn laid the overcoat and dinner suit across a chair and then went methodically through a suitcase and the drawers of a tallboy: there, wrapped in a sock, he came upon a flick-knife. He turned, with it in his hand, and found Leonard staring at him.

"This," Alleyn said, "is illegal. Where did you get it?"

"I picked it up," Leonard said, "in the street. Illegal, is it? Fancy."

"I shall take care of it."

Leonard whispered something to Moppett, who laughed immoderately and said: "Oh, Lord!" in a manner that contrived to be disproportionately offensive.

Alleyn then sat at a small desk in a corner of the room. He removed Leonard's pocketbook from his dinner jacket and examined the contents, which embraced five pounds in notes and a photograph of Miss Ralston in the nude. They say that nothing shocks a police officer, but Alleyn found himself scandalized. He listed the contents of the pocketbook and wrote a receipt for them, which he handed, with the pocketbook, to Leonard.

"'I don't expect to be long over this," he said. "In the meantime I should like a word with you, if you please, Miss Ralston."

"What for?" Leonard interposed quickly, and to Moppett: "You don't have to talk to him."

"Darling," Moppett said. "Manners! And I'll have you know I'm simply dying to talk to the—Inspector, is it? Or Super? I'm sure it's Super. Do we withdraw?"

She was stretched across the foot of the bed with her chin in her hands: a "lost girl," Alleyn thought, adopting the Victorian phrase, if ever I saw one.

He walked over to the window and was rewarded by the sight of Inspector Fox seated in a police car in Miss Cartell's drive. He looked up. Alleyn made a face at him and crooked a finger. Fox began to climb out of the car.

"If you don't mind," Alleyn said to Moppett, "we'll move into the passage."

"Thrilled to oblige," Moppett said. Drawing Leonard's gown tightly about her she walked round the screen and out of the door.

Alleyn turned to Leonard, "I shall have to ask you," he said, "to stay here for the time being."

"It's not convenient."

"Nevertheless you will be well advised to stay. What is your address in London?"

"76 Castlereagh Walk S.W. 14. Though why—"

"If you return there," Alleyn said, "you will be kept under observation. Take your choice."

He followed Moppett into the passage. He found her arranging her back against the wall and her cigarette in the corner of her mouth. Alleyn could hear Mr. Fox's bass voice rumbling downstairs.

"What can I do for you, Super?" Moppett asked with the slight smile of the film underworldling.

"You can stop being an ass," he rejoined tartly. "I don't know why I waste time telling you this, but if you don't you may find yourself in serious trouble. Think that one out, if you can, and stop smirking at me,"

Alleyn said, rounding off what was possibly the most professional speech of his career.

"Oi!" said Moppett. "Who's in a naughty rage?"

Alleyn heard Miss Cartell's edgeless voice directing Mr. Fox upstairs. He looked over the bannister and saw her upturned face, blunt, red and vulnerable. His distaste for Moppett was exacerbated. There she stood, conceited, shifty and complacent as they come, without scruple or compassion. And there belowstairs was her guardian, wide open to anything this detestable girl liked to hand out to her.

Fox could be heard saying in a comfortable voice: "Thank you very much, Miss Cartell. I'll find my own way."

"More Force?" Moppett remarked. "Delicious!"

"This is Inspector Fox," Alleyn said as his colleague appeared. He handed Leonard's dinner suit and overcoat to Fox. "General routine check," he said, "and I'd like you to witness something I'm going to say to Miss Mary Ralston."

"Good afternoon, Miss Ralston," Fox said pleasantly. He hung Leonard's garments over the bannister and produced his notebook. The half-smile did not leave Moppett's face but seemed, rather, to remain there by a sort of oversight.

"Understand this," Alleyn continued, speaking to Moppett. "We are investigating a capital crime and I have, I believe, proof that last night the cigarette case in question was in the possession of that unspeakable young man of yours. It was found by Mr. Cartell's body and Mr. Cartell has been murdered."

"Murdered!" she ejaculated. "He *hasn't!*" And then she went very white round the mouth. "I can't believe you," she said. "People like him don't get murdered. Why?"

"For one of the familiar motives," Alleyn said. "For knowing something damaging about someone else. Or threatening to take action against somebody. Financial troubles. Might be anything."

"Auntie Con said it was an accident."

"I daresay she didn't want to upset you."

"Bloody dumb of her!" Moppett said viciously.

"Obviously you don't feel the same concern for her. But if you did, in the smallest degree, you would answer my questions truthfully. If you've any sense, you'll do so for your own sake."

"Why?"

"To save yourself from the suspicion of something much more serious than theft."

She seemed to contract inside Leonard's dressing-gown. "I don't know what you mean. I don't know anything about it."

Alleyn thought: Are these two wretched young no-goods in the fatal line? Is that to be the stale, deadly familiar end?

He said: "If you stole the cigarette case, or Mr. Leiss stole it, or you both stole it in collusion, and, if, for one reason or another, you dropped it in the ditch last night, you will be well advised to say so."

"How do I know that? You're trying to trap me."

Alleyn said patiently: "Believe me, I'm not concerned to trap the innocent. Nor, at the moment, am I primarily interested in theft."

"Then you're trying to bribe me."

This observation, showing as it did a flash of perception, was infuriating.

"I can neither bribe nor threaten," he said. "But I can warn you, and I do. You're in a position of great danger. You, personally. Do you know what happens to people who withhold evidence in a case of homicide? Do you know what happens to accessories before the fact of such a crime? *Do you?*"

Her face crumpled suddenly like a child's and her enormous shallow eyes overflowed.

"All right," she said. "All right. I'll tell you. But it wasn't anything. You've got it all wrong. It was—"

"Well?"

"It was all a mistake," Moppett whispered.

The bedroom door opened and Leonard came out in his violet pajamas.

"You keep your great big beautiful trap shut, honey," he said. He stood behind Moppett, holding her arms. He really would, Alleyn had time to consider, do rather well in a certain type of film.

"Mr. Leiss," he said, "will you be kind enough to take yourself out of this?"

But, even as he said it, he knew it was no good. With astonishing virtuosity Moppett, after a single ejaculation of pain and a terrified glance at Leonard, leant back against him, falling abruptly into the role of seductive accessory. The tears still stood in her eyes and her mouth twitched as his fingers bit into her arm. She contrived a smile.

"Don't worry, darling," she said, rubbing her head against Leonard. "I'm not saying a thing."

"That's my girl," said Leonard savagely.

" 3 "

"Not," Mr. Fox remarked as they drove away, "the type of young people you'd expect to find in this environment."

"Not County, you think?" Alleyn returned.

"Certainly not," Fox said primly. "Leiss, now—a bad type that. Wide boy. Only a matter of time before he's inside for a tied stretch. But the young lady's a different story. Or ought to be," Fox said after a pause. "Or ought to be," he repeated heavily.

"The young lady," Alleyn said tartly, "is a young stinker. Look, Fox! There are threads of the Period cigarette tobacco in Leiss's pocket. Bob Williams'll lay on a vacuum cleaner, I daresay. Go through the pockets and return the unspeakable garments, will you? And check his dabs from the oddments in the pockets. To my mind, there's no doubt they pinched the cigarette case. Suppose Cartell or Period or both cut up rough? What then?"

"Ah," Fox said. "Exactly. And suppose Mr. Cartell threatend to go to the police and they set the trap for him and accidentally dropped the case in doing it?"

"All right. Suppose they did. Now as to their actions on the scene of the crime, we've got that pleasant child, Nicola Maitland-Mayne, for a witness; but she was in the throes of young love and may have missed one or two tricks. I'll check with her young man, although he was probably further gone than she. All right. I'll drop you at the Station and return to the genteel assault on My. Pyke Period. He'll have lunched by now. What about you?"

"Or you, Mr. Alleyn, if it comes to that."

"I think I'll press on, Br'er Fox. Get yourself a morsel of cheese and pickle at the pub and see if there's anything more to be extracted from that cagey little job, Alfred Belt."

"As a matter of fact," Fox confessed, "Mr. Belt and Mrs. Mitchell, the cook, who seems to be a very superior type of woman, suggested I should drop in for a snack later in the day. Mrs. Mitchell went so far as to indicate she'd set something cold aside."

"I might have known it," Alleyn said. "Meet you at the Station at fiveish." The car pulled up at Mr. Pyke Period's gate and he got out, arranging for it to pick him up again in half an hour.

Mr. Period received him fretfully in the drawing-room. He was evidently still much perturbed and kept shooting unhappy little glances out of the corners of his eyes. Alleyn could just hear the stutter of Nicola's typewriter in the study.

"I can't settle to anything. I couldn't eat my lunch. It's all too difficult and disturbing," said Mr. Period.

"And I'm afraid I'm not going to make it any easier," Alleyn rejoined. He waited for a moment and decided to fire point-blank. "Mr. Period," he said, "will you tell me why you wrote two letters of condolence to Miss Cartell, why they are almost exactly the same, and why the first was written and sent to her before either of you had been informed of her brother's death?"

There was nothing to be learnt from Mr. Period's face. Shock, guilt, astonishment, lack of comprehension or mere deafness might have caused his jaw to drop and his eyes to glaze. When he did speak it was politely and conventionally. "I beg your pardon? What did you say?"

Alleyn repeated his question. Mr. Period seemed to think it over. After a considerable pause he said flatly: "But I didn't."

"You didn't what?"

"Write twice. The thing's ridiculous."

Alleyn drew the two letters from his pocket and laid them before Mr. Period, who screwed his glass in his eye and stooped over them. When he straightened up, his face was the colour of beetroot. "There has been a stupid mistake," he said.

"I'm afraid I must ask you to explain it."

"There's nothing to explain."

"My dear Period!" Alleyn ejaculated.

"Nothing! My man must have made a nonsense."

"Your man didn't, by some act of clairvoyance, anticipate a letter of condolence, and forge a copy and deliver it to a lady before anyone knew she was bereaved?"

"There's no need to be facetious," said Mr. Period.

"I couldn't agree with you more. It's an extremely serious matter."

"Very well," Mr. Period said angrily. "Very well! I ah—I—ah—I had occasion to write to Connie Cartell about something else. Something entirely different and extremely private."

Astonishingly he broke into a crazy little laugh which seemed immediately to horrify him. He stared wildly at Alleyn. "I—ah—I must have—" He stopped short. Alleyn would have thought it impossible for him to become redder in the face, but he now did so. "The wrong letter," he said, "was put in the envelope. Obviously."

"But that doesn't explain . . . Wait a bit!" Alleyn exclaimed. "Come!" he said after a moment. "Perhaps sense does begin to dawn after all. Tell me, and I promise I'll be as discreet as may be, has anybody else of your acquaintance been bereaved of a brother?"

Mr. Period's eyeglass dropped with a click. "In point of fact," he said unhappily, "yes."

"When?"

"It was in yesterday's—ah! I heard of it yesterday."

"And wrote?"

Mr. Period inclined his head.

"And the letter was . . ." Alleyn wondered how on earth his victim's discomfiture could be reduced, and decided there was nothing much to be done about it. "The letters were identical?" he suggested. "After all, why not? One can't go on forever inventing consolatory phrases."

Mr. Period bowed and was silent. Alleyn hurried on. "Do you mind giving me, in confidence, the name of the—" It was difficult to avoid a touch of grotesquery. "The other bereaved sister?"

"Forgive me. I prefer not."

Remembering there was always Nicola and the *Daily Telegraph,* Alleyn didn't press the point.

"Perhaps," he said, "you wouldn't mind telling me what the missing letter was about: I mean, the one that you intended for Miss Cartell?"

"Again," Mr. Period said with miserable dignity, "I regret." He really looked as if he might cry.

"Presumably it has gone to the other bereaved sister? The wrong letter in the right envelope, as it were?"

Mr. Period momentarily closed his eyes as if overtaken by nausea and said nothing.

"You know," Alleyn went on very gently, "I have to ask about these things. If they're irrelevant to the case I can't tell you how completely and thankfully one puts them out of mind."

"They are irrelevant," Mr. Period assured him with vehemence. "Believe me, believe me, they *are. Entirely* irrelevant! My dear Alleyn—really—I promise you. There now," Mr. Period concluded with crackpot gaiety, " 'nuff said! Tell me, my dear fellow, you did have luncheon? I meant to suggest . . . but this frightful business puts everything out of one's head. *Not,* I hope, at our rather baleful little pub?"

He babbled on distractedly. Alleyn listened in the hope of hearing something useful, and, this not being the case, brought him up with a round turn.

He said: "There's one other thing. I understand that Lady Bantling drove you home last night?"

Mr. Period gaped at him. "But, of course," he said at last. "Dear Désirée! So kind. Of course! Why?"

"And I believe," Alleyn plodded on, "that after you had left her she didn't at once return to Baynesholme, but went into your garden and from there conducted a duologue with Mr. Cartell, who was looking out of his bedroom window. Why didn't you tell me about this?"

"I don't—really, I don't know."

"But I think you do. You looked through your own bedroom window and asked if anything was the matter."

"And nothing was!" Mr. Period ejaculated with a kind of pale triumph. "Nothing! She said so! She said—"

"She said: 'Nothing in the wide world. Go to bed, darling.'"

"Precisely. So exuberant, always!"

"Did you hear anything of the conversation?"

"Nothing!" Mr. Period ejaculated. "Nothing at all! But nothing. I simply heard their voices. And in my opinion she was just being naughty and teasing poor old Hal."

As Mr. Period could not be dislodged from this position Alleyn made his excuses and sought out Nicola in the study.

She was able to find a copy of yesterday's *Telegraph*. He read through the obituary notices.

"Look here," he said, "your employer is in a great taking-on about his correspondence. Did you happen to notice what mail was ready to go out yesterday evening?"

"Yes," Nicola said. "Two letters."

"Local addresses?"

"That's right," she said uneasily.

"'Mind telling me what they were?"

"Well—I mean . . ."

"All right. Were they to Miss Cartell and Désirée, Lady Bantling?"

"Why ask me," Nicola said, rather crossly, 'if you alread know?"

"I was tricking you, my pretty one, oiled Hawkshaw the detective."

"Ha-ha, very funny . . . I suppose," Nicola sourly remarked.

"Well, only fairly funny." Alleyn had wandered over to the corner of the room that bore Mr. Period's illuminated genealogy. "He seems woundily keen on begatteries," he muttered. "Look at all this. Hung up in a dark spot for modesty's sake, but framed and hung up, all the same. It's not an old one. Done at his cost, I'll be bound."

"How do you know?"

"If you keep on asking 'feed' questions you must expect to be handed the pay-off line. By the paper, gilt and paint."

"Oh."

"Where's Ribblethorpe?"

"Beyond Baynesholme, I think."

"The Pyke family seems to have come from there."

"So I've been told," Nicola sighed, "and at some length, poor lamb. He went on and on about it yesterday after luncheon. I think he was working something off."

"Tell me again about the conversation at lunch."

Nicola did so and he thanked her.

"I must go," he said.

"Where to?"

"Oh—up and down in the world seeking whom I may devour. See you later, no doubt."

As he left the house Alleyn thought: That was all pretty bloody facetious, but the girl makes me feel young. And as he got into the police car he added to himself: But so, after all, does my wife. And that's what I call being happily married.

"To Baynesholme," he added, to his driver. On the way there, he sat with his hat cocked forward, noticing that spring was advancing in the countryside and wondering what Désirée Ormsbury, as he remembered her, would look like after all these years. Pretty tough, I daresay, what with one thing and another, he supposed; and when he was shown into her boudoir and she came forward to greet him, he found he had been right.

Désirée was wearing tight pants and an Italian shirt. The shirt was mostly orange and so were her hair and lipstick. Her make-up generally was impressionistic rather than representational and her hands quite desperately haggard.

But when she grinned at him there was the old raffish, disreputable charm he remembered so well, and he thought: "She's formidable, still."

"It *is* you, then," she said hoarsely. "I wasn't sure if it was going to be you or your brother—George, was he?—who'd turned into a policeman."

"I wonder at your remembering either of us."

"I do, though. But of course George turned into a baronet. You're Rory, the dashing one."

"You appall me," Alleyn said.

"You don't look all that different. I wish I could say as much for myself. Shall we have a drink?"

"Not me, thank you," Alleyn said, rather startled. He glanced at a clock: it was twenty to three.

"I've only just had lunch," she explained. "I thought brandy might be rather a thing. Where did you have lunch?" She looked at him. "Wait a moment, will you? Sorry. I won't be long. Have a smoke." She added over her shoulder as she walked away: "I'm not trying to escape."

Alleyn lit a cigarette and looked about him. It was a conventional country-house boudoir, with incongruous dabs of Désirée scattered about it in the form of "dotty" bits of French porcelain and one astonishing picture of a nude sprouting green bay leaves and little flags.

There were photographs of Andrew Bantling and a smooth-looking youngish man whom Alleyn supposed must be Désirée's third husband. It was a rather colourless photograph but he found himself looking at it with a sense of familiarity. He knew the wide-set eyes were grey rather than blue and that the mouth, when smiling, displayed almost perfect teeth. He knew he had heard the voice: a light baritone, lacking colour. He knew he had at some time encountered this man but he couldn't remember where or when.

"That's Bimbo," said Désirée, returning. "My third. We've been married a year." She carried a loaded tray. "I thought you were probably hungry," she said, putting it on her desk. "You needn't feel awkward," she added. She strolled off and lit a cigarette. "Do have it, for God's sake, after all my trouble getting it. If I'm arrested, I promise I won't split on you. Eat up."

"Since you put it like that," Alleyn rejoined, "I shall, and very gratefully." He sat down to chicken aspic and salad, bread, butter, cheese, a bottle of lager and something in an oversized cocktail glass.

"Dry martini," Désirée said. She herself had a generously equipped brandy glass. She picked up a magazine and disappeared into a sofa. "Is that all right?"

By the smell he supposed it to be made up of nine parts gin to one of French. He therefore tipped it quickly into a vase of flowers on the desk and poured out the lager. The chicken aspic was quite excellent.

"Andrew tells me," Désirée said, "that you seem to think Hal was murdered."

"Yes, I do."

"It appears so unlikely, somehow. Unless somebody did it out of irritation. When we were married, I promise you I felt like it often enough. Still, being rid of him I no longer do—or did. If you follow me."

"Perfectly," said Alleyn.

"Andrew says it's all about a kind of booby-trap, he thinks. Is that right?"

"That's right."

"I expected," Désire said after a pause, "that it would be you asking me the questions."

"If you fill my mouth with delectable food, how can I?"

"Is it good? I didn't have any. I never fancy my lunch except for the drinks. *Was* Hal murdered? Honestly?"

"I think so."

There was a longish silence and then she began to talk about people they had both known and occasions when they had met. This went on for some time. In her offhand way she managed to convey an implicit familiarity. Presently she came up behind him. He could smell her scent, which was sharp and unfamiliar. He knew she was trying to get him off balance, to make him feel vulnerable, sitting there eating and drinking. He also knew, as certainly as if she had made the grossest of advances, that she was perfectly ready for an unconventional interlude. He wondered where her Bimbo had taken himself off to and if Andrew Bantling was in the house. He continued sedately to eat and drink.

"My Bimbo," she said as if he had spoken aloud, "is having his bit of afternoon kip. We were latish last night. One of my parties. Quite a pure one, but I suppose you know about that."

"Yes, it sounded a huge success," Alleyn said politely. He laid down his knife and fork and got up. "That was delicious," he said. "Thank you *very* much, jolly kind of you to think of it."

"Not at all," she murmured, coming at him with cigarettes and a lighter and an ineffable look.

"May we sit down?" Alleyn suggested and noticed that she took a chair facing a glare of uncompromising light: she was evidently one of those rare ugly, provocative women who can't be bothered taking the usual precautions.

"I've got to ask you one or two pretty important questions," Alleyn said. "And the first is this. Have you by any chance had a letter from Mr. Pyke Period? This morning, perhaps?"

She stared at him. "Golly, yes! I'd forgotten all about it. He must be dotty, poor lamb. How did you know?"

Alleyn disregarded this question. "Why dotty?" he asked.

"Judge for yourself."

She put a hand on his shoulder, leant across him and pulled out a drawer in her desk, taking her time about it. "Here it is," she said and dropped a letter in front of him. "Go on," she said. "Read it."

It was written in Mr. Period's old-fashioned hand, on his own letter paper.

MY DEAR:

Please don't think it too silly of me to be fussed about a little thing, but I can't help feeling that you might very naturally have drawn a quite unwarrantable conclusion from the turn our conversation took today. It really is a little *too* much to have to defend one's own ancestry, but I care enough about such matters to feel I must assure you that mine goes back as far as I, or anyone else, might wish. I'm afraid Hal, poor dear, has developed a slight *thing* on the subject. But, never mind! I don't! Forgive me for bothering you, but I know you will understand.

As ever,
P.P.P.

"Have you any idea," Alleyn said, "what he's driving at?"

"Not a notion. He dined here last night and was normal."

"Would you have expected another sort of letter from him?"

"Another sort? What sort? Oh! I see what you mean. About Ormsbury, poor brute? He's dead, you know."

"Yes."

"With P.P.'s passion for condolences it would have been more likely. You mean he's done the wrong thing? So, who was meant to have this one?"

"May I at all events keep it?"

"Do if you want to."

Alleyn pocketed the letter. "I'd better say at once that you may have been the last person to speak to Harold Cartell, *not* excepting his murderer."

She had a cigarette ready in her mouth and the flame from the lighter didn't waver until she drew on it.

"How do you make that out?" she asked easily. "Oh, I know. Somebody's told you about the balcony scene. Who? Andrew, I suppose, or his girl. Or P.P., of course. He cut in on it from his window."

"So you had a brace of Romeos in reverse?"

"Like hell I did. Both bald, and me, if we face it, not quite the dewy job either."

Alleyn found himself at once relishing this speech and knowing that she had intended him to have exactly that reaction.

"The dewy jobs," he said, "have their limitations."

"Whereas for me," Désirée said, suddenly overdoing it, "the sky's the limit. Did you know that?"

He decided to disregard this and pressed on. "Why," he asked, "having deposited Mr. Period at his garden gate, did you leave the car, cross the ditch and serenade Mr. Cartell?"

"I saw him at his window and thought it would be fun."

"What did you say?"

"I think I said: 'But soft, what light from yonder window breaks?'"

"And after that?"

"I really don't remember. I pulled his leg a bit."

"Did you tell him you were on the warpath?"

There was a fractional pause before she said: "Well, I must say P.P. has sharp ears for an elderly gent. Yes, I did. It meant nothing."

"And did you tell him to watch his step?"

"Why," asked Désirée, "don't we just let you tell me what I said and leave it at that?"

"Did you tackle him about that boy of yours?"

"All right," she said, "yes, I did!" And then: *"They* didn't tell you? Andy and the girl? Have you needled it out of them, you cunning fellow?"

"I'm afraid," Alleyn prevaricated, "they were too far up the lane and much too concerned with each other to be reliable witnesses."

"So P.P.——" She leant forward and touched him. "Look," she said, "I honestly don't remember what I said to Hal. I'd had one or two little drinks and was a morsel high." She waited for a moment and then, with a sharpness that she hadn't exhibited before, said: "If it was a booby-trap, I hadn't a chance to set it, had I? Not in full view of those two lovebirds."

"Who told you about the booby-trap?"

"P.P. told Andy, and Andy told me. . . . And I drove straight here, to Baynesholme, arriving at twenty-five to twelve. The first couple got back soon afterwards. From then on, I was under the closest imaginable observation. Isn't that what one calls a watertight alibi?"

"I shall be glad," Alleyn said, "to have it confirmed. How do you know you got back at 11:35?"

"The clock in the hall. I was watching the time because of the treasure hunt."

"Who won?"

"Need you ask? The Moppett and her bully. They probably cheated in some way."

"Really? How, do you suppose?"

"They heard us plotting about the clues in the afternoon. The last one led back to the loo tank in the downstairs cloakroom."

"Here?"

"That's right. Most of the others finally guessed it, but they were too late. Andrew and Nicola didn't even try, I imagine."

"Any corroborative evidence, do you remember?"

"Of my alibi?"

"Of your alibi," Alleyn agreed sedately.

"I don't know. I think I called out something to Bimbo. He might remember."

"So he might. . . . About last night's serenade to your second husband: did you introduce the subject of your son's inheritance?"

She burst out laughing; she had a loud, formidable laugh like a female Duke of Wellington. "Do you know," she said, "I believe I did. Something of the sort. Anything to get a rise."

"He called on you yesterday afternoon, didn't he?"

"Oh, yes," she said quickly. "About Flash Len and a car. He was in a great taking-on, poor pet."

"And on that occasion," Alleyn persisted, "did you introduce the subject of the inheritance?"

"Did we? Yes, so we did. I told Hal I thought he was behaving jolly shabbily, which was no more than God's truth."

"What was his reaction?"

"He was too fussed to take proper notice. He just fumed away about the car game. . . . Your spies *have* been busy," she added. "Am I allowed to ask who told you? Wait a bit, though. It must have been Sergeant Noakes. What fun for him."

"Why was Cartell so set against the picture-gallery idea?"

"My dear, because he was what he was. Fuddy-duddy-plus. It's a bore, because he's Andy's guardian."

"Any other trustees?"

"Yes. P.P."

"What does he think?"

"He thinks Andy might grow a beard and turn beat, which he doesn't dig. Still, I can manage my P.P. . . . Boo wouldn't have minded."

"Boo?"

"Bobo Bantling. My first. Andy's papa. *You* knew Boo. Don't be so stuffy."

Alleyn, who did in fact remember this singularly ineffectual peer, made no reply.

"*And* I may add," Lady Bantling said, apparently as an afterthought, "Bimbo considered it a jolly good bet. And he's got a flair for that sort of thing, Bimbo has. As a matter of fact Bimbo offered—" She broke off and seemed to cock an ear. Alleyn had already heard steps in the hall. "Here, I do believe, he is!" Désirée exclaimed and called out loudly: "Bimbo!"

"Hullo!" said a distant voice, rather crossly.

"Come in here, darling."

The door opened and Bimbo Dodds came in. Alleyn now remembered where he had seen him.

" 4 "

The recognition, Alleyn felt sure, was mutual, though Bimbo gave no sign of this. They had last met on the occasion of a singularly disreputable turn-up in a small but esoteric night club. There had been a stabbing, subsequent revelations involving a person of consequence, and a general damping-down process ending in a scantily publicized conviction. Benedict Arthur Dodds, Alleyn recollected, had been one of a group of fashionable gentlemen who had an undercover financial interest in the club which had come to an abrupt and discreditable end and an almost immediate reincarnation under another name. Bimbo had appeared briefly in court, stared at coldly by the magistrate, and was lucky to escape the headlines. At the time, Alleyn recollected, Bimbo was stated to be an undischarged bankrupt. It was before his marriage to Désirée.

She introduced them. Bimbo, who had the slightly mottled complexion of a man who has slept heavily in the afternoon, nodded warily and glanced at the tray. His right hand was neatly bandaged and he did not offer it to Alleyn.

"The Super and I, darling," Désirée said, "are boy-and-girl chums. He was starving and I've given him a snack. He's jolly famous nowadays, so isn't it nice to have him grilling us?"

"Oh, really?" said Bimbo. "Ha-ha. Yes."

"You must answer all his questions very carefully because it seems as if Hal was murdered. Imagine!"

Interpreting this speech to be in the nature of a general warning, Alleyn said: "I wonder if I may have a word with you, Mr. Dodds." And to Désirée: "Thank you so much for my delicious luncheon-without-prejudice."

For a split second she looked irritated, and then she said: "Not a bit. Do I gather that you want to go into a huddle with my husband?"

"Just a word," Alleyn said equably, "if we may. Perhaps somewhere else . . . ?"

"Not at all. I'll go and snip the deadheads off roses—except that there aren't any roses and it's the wrong time of the year."

"Perhaps you could get on with your embroidery," said Alleyn, and had the satisfaction of seeing her blink.

"Suppose," she suggested, "that you adjourn to Bimbo's study. Why not?"

"Why not?" Bimbo echoed, without cordiality.

As Alleyn passed her on his way out, she looked full in his face. It was impossible to interpret her expression, but he'd have taken a long bet that she was worried.

Bimbo's study turned out to be the usual sporting-print job with inherited classics on the shelves, together with one or two paperbacks looking like Long Acre in its more dubious reaches. Bimbo, whose manner was huffy and remote, said: "This is a very unpleasant sort of thing to happen."

"Yes, isn't it?"

"Anything we can do, of course."

"Thank you very much. There are one or two points," Alleyn said without refurbishing the stock phrases, "that I'd like to clear up. It's simply a matter of elimination, as I'm sure you'll understand."

"Naturally," said Bimbo.

"Well, then. You'll have heard that Mr. Cartell's body was found in a trench that has been dug in Green Lane, the lane that runs past Mr. Period's garden. Did you drive down Green Lane at any time last evening?"

"Ah—" Bimbo said. "Ah—let me think. Yes, I did. When going round the clues."

He paused while Alleyn reflected that this was a fair enough description of his own preoccupation.

"The clues for the treasure hunt?" he said. "When?"

"That's right. Oh, I don't know. About half-past ten. Might be later. I simply drove over the territory to see how they were all getting on."

"Yes, I see. . . . Was there anybody in the lane?"

"Actually," Bimbo said casually, "I don't remember. Or do I? No, there wasn't."

"Did you get out of the car?"

"Did I? I believe I did. Yes. I checked to make sure the last clue was still there."

"If you don't know what to do, think it over in the loo."

"Quite. Was it still there this morning?" Bimbo asked sharply.

"When did you get back?"

"Here? I don't know exactly."

"Before Lady Bantling, for instance?"

"Oh, yes. She drove old Period home. That was later. I mean, it was while I was out. I mean, we were both out, but I got home first."

"You saw her come in?"

"I really don't remember that I actually *saw* her. I heard her, I think. I was looking round the ballroom to see everything was all right."

"Any idea of the time?"

"I'm afraid I really wasn't keeping a stopwatch on our movements. It was before twelve, because they were all meant to be back by midnight."

"Yes, I see. And did you leave the house again?"

"I did not."

"I believe there was some sort of dogfight."

"My God, yes! Oh, I see what you mean. I went out with the others to the terrace and dealt with it. That ghastly bitch—" Here Bimbo made one or two extremely raw comments upon Pixie.

"She bit you, perhaps?"

"She certainly did," Bimbo said, nursing his hand.

"Very professional bandage."

"I had to get the doctor."

"After the party?"

"That's right. I fixed it up myself at the time, but it came unstuck."

"You tied it up?"

Bimbo stared at him. "I did. I went to a bathroom,

where there's a first-aid cupboard, and stuck a bandage on. Temporarily."

"How long did this take you, do you know?"

"I don't know. How the hell should I?"

"Well—at a guess."

"Quite a time. It kept oozing out, but in the end I fixed it. Quite a time, really. I should think all of twenty minutes before I rejoined the party. Or more. Some bloody mongrel tore my trousers and I had to change."

"Maddening for you," Alleyn said sympathetically. "Tell me: you are a member of the Hacienda Club?"

Bimbo went very still. Presently he said: "I simply cannot conceive what that has to do with anything at issue."

"It has, though," Alleyn said cheerfully. "I just wondered, you see, whether you'd ever run into Leonard Leiss at the Hacienda. His name's on their list."

"I certainly have not," Bimbo said. He moved away. Alleyn wondered whether he was lying.

"I'm no longer a member, and I've never seen Leiss, to my knowledge," Bimbo said, "until yesterday. He got himself asked to our party. In my opinion he's the rock-bottom. A frightful person."

"Right. So that settles that. Now, about the business of your stepson and the Grantham Gallery."

He gave Bimbo time to register the surprise that this change in tactics produced. It was marked by a very slight widening of the eyes and recourse to a cigarette case. Alleyn sometimes wondered how much the cigarette-smoking person scored over an abstainer when it came to police investigations.

"Oh, that!" Bimbo said. "Yes, well, I must say I think it's quite a sound idea."

"You talked it over with Bantling?"

"Yes, I did. We went into it pretty thoroughly. I'm all for it."

"To the extent of taking shares in it yourself?"

Bimbo said airily: "Even that. Other things being equal."

"What other things?"

"Well—fuller inquiries and all that."

"And the money of course?"

"Of course."

"Have you got it?" Alleyn asked calmly.

"I must say!" Bimbo ejaculated.

"In police inquiries," Alleyn said, "no question is impertinent, I'm afraid."

"And I'm afraid I disagree with you."

"Would you mind telling me if you are still an undischarged bankrupt?"

"I mind very much, but the answer is no. The whole thing was cleared up a year ago."

"That would be at the time of your marriage, I think?"

Bimbo turned scarlet and said not a word.

"Still," Alleyn went on after a slight pause, "I suppose the Grantham Gallery plan will go forward now, don't you?"

"I've no idea."

"No reason why it shouldn't, one imagines, unless Mr. Period, who's a trustee, objects."

"In any case it doesn't arise."

"No?"

"I mean it's got nothing to do with this ghastly business."

"Oh, I see. Well, now," Alleyn said briskly, "I fancy that's about all. Except that I ought to ask you if there's anything in the wide world you can think of that could be of help to us."

"Having no idea of the circumstances I can hardly

be expected to oblige," Bimbo said with a short laugh.

"Mr. Cartell's body was found in the open drain outside Mr. Period's house. He had been murdered. That," Alleyn lied, "is about all anyone knows."

"How had he been murdered?"

"Hit on the head, it appears, and smothered."

"Poor old devil," said Bimbo. He stared absently at his cigarette. "Look!" he said. "Nobody likes to talk wildly about a thing like this. I mean it just won't do to put a wrong construction on what may be a perfectly insignificant detail, will it?"

"It's *our* job to forget insignificant details."

"Yes, I know. Of course. All the same—"

"Mr. Dodds, I really think I can promise you I won't go galloping down a false trail with blinkers over my eyes."

Bimbo smiled. "O.K.," he said. "Fair enough. No doubt I'm behaving like the original Silly Suspect or something. It's just that, when it comes to the point, one doesn't exactly fancy trotting out something that may turn out to be—well—"

"Incriminating?"

"Well, exactly. Mind you, in principle, I'm for weighing-in with the police. We bellyache about them freely enough but we expect them to protect us. Of course everybody doesn't see it like that."

"Not everybody."

"No. And anyway with all the rot-gut that the long-haired gentry talk about understanding the thugs, it's up to the other people to show the flag."

Disregarding a certain nausea in the region of his midriff, Alleyn said: "Quite."

Bimbo turned away to the window and seemed to be contemplating the landscape. Perhaps because of this, his voice had taken on a different perspective.

"Personally," Alleyn heard him say, "I'm in favour of capital punishment."

Alleyn, who was one of an extremely small minority among his brother-officers, said: "Ah, yes?"

"Anyway, that's nothing to do with the point at issue," Bimbo said, turning back into the room. "I don't know why I launched out like this."

"We can forget it."

"Yes, of course."

"You were going to tell me . . . ?"

"Yes, I was. It's about this bloody fellow Leiss and his ghastly girl. They hung on to the bitter end of the party, of course. I've never seen anybody drink more or show it less, I'll say that for them. Well, the last car was leaving—except his bit of wreckage—and it was about two o'clock. I thought I'd give them the hint. I collected his revolting overcoat and went to hunt them out. I couldn't find them at first, but I finally ran them down in my study, here, where they had settled in with a bottle of champagne. They were on the sofa with their backs to the door and didn't hear me come in. They were pretty well bogged down in an advanced necking party. He was talking. I heard the end of the sentence." Bimbo stopped and frowned at his cigarette. "Of course, it may not mean a damn' thing." He looked at Alleyn, who said nothing.

"Well, for what it's worth," Bimbo went on. "He said: 'And that disposes of Mr. Harold Cartell for keeps.' And she said something like: 'When do you think they'll find it?' and he said: 'In the morning, probably. Not windy, are you? For Christ's sake, keep your head: we're in the clear.' "

CHAPTER SIX

Interlude

With this piece of reportage, spurious or not as the case might prove to be, it appeared that Bimbo had reached saturation point as a useful witness. He had nothing more to offer. After noticing that a good deal of un-opened mail lay on the desk, including several bills and a letter from a solicitor, addressed to Benedict Arthur Dodds, Alleyn secured Bimbo's uneasy offer to sign a statement and took his leave.

"Please don't move," Alleyn said politely, "I can find my way out." Before Bimbo could put himself in motion, Alleyn had gone out and shut the study door behind him.

In the hall, not altogether to his surprise, he found Désirée. She was, if anything, a little wilder in her general appearance, and Alleyn wondered if this was to be attributed to another tot of brandy. But in all other respects she seemed to be more or less herself.

"Hullo," she said. "I've been waiting for you. There's a sort of *crise*."

"What sort?"

"It may not be a *crise* at all, but I thought I'd better tall you. I really feel a bit awkward about it. I seem to have made a clanger, showing you P.P.'s funny letter. It wasn't meant for me."

"Who was it meant for?"

"He wouldn't say. He's just rung up in a frightful taking-on, asking me to throw it on the fire and forget about it. He went on at great length, talking about his grand ancestors and I don't know what else."

"You didn't tell him I'd seen the letter?"

Désirée looked fixedly at him. "No," she said. "I didn't, but I felt like a housemaid who's broken a cup. Poor P.P. What can it all be about? He is so fussed— you can't imagine."

"Never mind," Alleyn said, "I daresay it's only his overdeveloped social sense."

"Well, I know. All the same . . ." She put her hand on his arm. "Rory," she said, "if you don't awfully mind, *don't* tell him I gave you the letter. He'd think me such a *sweep*."

At that moment Alleyn liked her very much. "I won't tell him," he said carefully, "unless I have to. And for your part, I'll be obliged if *you* don't tell him, either."

"I'm not likely to, am I? And anyway, I don't quite see why the promises about this letter should all be on my side."

"It may be important."

"All right, but I can't think how. You've got it. Are you going to use it in some way?"

"Not if it's irrelevant."

"I suppose it's no good asking you to give it back to me. No, I can see it's not."

"It isn't, really, Désirée," Alleyn said, using her name for the first time. "Not till I make quite sure it's of no account. I'm sorry."

"What a common sort of job you've got. I can't think how you do it." She gave one of her harsh barks of laughter.

He looked at her for a moment. "I expect that was a very clever thing to say," he said. "But I'm afraid it makes no difference. Good-bye. Thank you again for my lunch."

When he was in the car he said: "To Ribblethorpe. It's about five miles, I think. I want to go to the parish church."

It was a pleasant drive through burgeoning lanes. There were snowdrops in the hedgerows and a general air of freshness and simplicity. Désirée's final observation stuck in his gullet.

Ribblethorpe was a tiny village. They drove past a row of cottages and a shop-post-office and came to a pleasant if not distinguished church with a big shabby parsonage beyond it.

Alleyn walked through the graveyard and very soon found a Victorian headstone to FRANCES ANN PATRICIA, INFANT DAUGHTER OF ALFRED MOLYNEUX PIERS PERIOD ESQUIRE AND LADY FRANCES MARY JULIA, HIS WIFE. SHE IS NOT DEAD BUT SLEEPETH. Reflecting on the ambiguity of the quotation, Alleyn moved away and had not long to search before he found carved armorial bearings exactly similar to those in Mr. Period's study. These adorned the grave of Lord Percival Francis Pykke, who died in 1701 and had conferred sundry and noble benefits upon this parish. The name recurred pretty regularly up and down the graveyard from Jacobean times onward. When he went into the church it was the same story. Armorial fish, brasses and tablets all confirmed the eminence of innumerable Pykes.

Alleyn was in luck. The baptismal register was not locked away in the vestry but chained to a carved desk, hard by the font. In the chancel a lady wearing an apron and housemaid's gloves was polishing brasses. Her hat, an elderly toque, had been, for greater ease, lifted up on her head—giving her a faint air of recklessness. He approached her.

"I wonder," Alleyn said, "if I may look in the baptismal register? I'm doing a bit of extremely amateurish research. I'll be very careful."

"Oh, rather!" said the lady, jollily. "Do. My husband's over at Ribblethorpe-Parva with the Mothers, or he'd help like a shot. I don't know if I——"

"Thank you so much but it's really quite a simple job," Alleyn said hastily. "Just a family thing, you know."

"We haven't been here long: only three months, so we're not up in the antiquities." The Rector's wife, as Alleyn supposed she must be, gave a final buffet with her polisher, tossed her head at her work in a jocular manner, bobbed to the altar and made for the vestry. "I'm Mrs. Nicholls," she said. "My husband followed dear old Father Forsdyke. You'll find all the entries pretty erratic," she added over her shoulder. "Father Forsdyke was a saint but as vague as could be. Over ninety when he died, rest his soul." She disappeared. Somehow, she reminded him of Connie Cartell.

The register was bound in vellum and bore the Royal Arms on its cover. Its pages were divided into columns headed *When Baptised, Child's Christian Name, Parents' Names, Abode, Quality, Trade or Profession* and *By Whom Performed*. It had been opened at July 1874.

How old was Mr. Pyke Period? Fifty-eight? Over sixty? Difficult to say. Alleyn started his search at the first entry in 1895. In that year the late Mr. Forsdyke was already at the helm and, although presumably not much over thirty, pretty far advanced in absence-of-mind. There was every sort of mistake and erasure, Mr. Forsdyke madly representing himself by turns as "Officiating Priest," "Infant," "Godmother," and in one entry as *Abode*. These slips were sometimes corrected by himself, sometimes by another person and sometimes not at all. In several places, the sponsors appeared under *Quality, Trade or Profession,* in others they were crammed in with the parents. In one respect, however, all was consistency. Where a male Pyke was in question the *Quality* was invariably "Gentleman."

At the bottom of a particularly wild page in the year 1897, Alleyn found what he wanted. Here on May 7th (altered to 5th) was baptised Frances Ann Patricia, daughter of Alfred Molyneux Piers Period and Lady Frances Mary Julia Period *née* Pyke, with a huddle of amended sponsors. In another hand, crammed in under Frances Ann Patricia, a second infant had been entered: Percival Pyke. Brackets had been added, enclosing the word "Twins."

It would seem that, on the occasion of his baptism, Mr. Pyke Period had fallen a victim to the Rector's peculiarity and had been temporarily neglected for his twin sister who, Alleyn remembered from her headstone, had died in infancy.

He spent a long time over this additional entry, using a strong pocket lens. He would have been very glad to remove the page and give it the full laboratory treatment. As it was he could see that a fine-pointed steel nib had been used and he noted that such another nib was rusting in the pen on the desk which also carried an old-fashioned inkpot. The writing was in a copperplate style, without character and rather laborious.

Praying that Mrs. Nicholls was engaged in further activities in the vestry, Alleyn slipped out to the car and took a small phial from his homicide kit. Back at the font—and hearing Mrs. Nicholls, who was an insecure mezzo, distantly proclaiming that she ploughed the fields and scattered—he let fall a drop from the phial on the relevant spot. The result was not as conclusive as the laboratory test would have been, but he would have taken long odds that the addition had been made at a different time from the main entry. Trusting that if anybody looked at this page they would conclude that some sentimentalist had let fall a tear over the infant in question, Alleyn shut the register.

The Rector's wife returned without her apron and with her hat adjusted. "Any luck?" she asked.

"Thank you," Alleyn said. "Yes, I think so. I find these old registers quite fascinating. The same names recurring through the years—it gives one such a feeling of continuity: the quiet life of the countryside. You seem to have had a steady progression of Pykes."

"One of the oldest families, *they* were," said the Rector's wife. "Great people in their day by all accounts."

"Have they disappeared?"

"Oh, yes. A long time ago. I think their manor house was burnt down in Victorian times and I suppose they moved away. At all events the family died out. There's a Mr. Period over at Little Codling, who I believe was related, but I've been told he's the last. Rather sad."

"Yes, indeed," Alleyn said.

He thanked her again and said he was sorry to have bothered her.

"No bother to me," she said. "As a matter of fact we had someone else in, searching the register, a few weeks ago. A lawyer I think he was. Something to do with a client, I daresay."

"Really? I wonder," Alleyn improvised, "if it was my cousin." He summoned the memory of Mr. Cartell, dreadfully blurred with mud. "Elderly? Slight? Baldish with a big nose? Rather pedantic old chap?"

"I believe he was. Yes, that exactly describes him. Fancy!"

"He's stolen a march on me," Alleyn said. "We're amusing ourselves hunting up the family curiosities." He put something in the church maintenance box and took his leave. As he left the church a deafening rumpus in the lane announced the approach of an antique motor car. It slowed down. The driver looked with great interest at Alleyn and the police car. He then accelerated and rattled off down the lane. It was Mr. Copper in the Bloodbath.

" 2 "

"If there's one thing I fancy more than another, Mrs. Mitchell," said Inspector Fox, laying down his knife and fork, "it's a cut of cold lamb, potato salad and a taste of cucumber relish. If I may say so, your cucumber relish is something particular. I'm very much obliged to you. Delicious."

"Welcome, I'm sure," said Mrs. Mitchell. "I've got a nephew in the Force, Mr. Fox, and from what he says it's the irregular meals that tells in the end. Worse than the feet, even, my nephew says; and his are a treat, believe you me. Soft corns! Well! Like red-hot coals, my nephew says."

Alfred cleared his throat. "Occupational disabilities!" he generalized. "They happen to the best of us, Mrs. M."

"That's right." Look at my varicose veins. I don't mean literally," Mrs. Mitchell added with a jolly laugh, in which Fox joined.

"Well, now," he said. "I mustn't stay here gossiping all the afternoon or I'll have the Superintendent on my tracks."

"Here we are, acting as pleasant as you please," Mrs. Mitchell observed, "and all the while there's this wicked business hanging over our heads. You know? In a way I can't credit it."

"Naturally enough, Mrs. M.," Alfred pointed out. "Following, as we do, the even tenor of our ways, the concept of violence is not easily assimilated. Mr. Fox appreciates the point of view, I feel sure."

"Very understandable. . . . I suppose," Fox suggested, "you might say the household had ticked over as comfortably as possible ever since the two gentlemen decided to join forces."

There was a brief silence broken by Mrs. Mitchell. "In a manner of speaking, you might," she concluded, "although there have been—well . . ."

"Exterior influences," Alfred said, remotely.

"Well, exactly, Mr. Belt."

"Such as?" Fox suggested.

"Since you ask me, Mr. Fox, such as the dog and the Arrangement. And the connections," Mrs. Mitchell added.

"Miss Mary Ralston, for instance?"

"You took the words out of my mouth."

"We mustn't," Alfred intervened, "give too strong an impression, Mrs. M."

"Well, I daresay we mustn't, but you have to face up to it. The dog is an animal of disgusting habits, and that young lady's been nothing but a menace ever since the Arrangement was agreed upon. You've said it yourself, Mr. Belt, over and over again."

"A bit wild, I take it," Fox ventured.

"Blood," Mrs. Mitchell said sombrely, "will tell. Out of an Orphanage—and why there, who knows?"

"As Mr. Cartell himself realized," Alfred said. "I heard him make the observation last evening, though he didn't frame it in those particular terms."

"Last evening? Really? Cigarette, Mrs. Mitchell?"

"Thank you, Mr. Fox." Alfred and Mrs. Mitchell exchanged a glance. A bell rang.

"Excuse me," Alfred said. "The study." He went out. Fox, gazing benignly upon Mrs. Mitchell, wondered if he detected a certain easing-up in her manner.

"Mr. Belt," she said, "is very much put about by all this. He don't show his feelings, but you can tell."

"Very natural," Fox said. "So Mr. Cartell didn't find

himself altogether comfortable about Miss Ralston?" he hinted.

"It couldn't be expected he should take to her. A girl of that type calling him 'Uncle,' and all. As for our gentleman—well!"

"I can imagine," Fox said, cozily. "Asking for trouble." He beamed at her. "So there were words?" he said. "Well, bound to be, when you look at the situation, but I daresay they didn't amount to much, the deceased gentleman being of such an easy-going nature, from all accounts."

"I'm sure I don't know who gave you that idea, Inspector," Mrs. Mitchell ejaculated. "I'd never have called him that, never. Real old bachelor and a lawyer into the bargain. Speak no ill, of course, but speak as you find all the same. Take last evening. There was all this trouble over our gentleman's cigarette case."

Fox allowed her to tell him at great length about the cigarette case.

". . . So," Mrs. Mitchell said after some minutes, "Mr. Cartell goes over to the other house, and by all accounts (though that Trudi, being a foreigner, can't make herself as clear as we would have wished) tackles Miss Moppett and as good as threatens her with the police. Hand back the case and give up her fancyboy Or Else. Accordin' to Trudi, who dropped in last evening."

Fox made clucky noises. Alfred returned to fetch his cap.

"Bloody dog's loose again," he said angrily. "Bit through her lead. Now, I'm told I've got to find her because of complaints in the village."

"What will he do with her?" Mrs. Mitchell wondered.

"I know what I'd do with her," Alfred said viciously. "I'd gas her. Well, if I don't see you again, Mr. Fox . . ."

Fox remarked that he had no doubt that they would meet.

When Alfred had gone Mrs. Mitchell said: "Mr. Belt feels strongly on the subject. I don't like to think of destroying the dog, I must say. I wonder if my sister would like her for the kiddies. Of course with her out of the way and the other matter settled, it will seem more like old times." She covered her mouth with her hand. "That sounds terrible. Don't take me up wrong, Mr. Fox, but we was all very comfortably situated before and therefore sorry to contemplate making a change."

"Were you thinking of it? Giving notice?"

"Mr. Belt was. Definitely. Though reluctant to do so, being he's stayed all his working life with our gentleman. However, he spoke to Mr. Period on the subject, and the outcome was promising."

Mrs. Mitchell enlarged upon this theme at some length. "Which was a relief to all concerned," she ended, "seeing we are in other respects well situated, and the social background all that you could fancy. Tonight, for instance, there's the Church Social, which we both attend regular and will in spite of everything. But after what passed between him and Mr. Cartell over the missing article, nothing else could be expected. Mr. Belt," Mrs. Mitchell added, "is a man who doesn't forget. Not a thing of that sort. During the war," she added obscurely, "he was in the. signalling."

The back doorbell rang and Mrs. Mitchell attended it. Fox could hear, but not distinguish, a conversation in which a male voice played the predominant part. He strolled to an advantageous position in time to hear Mrs. Mitchell say, "Fancy! I wonder why!" and to see a man in a shabby suit who said: "Your guess is as good as mine. Well, I'll be on my way."

Fox returned to his chair and Mrs. Mitchell re-entered.

"Mr. Copper from the garage," she said. "To inquire about the Church Social. He saw your Superintendent coming out of Ribblethorpe Church. I wonder why."

Fox said Superintendent Alleyn was much interested in old buildings, and, with the inner calm that characterized all his proceedings, took his leave and went to the Little Codling constabulary. Here he found Superintendent Williams with his wife's vacuum cleaner. "Not the Yard job," Williams said cheerfully, "but it's got a baby nozzle and should do."

They gave Leonard Leiss's dinner suit and overcoat a very thorough going-over, extracting soil from the excavations and enough of Mr. Period's Turkish cigarette tobacco to satisfy, as Fox put it, a blind juryman in a total eclipse.

They paid particular attention to Leonard's wash-leather gloves, which were, as Nicola had suggested, on the dainty side.

"Soiled," Williams pointed out, "but he didn't lift any planks with those on his hands." Fox wrote up his notes and, in a reminiscent mood, drank several cups of strong tea with the Superintendent and Sergeant Noakes, who was then dispatched to return the garments to their owner.

At five o'clock Alleyn arrived in the police car and they all drove to the mortuary at Rimble. It was behind the police station and had rambling roses trained up its concrete walls. Here they found Sir James Curtis, the Home Office Pathologist, far enough on with his autopsy on Harold Cartell's body to be able to confirm Alleyn's tentative diagnosis. The cranial injuries were consistent with a blow from the plank. The remaining multiple injuries were caused by the drainpipe falling on the body and ramming it into the mud. The actual cause of death had been suffocation. Dr. Elkington was about to leave and they all stood looking down at what was left of Mr. Cartell. The face was now cleaned. A knowledgeable, faintly supercilious, expression lay about the mouth and brows.

In an adjoining shed, Williams had found temporary storage for the planks, the lantern and the stanchion. Here, Detective-Sergeants Thompson and Bailey were to be found, having taken further and more extensive photographs.

"I'm a bit of a camera-fiend myself and they've been using my darkroom," said Williams. "We're getting the workmen to bring the drainpipe along in their crane-truck. Noakes'll come back with them and keep an eye on it, but these chaps of yours tell me they got what they wanted on the spot."

Alleyn made the appropriate compliments, which were genuine, indeed. Williams was the sort of colleague that visiting Superintendents yearn after, and Alleyn told him so.

Bailey, a man of few words, great devotion and mulish disposition, indicated the two foot-planks which had been laid across packing cases, underside up.

"Hairs," he said. "Three. Consistent with deceased's."

"Good."

"There's another thing." Bailey jerked his finger at a piece of microphotographic film and a print laid out under glass on an improvised bench. "The print brings it up. Still wet, but you can make it out. Just."

The planks were muddy where they had dug into the walls of the ditch, but at the edges and ten inches from the ends of microphotograph showed confused traces. Alleyn spent some time over them.

"Yes," he said. "Gloved hands, I don't mind betting. Big, heavy gloves." He looked up at Bailey. "It's a rough undersurface. If you can find as much leather as would go in the eye of a needle we're not home and dry but we may be in sight. Which way were they carried here?"

"Underside up," Bailey said.

"Right. Well, you can but try."

"I have, Mr. Alleyn. Can again."

"Do," said Alleyn. He was going over the undersurface of the planks with his lens. "Tweezers," he said.

Bailey put a pair in his hand and fetched a sheet of paper.

"Have a go at these," Alleyn said and dropped two minute specks on the paper. "They may be damn'-all but it looks as if they might have rubbed off the seam of a heavy glove. *Not* wash leather, by the way. Strong hide—and . . . Look here."

He had found another fragment. "String," he said. "Heavy leather and string."

"You got to have the eyes for it," Detective-Sergeant Thompson said to nobody in particular.

During the brief silence that followed this pronouncement, the unmistakable racket of a souped-up engine made itself heard.

"That," Mr. Fox observed, "sounds like young Mr. Leiss's sports car."

"Stopping," Williams observed.

"Come on, Fox," Alleyn said. They went out to the gate. It was indeed Mr. Leiss's sports car, but Mr. Leiss was not at the wheel. The car screamed to a halt, leaving a trail of water from its radiator. Moppett, wearing a leather coat and jeans, was leaning out of the driving window.

With allowances for her make-up, which contrived to look both dirty and extreme, Alleyn would have thought she was pale. Her manner was less assured than it had been: indeed, she seemed to be in something of an emotional predicament.

"Oh, good," she said. "They told me you might be here. Sorry to bother you."

"Not at all," Alleyn said. Moppett's fingers, over-fleshed, sketchily nail-painted and stained with nicotine, moved restlessly on the driving wheel.

"It's like this," she said. "The local cop's just brought Lenny's things back: the overcoat and dinner suit."

"Yes?"

"Yes. Well, the thing is, his gloves are missing."

Alleyn glanced at Fox.

"'I beg your pardon, Miss Ralston," Fox said, "but I saw to the parcel myself. The gloves were returned. Cream wash leather, size seven."

"I don't mean those," Moppett said. "I mean his driving gloves. They're heavy leather ones with string backs. I ought to know. I gave them to him."

" 3 "

"Suppose," Alleyn suggested, "you park your car and we get this sorted out."

"I don't want to go in there," Moppett said with a sidelong look at the mortuary. "That's the dead-place, isn't it?"

"We'll use the Station," Alleyn said, and to that small yellowwood office she was taken. The window was open. From a neighbouring garden came an insistent chatteration of birdsong and the smell of earth and violets. Fox shut a side door that led into the yard. Moppett sat down.

"Mind if I smoke?" she said.

Alleyn gave her a cigarette. She kept her hands in her pockets while he lit it. She then began to talk rapidly in a voice that was pitched above its natural level.

"I can't be long. Lennie thinks I'm dropping the car at the garage. It's sprung a leak," she added unnecessarily, "in its waterworks. He'd be livid if he knew I was here. He's livid anyway about the gloves. He swears they were in his overcoat pocket."

Alleyn said: "They were not there when we collected the coat. Did he have them last night, do you know?"

"He didn't wear them. He wore his other ones. He's jolly fussy about his gloves," said Moppett. "I tell him Freud would have had something to say about it. And now I suppose I'll get the rocket."

"Why?"

"Well, because of yesterday afternoon. When we were at Baynesholme. We changed cars," Moppett said, without herself changing colour, "and I collected his overcoat from the car he decided not to buy. He says the gloves were in the pocket of the coat."

"What did you do with the coat?"

"That's just what I can't remember. We drove back to Auntie Con's to dine and change for the party, and our things were still in the car. His overcoat and mine. I suppose I bunged the lot out while he went off to buy cigarettes."

"You don't remember where you put the overcoat?"

"I should think I just dumped it in the car. I usually do."

"Mr. Leiss's coat was in his wardrobe this morning."

"That's right. Trudi put it there, I expect. She's got a letch for Lennie, that girl. Perhaps she pinched his gloves. And now I come to think of it," Moppett said, "I wouldn't mind betting she did."

"Did you at any time wear the gloves yourself?"

After a longish silence Moppett said: "That's funny. Lennie says I did. He says I pulled them on during the drive from London yesterday morning. I don't remember. I might or I might not. If I did I just don't know where I left them."

"Did he wear his overcoat when you returned to Baynesholme for the party?"

"No," Moppett said, quickly. "No, he didn't. It was rather warm." She got to her feet. "I ought to be going back," she said. "You don't have to tell Lennie I came, do you? He's a bit tricky about that sort of thing."

"What sort of thing?"

"Well—you know."

"I'm afraid I don't know."

She watched him for a second or two: then, literally, she bared her teeth at him. It was exactly as if she had, at the same time, laid back her ears. "You're lying," she said. "I know. You've found them, and you're sticking to them. I know the sort of things you do."

"That statement," Alleyn said mildly, "is utter nonsense, and you will create an extremely bad impression if you persist in it. You have reported the loss of the gloves and the loss has been noted. Is there anything else you would like to discuss?"

"My God, no!" she said and walked out of the Station. They heard her start up the car and go roaring off down the lane.

"Now, what do we make of that little lot?" Fox asked.

"What we have to *do* is find the damn' gloves."

"He'll have got rid of them. Or tried to. Or else she really has lost them and he's dead-scared we'll pick them up. That'd be a good enough reason for him giving her the works."

"Hold on, Br'er Fox. You're getting yourself wedded to a bit of hearsay evidence."

"Am I?"

"We've only her word that he's giving her fits."

"That's right," Fox agreed in his rather heavy way. "So we have." He ruminated for a short time. "Opportunity?" he said.

"They collared a bottle of their host's champagne and set themselves up in his study. He had to turf them out, I gather, at the tag end of the party. And, by the way, he handed Leiss his overcoat, so that bit was a lie. I imagine they could have nipped off and back again without much trouble. It may interest you to learn, Br'er Fox, that when they were discovered by Bimbo Dodds, Mr. Leiss was assuring his girl friend that Mr. Cartell was disposed of and she had no need to worry."

"Good gracious."

"Makes you fink, don't it?"

"When was this?"

"Dodds thinks it was about two A.M. He, by the way, is the B. A. Dodds who was mixed up in the night club affair that later became the Hacienda case and Leonard Leiss is a member of the Hacienda."

"Fancy!"

"Of course he may have invented the whole story. Or mistaken the implication."

"Two A.M. *About*. The only firm time we've got out of the whole lot," Fox grumbled, "is one A.M. According to everybody, the deceased always took the dog out at one. Mr. Belt and Mrs. Mitchell reckon he used to wait till he heard the church clock. The last car from the treasure hunt was back at Baynesholme by midnight. Yes," Fox concluded sadly, "it was an open field all right."

"Did either Alfred or Mrs. Mitchell hear anything?"

"Not a thing. They're both easy sleepers. Alfred," Fox sighed, "was thinking of turning in his job, and she was thinking of following suit."

"Why?"

"He reckoned he couldn't take the new setup. The bitch worried him. Not even clean, Mrs. Mitchell says. And the deceased seems to have suggested that Alfred

might have had something to do with the missing cigarette case, which, Mrs. Mitchell says, Alfred took great
exception to. They were both very upset, because
they've been there so long and didn't fancy a change at
their time of life. Alfred went so far as to tell Mr.
Period that it was either them or Mr. Cartell."

"When did he do that, Fox?"

"Last evening. Mr. Period was horribly put out
about it, Mrs. Mitchell says. He made out life wouldn't
be worth living without Alfred and her. And he practically undertook to terminate Mr. Cartell's tenancy.
They'd never known him to be in such a taking-on.
Quite frantic, was the way she put it."

"Indeed? . . . I think he cooked the baptismal register, all right, Fox, and I think Mr. Cartell rumbled it,"
Alleyn said, and described his visit to Ribblethorpe.

"Now, isn't that peculiar behaviour!" Fox exclaimed. "A gentleman going to those lengths to make
out he's something he is not. You'd hardly credit it."

"You'd better, because I've a strong hunch that this
case may well turn about Mr. Period's obsession. And
it is an obsession, Br'er Fox. He's been living in a
world of fantasy, and it's in danger of exploding over
his head."

"Lor!" Fox remarked, comfortably.

"When you retire in fifty years' time," Alleyn said
with an affectionate glance at his colleague, "you must
write a monograph on *Snobs I Have Known*. It's a
fruitful field and it has yet to be exhausted. Shall I tell
you what I think might be the Period story?"

"I'd be obliged," said Fox.

"Well, then. A perfectly respectable upper-middle-
class origin. A natural inclination for grandeur and a
pathologically sensitive nose for class distinctions. Money, from whatever source, at an early enough age to
provide the suitable setting. Employment that brings
him in touch with the sort of people he wants, God

save the mark, to cultivate. And all this, Br'er Fox, in, let us say, the twenties, when class distinctions were comparatively unjolted. It would be during this period—what a name he's got, to be sure!—that a fantasy began to solidify. He became used to the sort of people he had admired, felt himself to be one of them, scarcely remembered his natural background and began to think of himself as one of the nobs. The need for justification nagged at him. He's got this unusual name. Somebody said: 'By the way, are you any relation to the Period who married one of the Ribblethorpe Pykes?' and he let it be thought he was. So he began to look into the Ribblethorpe Pykes and Periods and found that both sides have died out. It would be about now that 'Pyke' was adopted as a second name—not hyphenated, but always used. He may have done it by deed poll. That, of course, can be checked. And—well, there you are. I daresay that by now he'd persuaded himself he was all he claimed to be and was happily established in his own fairy tale until Cartell, by some chance, was led to do a little private investigation and, being exasperated beyond measure, blew the gaff at yesterday's luncheon party. And if that," Alleyn concluded, "is not an excursion into the hateful realms of surmise and conjecture, I don't know *what* it is."

"Silly," Fox said. "If true. But it makes you feel sorry for him."

"Does it? Yes, I suppose it does."

"Well, it does me," Fox said uneasily. "What's the next move, Mr. Alleyn?"

"We'll have to try to find those blasted gloves."

"Where do we start?"

"Ask yourself. We're told by the unspeakable Moppett that she wore them when they drove from London to Little Codling. They might have been dropped at Miss Cartell's, Mr. Period's, or Baynesholme. They might be in the pocket of the Scorpion. They might have been burnt or buried. All we know is that it's odds-on the planks were shifted, with homicidal intent, by someone who was probably wearing leather and string gloves, and that Leonard Leiss, according to his fancy-girl, is raising merry hell because he's lost such a pair. So, press on, Br'er Fox. Press on."

"Where do we begin?"

"The obvious place is Miss Cartell's. The Moppett *says* she dumped their overcoats there, and that the gloves were in Leiss's pocket. I don't want Miss Cartell to think we're hounding her treasured ward, because if she does think that, she perfectly capable of collaborating with Leiss or the Moppett herself or Lord knows who, out of pure protective hennery. She's a fool of a woman, Lord help her. I tell you what, Fox. You do your well-known stuff with Trudi—and make it jolly careful. Then try your hand with the Period household, which evidently, as far as the staff is concerned, has been nicely softened-up by you."

"They're going out this evening," Fox said. "Church Social. They'll be in great demand, I daresay."

"Damn. All right, we'd better let them go. And, if that fails, we'll have to ask at Baynesholme. What's the matter?"

Fox was looking puffy—a sure sign, in that officer, of embarrassment.

"Well, Mr. Alleyn," he said, "I was just thinking."

"Thinking what?"

"Well, there's one aspect of the case which of course you've considered, so I'm sure there's no need to mention it. But since you ask me, there's the other young couple. Mr. Bantling and Miss Maitland-Mayne."

"I know. They were canoodling in the lane until after the other couples went back to Baynesholme, and might therefore have done the job. So they might, Br'er Fox. So, indubitably, they might."

"It'd be nice to clear them up."

"Your ideas about what would be nice vary between a watertight capital charge and cold lamb with cucumber relish. But it would be nice, I agree."

"You may say, you see, that as far as the young man is concerned, somebody else's defending counsel, with his back to the wall, could talk about motive."

"You may indeed."

"Mind, as far as the young lady's concerned, the idea's ridiculous. I think you said they met for the first time yesterday morning."

"I did. And apparently took to each other at first sight. But, I promise you, you're right. As far as the young lady is concerned I really do believe the idea's ridiculous. As for Master Andrew Bantling, he's a conventionally dressed chap. I can't think that his rig was topped off by a pair of string-backed hacking gloves. All right," Alleyn said, raising a finger. "Could he, by some means, have got hold of Leiss's gloves? When? At Baynesholme? There, or at Mr. Period's? Very well! So he drove his newly acquired girlfriend to the lane, confided his troubles to her, put on Leiss's gloves and asked her to wait a bit while he rearranged the planks."

"Well, there you are!" Fox exclaimed. "Exactly. Ridiculous!" He nodded once or twice and then said: "Where is he? Not that it matters."

Alleyn looked at his watch.

"I should think," he said, "he's on the main London highway with Nicola Maitland-Mayne. God bless my soul!" he ejaculated.

"What's up, Mr. Alleyn?"

"Do you know, I believe she's taking him to show one of his paintings to Troy. Tonight. She asked me if I thought Troy would mind. This was before the case had developed. I don't mind betting she sticks to it."

In this supposition he was entirely right.

" 4 "

"She's not a Scorpion," Andrew remarked as he negotiated a conservative overtake, "but she goes, bless her tiny little horsepower. It feels to me, Nicola, that we have been taking this trip together much more often than twice. Are you ever called 'Nicky'?"

"Sometimes."

"I don't really take to abbreviations, but I shall think about it. Better than 'Cola,' which sounds like a commercial."

"I am never called 'Cola.' "

"That's right. One must draw the line somewhere, must not one?"

Conscious of an immense and illogical wave of happiness, Nicola looked at him. Why should his not singularly distinguished profile be so pleasing to her? Was it the line of the jaw, about which she seemed to remember lady novelists make a great to-do? Or his mouth, which she supposed should be called generous? It was certainly amusing.

"What's the matter?" he asked.

"Nothing. Why?"

"You were looking at me," Andrew said, keeping a steady eye on the road.

"Sorry."

"Not at all. Dear Nicola."

"Don't go too fast."

"I'm not. She won't do more than fifty. Oh, I beg your pardon. I see what you mean. All right, I won't. But my aim, as I thought I had indicated, is not an immediate, snappy little affair with no bones broken. Far from it."

"I see."

"Tell me, if you don't mind, what you think of my people. No holds barred. It's not an idle question."

"I like your mama."

"So do I, but of course one ought to point out her legend which I expect you're familiar with, anyway. Most of it's fairly true. She's an outrageous woman really."

"But kind. I set great store by kindness."

"Well, yes. As long as she doesn't get stuck into a feud with somebody. She's generous and you can talk to her about anything. You may get a cockeyed reaction but it'll be intelligent. I dote on her."

"Are you like her?"

"I expect so, but less eccentric in my habits. I'm of a retiring disposition, compared to her, and spend most of my spare time painting, which makes me unsociable. I know I don't look like it, but I'm a serious painter."

"Well, of course. Are you very modern? All intellect, paint droppings and rude shapes?"

"Not really. You'll have to see."

"By the way, the Cid says Troy would be delighted if we'd call. To show her your work."

"The Cid?"

"Superintendent Alleyn, C.I.D. Just my girlish fun."

"I can take it if he can," Andrew said kindly. "But you know I doubt, really, if I dare show her anything. Suppose she should find it tedious and sterile?"

"She will certainly say so."

"That's what I feared. She takes pupils, doesn't she? Very grand ones with genius dripping out of their beards?"

"That's right. Would you like her to take you?"

"Lord, Lord!" Andrew said. "What a notion!"

"If it's not a question in bad taste, will you be able to get the Grantham Gallery, now, as you hoped?"

"I wanted to talk to you about it. I think I might, you know. I don't imagine P.P. will raise the same objections. I talked to him about it yesterday morning."

Remembering what Mr. Period had said about these plans, Nicola asked Andrew if he didn't think there would be some difficulty.

"Oh, I don't, really. He talked a lot of guff about tradition and so on but I'm sure he'll be reasonable. He's different from Hal. *He* was just being bloody-minded because I wanted to leave the Brigade and because he was bloody-minded anyway, poor old Hal. All the same, I wish I hadn't parted from him breathing hell-fury. Seeing what's happened. He wasn't such a bad old stinker," Andrew reflected. "Better than Bimbo, anyway. What, by the way, did you think of Bimbo?"

"Well—"

"Come on. Honestly."

"There wasn't anything *to* think. Just a rather negative, fashionable, ambiguous sort of person."

"I simply can't imagine what persuaded my Mama to marry him. Well, I suppose I can, really." Andrew hit his closed fist once upon the driving wheel. "Still, don't let's talk about that."

He drove on for some minutes in silence while Nicola tried to sort out her desperate misgivings. "Andrew," she said at last, and because he answered "What, dear?" so gently, and with such an old-fashioned air, found herself at a complete disadvantage.

"Look," she said. "Have you thought—I know it's fantastic—but have you . . . ?"

"All right," Andrew said. "I know. Have I thought that Hal's death is a material advantage to me and that your Cid probably knows it? Yes, I have. Strangely enough, it doesn't alarm me. Nicola, it's not fair to wish all this business on you. Here I am, doing nothing but talk about me and setting myself up as an insufferable egoist, no doubt. Am I boring you very much?"

"No," Nicola said truthfully. "You're not doing that. You're talking about yourself, which is the usual thing."

"My God!" Andrew ejaculated. "How very chastening."

"This time it's a bit different."

"Is it? How much?"

"No," Nicola said. "Don't let's rush our fences. We only met yesterday morning. Everything's being precipitated like one of those boring chemical experiments. Don't let's pay too much attention."

"Just as you like," he said huffily. "I was going to ask if you'd dine with me. Is that too precipitate?"

"I expect it is, really, but I'd like to. Thank you, Andrew. I have a motive."

"And what the hell is that?"

"I did mention it before. I'm going to visit Troy Alleyn this evening, and I wondered if you'd come with me and show her a picture. As I told you, the Cid says she'd be delighted."

Andrew was silent for a moment and then burst out laughing. "Well, I must say!" he ejaculated. "As one of the suspects in a murder charge—yes, I am, Nicola. You can't escape it—I'm being invited to pay a social call on the chief cop's wife. How dotty can you get?"

"Well, why not?"

"Will he be there? No, I suppose not. He'll be lying flat on his stomach in Green Lane looking for my boot-prints."

"So it's a date?"

"It's a date."

"Then, shall we collect your pictures? I live quite close to the Alleyns. Could you make do with an omelette in my flat?"

"Do you share it with two other nice girls?"

"No."

"Then I'd love to."

Nicola's flat was a converted studio off the Brompton Road. It was large and airy and extremely uncluttered. The walls were white and the curtains and chairs yellow. A workmanlike desk stood against the north window and a pot of yellow tulips on the table. There was only one picture, hung above the fireplace. Andrew went straight to it.

"Gosh," he said, "it's a Troy. And it's you."

"It was for my twenty-first birthday, last year. Wasn't it wonderful of her?"

There was a long silence. "Wonderful," Andrew said. "Wonderful." And she left him to look at it while she rang Troy Alleyn and then set to work in her kitchen.

They had cold soup, an omelette, white wine, cheese and salad, and their meal was extremely successful. They both behaved in an exemplary manner, and if their inclination to depart from this standard crackled in the air all round them, they contrived to disregard it. They talked and talked and were happy.

"It's almost nine o'clock," Nicola said. "We mustn't be too late at Troy's. She'll be delighted to see you, by the way."

"Will she?"

"Why did you leave your pictures in the car?"

"I don't know. Well, yes I do, but it doesn't matter. Wouldn't it be nice to stay here?"

"Come on," Nicola said firmly.

When they had shut the door behind them, Andrew took her hands in his, thanked her for his entertainment and kissed her lightly on the cheek.

"Here we go," he said.

They collected the canvases from the car and walked to the Alleyns' house, which was at the end of a blind street near Montpelier Square. It was such a natural and familiar thing for Nicola to take this evening walk that her anxieties left her, and by the time they reached their destination and Troy herself opened the door to them, she felt nothing but pleasure in their expedition.

Troy was wearing the black trousers and smock that meant she had been working. Her shortish dark hair capped a spare head and fell in a single lock across her forehead. Andrew stood to attention and carried his canvases as if they were something rather disgraceful that had been found in the guardroom.

"I'm in the studio," Troy said. "Shall we go there? It's a better light."

Andrew himself fell in and followed them.

There was a large charcoal drawing on the easel in Troy's studio: a woman with a cat. On the table where Troy had been working were other drawings under a strong lamp.

Andrew said: "Mrs. Alleyn, it's terribly kind of you to let me come."

"Why?" Troy said, cheerfully. "You're going to show me some work, aren't you?"

"Oh God!" Andrew said. "So Nicola tells me."

Troy looked at him in a friendly manner and began to talk about the subject of the drawing, saying how paintable and silly she was, always changing her hair and coming in the wrong clothes, and that the drawing was a study for a full-scale portrait. Andrew eased up a little.

Nicola said: "There are one or two things to explain."

"Not as many as you may think. Rory rang up an hour ago from Little Codling."

"Did he tell you about Andrew's stepfather?"

"Yes, he did. I expect," Troy said to Andrew, "it seems unreal as well as dreadful, doesn't it?"

"In a way it does. We—I didn't see much of him. I mean—"

"Andrew," Nicola said, "insists that the Cid has got him down among the suspects."

"Well, it's not for me to say," Troy replied, "but I didn't think it sounded like that. Let's have a look at your things."

She took her drawing off the easel and put it against the wall. Andrew dropped all his paintings on the floor with a sudden crash. "I'm frightfully sorry," he said.

"Come on," Troy said. "I'm not a dentist. Put it on the easel."

The first painting was a still life: tulips on a window sill in a red goblet with rooftops beyond them.

"Hul-lo!" Troy said and sat down in front of it.

Nicola wished she knew a great deal more about painting. She could see it was incisive, freely done and lively, with a feeling for light and colour. She realized that she would have liked it very much if she had come across it somewhere else. It didn't look at all amateur-ish.

"Yes, well of course," Troy said, and it was clear that she meant: "Of course you're a painter and you were right to show me this." She went on talking to Andrew, asking him about his palette and the conditions under which he worked. Then she saw his next canvas, which was a portrait. Désirée's flaming hair and cadaverous eyes leapt out of a flowery back-ground. She had sat in a glare of sunlight and the treatment was far from being conventional.

"My mum," Andrew said.

"You had fun with the colour, didn't you? Don't you find the eye-round-the-corner hell to manage in a three-quarter head? This one hasn't quite come off, has it? Look, it's that dab of pink that hits up. Now, let's see the next one."

The next and last one was a male torso uncompromisingly set against a white wall. It had been painted with exhaustive attention to anatomy. "Heavens!" Troy ejaculated. "You've practically skinned the man." She looked at it for some time and then said: "Well, what are you going to do about this? Would you like to work here once a week?"

After that Andrew was able to talk to her and did so with such evident delight that Nicola actually detected in herself a twinge of something that astonished her and gave an edge to her extreme happiness.

It was not until much later, when Troy had produced lager, and they were telling her about the Grantham Gallery project, that Nicola remembered Mr. Period.

"I think," she told Troy, "you're going to be approached by my new boss. He's writing a book on etiquette and his publishers want a drawing of him. He's rather shy about asking because you turned down one of his lordly chums. You know him, don't you? Mr. Pyke Period?"

"Yes, of course I do. He crops up at all the Private Views that he thinks are smart occasions. I'll be blowed if I'll draw him."

"I was afraid that might be your reaction."

"Well," Troy said, "there's no denying he really is a complete old phony. Do you know he once commissioned a pupil of mine to do a painting from some print he'd picked up, of a Georgian guardee making faces at a thunderstorm. He said it was one of his ancestors, and so it may have been, but after a lot of beating about the bush he made it quite clear that he wanted this job faked to look like an eighteenth-century portrait. My pupil was practically on the breadline at the time and I'm afraid the thing was done."

"Oh, dear!" Nicola sighed. "I know. It's there, in the library, I think. He's like that, but he's rather an old sweetie-pie, all the same. Isn't he, Andrew?"

"Nicola," said Andrew, "I daresay he is. But he's a terrible old donkey. And yet—I don't know. Is P.P. just plain silly? I doubt it. I rather think there's an element of low cunning."

"Childish, not low," Nicola insisted, but Andrew was looking at her with such a degree of affectionate attention that she was extremely flustered.

"Well," Andrew said. "Never mind, anyway, about P.P."

"I can't help it. He was so miserable all the afternoon. You know: trying to forge ahead with his tips on U-necessities, as he inevitably calls them, and then falling into wretched little trances. He really was in a bad state. Everything seemed to upset him."

"What sorts of things?" Troy asked. "Have some more lager?"

"No, thank you. Well, he kept singing in an extremely dismal manner. And then he would stop and turn sheet-white. He muttered something about 'No, no, I mustn't—better forget it,' and looked absolutely terrified."

"How very odd," Andrew said. "What was his song?"

"I don't remember—yes, I do!" Nicola exclaimed. "Of course I do! Because he'd done the same sort of thing yesterday, after lunch: hummed it and then been cross with himself. But it was different today. He seemed quite shattered."

"And the song?"

"It was the pop-song that ghastly Leonard kept whistling through his teeth at luncheon. He even sang a bit of it when they were looking at the cigarette case: *If you mean what I think you mean, O.K. by me. Things aren't always what they seem. O.K. by me.*"

"Not exactly a 'Period piece.' "

"It was all very rum."

"Did you happen to mention it to Rory?" Troy asked.

"No. I haven't seen him since it happened. And anyway, why should I?"

"No reason at all, I daresay."

"Look," Nicola said quickly, "however foolish he may be, Mr. Period is quite incapable of the smallest degree of hanky-panky—" She stopped short and the now familiar jolt of indefinable panic revisited her. "Serious hanky-panky, I mean," she amended.

"Good Lord, no!" Andrew said. "Of course he is. Incapable, I mean."

Nicola stood up. "It's a quarter to twelve," she said. "We must go, Andrew. Poor Troy!"

The telephone rang and Troy answered it. The voice at the other end said quite distinctly: "Darling?"

"Hullo," Troy said. "Still at it?"

"Very much so. Is Nicola with you?"

"Yes," Troy said. "She and Andrew Bantling."

"Could I have a word with her?"

"Here you are."

Troy held out the receiver and Nicola took it feeling her heart thud stupidly against her ribs.

"Hullo, Cid," she said.

"Hullo, Nicola. There's something that's cropped up here that you might just possibly be able to give me a line about. After I left you today, did you discuss our conversation with anybody?"

"Well, yes," she said. "With Andrew."

"Anyone else? Now don't go jumping to conclusions, there's a good child, but did Mr. Period want to know if you told me anything about his luncheon party?"

Nicola swallowed. "Yes, he did. But it was only, poor lamb, because he hates the idea of your hearing about the digs Mr. Cartell made at his snob-values. He was terribly keen to know if I'd told you anything about the baptismal register story."

"And you said you had told me?"

"Well, I had to, when he asked me point-blank. I made as little of it as I could."

"Yes. I see. One other thing—and it's important, Nicola. Do you, by any chance, know anything that would connect Mr. Period with a popular song?"

"A song! No—not—"

"Something about *O.K. by me?*"

CHAPTER SEVEN

Pixie

It had been five past eleven when Alleyn was summoned to the telephone. He and Fox, having struck a blank in respect to the gloves, had been mulling over their notes in the Codling pub when the landlord, avid with curiosity, summoned him.

"It's a call for you, sir," he said. "Local. I didn't catch the name. There's no one in the bar parlour, if that suits you."

Alleyn took the call in the bar parlour.

He said: "Alleyn here. Hullo?"

Mr. Pyke Period, unmistakable and agitated, answered. "Alleyn? Thank God! I'm so sorry to disturb you at this unconscionable hour. Do forgive me. The thing is there's something I feel I ought to tell—"

The voice stopped. Alleyn heard a bump, followed by a soft, heavier noise and then by silence. He waited for a moment or two. There was a faint definite click and, again, silence. He rang and got the "engaged" signal. He hung up and turned to find Fox at his side.

"Come on," he said. "I'll tell you on the way."

When they were clear of the pub he broke into a run, with Fox, heavy and capable, on his heels.

"Period," Alleyn said. "And it looks damn' fishy. Stopped dead in full cry. Characteristic noises."

The pub was in a side street that led into the Green at Mr. Period's end of it. There was nobody about and their footsteps sounded loud on the paving-stones. Connie Cartell's Pekingese was yapping somewhere on the far side of the Green. Distantly, from the parish schoolroom, came the sound of communal singing.

Only one room in Mr. Period's house was lit and that was the library. Stepping as quietly as the gravelled drive would permit, they moved towards the French windows. Bay trees stood on either side of the glass doors, which were almost but not quite shut.

Alleyn looked across the table Nicola had used, past her shrouded typewriter and stacked papers. Beyond, to his right, and against the window in the side wall, was Mr. Period's desk. His shaded lamp, as if it had been switched on by a stage manager, cast down a pool of light on that restricted area, giving it an immense theatricality. The telephone receiver dangled from the desk and Mr. Period's right arm hung beside it. His body was tipped forward in his chair and his face lay among his papers. The hair was ruffled like a baby's and from his temple a ribbon of blood had run down the cheekbone to the nostril.

"Doctor"—Alleyn said—"What's-his-name—Elkington."

Fox said: "Better use the other phone." He replaced the receiver very gingerly and went into the hall.

Mr. Period was not dead. When Alleyn bent over him, he could hear his breathing—a faint snoring sound. The pulse was barely perceptible.

Fox came back. "On his way," he said. "Will I search outside?"

"Right. We'd better not move him. I'll do the house."

It was perfectly quiet and empty of living persons. Alleyn went from room to room, opening and shutting doors, receiving the indefinable smells of long-inhabited places, listening, looking and finding nothing. Mrs. Mitchell's room smelt stuffily of hairpins and Alfred Belt's of boot polish. Mr. Period's bedroom smelt of hair lotion and floor polish, and Mr. Cartell's of blankets and soap. Nothing was out of place anywhere in Mr. Period's house. Alleyn returned to the library as Fox came in.

"Nothing," Fox said. "Nobody, anywhere."

"There's the instrument," Alleyn said.

It was the bronze paperweight in the form of a fish that Désirée had given Mr. Period. It lay on the carpet close to his dangling hand.

"I'll get our chaps," Fox said. "They're in the pub. Here's the doctor."

Dr. Elkington came in looking as if his professional manner had been fully extended.

"What now, for God's sake?" he said and went straight to his patient. Alleyn watched him make his examination, which did not take long.

"All right," he said. "On the face of it he's severely concussed. I don't think there's any extensive cranial injury but we'll have to wait. Half an inch either way and it'd have been a different matter. We'd better get him out of this. Where's that man of his—Alfred?"

"At a Church Social," said Alleyn. "We could get a mattress. Or what about the sofa in the drawing-room?"

"All right. Better than manhandling him all over the shop."

Fox and Alleyn carried Mr. Period into the drawing-room and propped him up on the sofa, Dr. Elkington supporting his head.

"Will he speak?" Alleyn asked Dr. Elkington.

"Might or might not. Your guess is as good as mine. There's nothing we can do at the moment. He may have to go to hospital. I'd better get a nurse. What's the story, if there is a story?"

"Somebody chucked a bronze paperweight at him. You'd better look at it. Don't touch it unless you have to. Fox will show you. I'm staying here. I'll let you know if there's a change."

"Attempted murder?" Dr. Elkington said, making a mouthful of it.

"I think so."

"For God's sake!" Dr. Elkington repeated. He and Fox went out of the room. Alleyn drew up a chair and watched Mr. Period.

His eyes were not quite closed and his breathing, though still markedly stertorous, seemed to be more regular. Alleyn heard Dr. Elkington at the telephone.

The doorbell rang. The other chaps, he thought. Fox would cope.

Mr. Period's eyes opened and looked, squintingly, at nothing.

"You're all right," Alleyn said, leaning towards him.

Dr. Elkington came back. "It's the paperweight sure enough," he said. "Trace of blood on the edge." He went to the sofa and took Mr. Period's hand in his.

"Don't worry," he said. "You're all right."

The flaccid lips parted. After an indeterminate noise a whisper drifted through them: *It was that song.*

"Song? What song?"

"He's deeply concussed, Alleyn."

"What song?"

"*Should have told Alleyn. Whistling. Such awfully bad form. Luncheon.*"

"What song?"

"*Couldn't—out of my head.*" Mr. Period whispered plaintively. "*So silly. 'O.K. by me.' So, of course. Recognized. At once.*" The sound faded and for a moment or two the lips remained parted. Then Mr. Period's own voice, uncannily articulate, said quite clearly: "May I speak to Superintendent Alleyn?"

"Yes," Alleyn said, holding up a warning hand. "Alleyn speaking."

"Just to tell you. Whistling. Recognized it. Last night. In the lane. Very wrong of me not to—Divided loyalties." There was a longish silence. Alleyn and Elkington stared absently at each other. *"O.K. by me,"* the voice sighed. *"So vulgar."*

The eyes closed again.

"This may go on for hours, Alleyn."

"How much will he remember when he comes round?"

"Everything probably, up to the moment he was knocked out. Unless there's a serious injury to the brain." Dr. Elkington was stooping over his patient. "Still bleeding a bit. I'll have to put in a couple of stitches. Where's my bag?" He went out. Fox was talking to the men in the hall. "We'll seal the library and cover the area outside the window."

"Do we search?" asked somebody. Williams, Alleyn decided.

"Better talk to the Chief."

Fox and Williams came in with Dr. Elkington, who opened his professional bag.

"Just steady his head, will you?" he asked Alleyn.

Holding Mr. Period's head between his hands, Alleyn said to Fox and Williams: "It looks as if the thing was thrown at him by somebody standing between the table and the French windows while he was ringing me up. I heard the receiver knock against the desk as it fell and I heard a click that might well have been made by the windows being pulled to. You're not likely to find anything on the drive. It's as dry as a bone and in any case the French doors are probably used continually. Whoever made the attack had time enough to effect a clean getaway before we came trundling in, but I think the best line we can take is to keep watch in case he's still hiding in the garden—Noakes and Thompson can do that—and Fox, you rouse up Miss Cartell's household. Somebody will have to stay here in case he speaks again. Bob, would you do that?"

"Right," said Superintendent Williams.

"I've got a call to London."

"To London?" Williams repeated.

"It may give us a line. Fox, I'll join you at Miss Cartell's. O.K?"

"O.K., Mr. Alleyn."

"And Bailey had better have a go at the paper-weight. I think it was probably on the table near the French windows. There are various piles of stacked papers, all but one weighed down. And one of the ashtrays has got two lipsticked butts in it. Miss Ralston and Leiss smoke Mainsails, Lady Bantling smokes Cafards and Mr. Period, Turkish. Ask him to look. Gloves!" Alleyn ejaculated. "If we could find those damn' gloves. Not that they are likely to have anything to do with this party, but we've a glove-conscious homicide on our hands, I fancy. All right. . . . Let's get cracking."

It was at this juncture—at a quarter to midnight—that he talked on the telephone to Nicola Maitland-Mayne.

Then he rejoined Elkington in the drawing-room.

"Has he said anything else?"

"No."

"Look here, Elkington, can you stick it here with Williams for a bit? We're fully extended, we can't risk the chance of missing anything he may say, and Williams will be glad of a witness. Somebody will relieve you as soon as possible."

"Yes, of course."

"Write it down, Bob, if he does speak. I'm much obliged to you both."

He was about to go when a sound, fainter than anything they had yet heard, came from the sofa. It wavered tenuously for a second or two and petered out. Mr. Period, from whatever region he at present inhabited, had been singing.

" 2 "

As Alleyn was about to leave the house, Detective Sergeant Bailey presented himself.

"There's a small thing," he said.

"What small thing?"

"There's nothing for us on the gravel outside the French windows, Mr. Alleyn, but I reckon there's something on the carpet."

"What?"

"Traces of ash. Scuffed into the carpet, I reckon, by one of those pin-point heels."

"Good man," Alleyn said. "Carry on." He let himself out and walked down the drive.

It was a dark night, overcast and rather sultry. As he approached the gates he became aware of a very slight movement in a patch of extremely black shadows cast by a group of trees. He stopped dead. Was it Thompson or Noakes, on to something and keeping doggo, or was it . . . ? He listened and again there was a rustle and the sound of heavy breathing. At this moment a spot of torchlight danced about the drive and Sergeant Noakes himself appeared from the opposite direction, having apparently crossed the lawn and emerged through Mr. Period's shrubs. He shone his light in Alleyn's face and said: "Oh, beg pardon, sir. There's nothing to be seen, sir, anywhere. Except dog prints. Two kinds."

Alleyn gestured silently towards the shadows. "Eh?" said Noakes. "What?" And then comprehensively: "Cor!"

There being no point after this in attempting any further concealment Alleyn said: "Look out, you ass," and switched on his own torchlight, aiming it at the shadows.

"On your toes, now," he said and advanced, Noakes with him.

He walked past a lowish thicket of evergreens, pointed his light into the depths beyond, and illuminated Alfred Belt with Mrs. Mitchell, transfixed in his arms.

"I'm sure I beg your pardon, sir," said Alfred.

Mrs. Mitchell said: "Oh dear; what a coincidence! What will the gentlemen be thinking," and tittered.

"What we'll be thinking," Alleyn said, "depends to a certain extent on what you'll be saying. Come out."

Alfred looked at his arms as if they didn't belong to him, released Mrs. Mitchell and advanced to the drive. "I should have thought, sir," he said with restraint, "that the circumstance was self-explanatory."

"We didn't return by the side gate," Mrs. Mitchell offered, "on account of my not fancying it after what has taken place."

"A very natural feminine reaction, sir, if I may say so."

"We were returning," said Mrs. Mitchell, "from the Church Social."

"Mrs. Mitchell has been presented with the long-service Girls' Friendly Award. Richly deserved. I was offering my congratulations."

"Jolly good," Alleyn said. "May I offer mine?"

"Thank you very much, I'm sure. It's a teapot," Mrs. Mitchell said, exhibiting her trophy.

"And of course, a testimonial," Alfred amended.

"Splendid. And you have spent the evening together?"

"Not to say together, sir. Mrs. Mitchell, as befitted the occasion, occupied the rostrum. I am merely her escort," said Alfred.

"The whole thing," Alleyn confessed, "fits together

like a jigsaw puzzle. What are you going to do next?"

"Next, sir?"

"Next."

"Well sir. As it's something of an event, I hope to persuade Mrs. Mitchell to join me in a nightcap, after which we will retire," Alfred said with some emphasis, "to our respective accommodations."

"Dog permitting," Mrs. Mitchell said abruptly.

"Dog?"

"Pixie, sir. She is still at large. There may be disturbances."

"Alfred," Alleyn said, "when did you leave Mr. Period?"

"Leave him, sir?"

"Tonight?"

"After I had served coffee, sir, which was at eight-thirty."

"Do you know if he was expecting a telephone call?"

"Not that I was aware," Alfred said. "He didn't mention it. Is anything the matter, sir, with Mr. Period?"

"Yes," Alleyn said, "there is. He has been the victim of a murderous assault, and is severely concussed."

"Oh, my Gawd!" Mrs. Mitchell ejaculated and clapped a hand over her mouth.

"My gentleman? Where is he? Here," Alfred said loudly, "let me go in!"

"By all means. You will find Dr. Elkington there and Superintendent Williams. Report to them, will you?"

"Certainly, sir," said Alfred.

"One other thing. When did you empty the ashtrays in the library?"

"After dinner, sir. As usual."

"Splendid. Thank you."

"Thank you, sir," Alfred said, automatically.

Alleyn saw them go in and himself crossed the Green to Miss Cartell's house. A belated couple, closely entwined, was making its way home, presumably from the Social. Otherwise all was quiet.

He found Fox in Miss Cartell's drawing-room with the household rounded up before him. On these occasions Fox always reminded Alleyn of a dependable sheepdog.

Connie herself was lashed into a dull purple robe, beneath the hem of which appeared the decent evidence of a sensible nightgown and a pair of extremely grubby slippers. Leonard Leiss was in trousers and shirt and Moppett in the négligé she had worn that morning. She was made up. Her pale lipstick had been smudged and her hair was dishevelled. She looked both sulky and frightened. Trudi, in a casque of hair curlers, but still fully dressed, seemed to be transfixed by astonishment.

Connie said: "Look here, this is all pretty ghastly, isn't it? How is he?"

"He's not conscious."

"Yes, but I mean, how *bad* is it?"

Alleyn said they were not sure how bad it was.

"Well, but what happened?" Connie persisted, looking resentfully at Inspector Fox. "We don't know anything. Turfing everybody out of bed and asking all these questions."

"Oh, do pipe down, Auntie," Moppett protested with some violence. "It's perfectly obvious what it's all about."

"It's not obvious to me."

"Fancy!" Leonard remarked offensively.

Fox said with forbearance: "Well now, Mr. Alleyn, we're getting on slowly. I've tried to explain the necessity, as a purely routine affair, for checking-up these good people's whereabouts."

"Certainly."

"Yes. Well it seems Miss Cartell has been at home this evening, apart from an interval when she took her little dog into the garden—"

"That's right," Connie interrupted indignantly. "And if it wasn't for that damned bitch, I'd have been in my bed an hour ago. And where's my Li? That's what I want to know. He's a valuable dog, and if anything's happened to him, chasing after that mongrel, I'll hold you responsible." She wrung her hands distractedly.

"The little dog," Fox explained, "has gone off for a romp."

Moppett laughed shrilly.

"What happened exactly?"

"I'll tell you what happened," Connie shouted. "I was going to bed and he asked for outies. He'd already had them once, so I might have known, but he kept on asking. So I took him down. No sooner were we in the garden than I saw that brute, and so did he. She went floundering off and he was out of my arms and after her before I could stop him. I'm a bit clumsy because of my thumb. Otherwise," she added, proudly, "he wouldn't have made it."

"Miss Cartell," Fox explained, "was in the garden, calling the little dog, when I arrived."

"There'll have to be an organized search," Connie blustered. "That's all. An organized search. I'm jolly sorry about P.P., but I can't help it."

"How long ago did this happen?"

"Did what happen?"

"The Pekingese business."

"How the hell should I know?" Connie said, rudely. "I seem to have been out there for hours. All over the village in this kit. Look at my feet! Nobody about, luckily. Not that I care. God knows where he's got to."

"What time did you go to bed?"

"I haven't been to bed."

"Well, when did you get ready to go to bed?"

"I don't know. Yes, I do. About nine o'clock."

"Early!" Alleyn remarked.

"I wanted to watch the telly. I like to be comfortable," said Connie.

"And did you watch your telly?"

"Started to, but it was a lot of guff about delinquent teenagers. I went to sleep. Li woke me. That's when he asked for outies."

"Well," Alleyn said, "we progress."

"If you've finished with me——"

"I'll have to ask you to wait a minute or two longer."

"My God!" Connie said and threw up her hands.

Alleyn turned to Moppett and Leonard.

"And neither of you, I gather, joined in the search."

Leonard stretched himself elaborately. "Afraid not," he said. "I understood it to be a routine party."

"I shouted up to you," Connie pointed out resentfully.

"So sorry," Moppett said. "I was in my bath."

"You hadn't washed your face," Alleyn observed.

"I don't clean my face in my bath."

"But you bathed?"

"Yes."

"When? For how long?"

"I don't know when, and I like to take my time."

"Fox?" Alleyn said. "Will you look in the bathroom?"

Fox made for the door.

"All right," Moppett said breathlessly. "I didn't have a bath. I was going to and I heard all the rumpus and Auntie shrieking for Li and I went to Lennie's room and said ought we to do anything and we got talking and then your friend Mr. Fox came and hauled us down here."

"And earlier? Before you thought of taking a bath?"

"We were talking."

"Where?"

"In my room."

Connie looked at her with a sort of despair. "Really, you two," she said like an automaton. "What Mr. Alleyn will think!" She looked anxiously at him. "I can vouch for them," she said. "They were both in. All the evening. I'd swear it."

"You were asleep with the television on, Miss Cartell."

"I'd have known if anyone went out. I always do. It was only a cat nap. They always bang the door. Anyway I heard them, talking and laughing upstairs."

"Can you help us, Trudi?" Alleyn asked.

"I do not know what is all happen," said Trudi. "I am at the priest's hall where is a party. I sing. Schuplatter dancing also I do."

"That'd sent them," said Leonard and laughed.

"I return at half-past eleven o'clock and I make my hair."

"Did you help in the search?"

"Please?"

"Did you help look for the little dog?"

"*Ach!* Yes. I hear the screech of Miss Cartell who is saying 'Come Li, come Li,' and I go."

"There you are!" Connie cried out with a sort of gloomy triumph about nothing in particular.

Leonard murmured: "You're wasting your time, chum."

Alleyn said: "I should like to know if there were any personal telephone calls during the day, Miss Cartell. Apart from routine domestic ones."

Connie stared at him distractedly. "I don't know," she said. "No. I don't think so. No. Not for me."

"For anyone else? Outgoing or incoming calls? Mr. Leiss?"

"I had a call to London," Leonard said. "I had to put off an urgent business engagement. Thanks to your keeping me here."

"It was a jolly long call," Connie said, obviously with thoughts of the bill.

"Who was it made to, if you please?"

"Fellow at my club," Leonard said grandly.

"The Hacienda?"

Leonard darted a venomous glance at him, leant back in his chair and looked at the ceiling.

"And that was the only call?" Alleyn continued.

"Far as I know," said Connie.

"Any messages?"

"Messages?"

"Notes? Word of mouth?"

"Not that I know," Connie said wearily.

"Please?" Trudi asked. "Message? Yes?"

"I was asking if anyone brought a letter, a written note, or a message."

"No, they didn't," Moppett loudly interrupted.

"But, yes, Miss. For you. By Mr. Belt."

"All right. *All* right," Leonard drawled. "She can't remember every damn' thing. It didn't amount to a row of beans—"

"One moment," Alleyn said, raising a finger. Leonard subsided. "So Belt brought you a message from Mr. Period. When, Miss Ralston?"

"I don't know."

"After tea," Trudi said.

"What was the message?"

"I didn't pay much attention. I don't remember," said Moppett.

"You don't have to talk," Leonard said. "Shut up." He began to whistle under his breath. Moppett nudged his foot and he stopped abruptly.

"What," Alleyn asked, "is that tune? Is it 'O.K. by Me'?"

"No idea, I'm afraid," Leonard said. Moppett looked deadly sick.

"Have you had the leak in the radiator mended?"

Moppett made a strange little noise in her throat.

"Miss Ralston," Alleyn said, "did you whistle late last night when you were near Mr. Period's garden gate?"

There was a kind of stoppage in the room as if a film had been halted at a specific point.

Moppett said: "You must be dotty. What do you mean—in the lane?"

"Like I told you. You don't have to say one single thing. Just keep your little trap shut, baby," said Leonard.

"Moppett!" Connie cried out. "Don't. Don't say anything, darling."

Moppett hurled herself at her guardian and clawed her like a terrified kitten. "Auntie Con!" she sobbed. "Don't let him! Auntie Con! I'm sorry. I don't know anything. I haven't done anything. Auntie Con!"

Connie enfolded her with a gesture that for all its clumsiness had something classic about it. She turned her head and looked at Alleyn with desperation.

"My ward," she said, "hasn't anything to tell you. Don't frighten her."

The front doorbell sounded loudly.

"I answer?" Trudi asked composedly.

"If you please," Alleyn said.

Leonard got up and walked away. Connie's large uncomely hand patted Moppett as if she were a dog. Voices sounded in the hall and an exclamation from Trudi.

"My God," Connie exclaimed, "what now?"

"Don't let them come," Moppett said. "Who is it? Don't let them come."

Connie put her aside. After a venomous and terrified look at Alleyn, Moppett joined Leonard at the far end of the room, noisily blowing her nose.

A strangulated yapping broke out and an unmistakable voice said: "Shut up, you little ass," and then, apparently to Trudi: "Well, just for a moment."

Désirée Bantling came in, followed by her husband. She was dressed in green and mink and carried the dishevelled and panting Pekingese.

"Hullo, Connie," she said. "Look what we've found!"

Connie made a plunge at her and gathered the dog into her arms in much the same way she had taken Moppett.

"Hullo, Rory," said Désirée, "still at it? Good evening," she added in the direction of Fox, Moppett and Leonard.

Bimbo said: "We picked him up out there having a high old time with the boxer bitch."

"She took another bite at poor Bimbo," Désirée said. "Same hand and all. It's becoming quite a thing with her. Show them, darling."

Bimbo, who had his left hand in his overcoat pocket, said: "Do shut up about it, darling."

"He's rather touchy on the subject," Désirée explained. "I can't think why."

"You bad boy," Connie said. The Pekingese licked her face excitedly.

"So, knowing you'd be in a fever, we roped him in. I fear she's seduced him, Connie," said Désirée.

"Is nature," Trudi observed. She was standing inside the door.

"And there," Désirée remarked with a grin, "you have the matter in a nutshell."

She gave a comprehensive glance round the room. "We're not staying," she said, "having had a pretty lethal evening. Sorry to interrupt. Come along, darling."

Alleyn said: "Just a minute, if you don't mind."

She looked at him in her leisurely unconcerned way. "What, again?" she remarked and sat down.

"Where exactly did you find the dog?"

With Pixie, it appeared, on the Green. It had taken Désirée and Bimbo some time to catch Li, and they must have looked, she said, pretty silly, if there'd been anyone to see them. She fitted a cigarette into a holder. Her beautiful gloves were dirty.

"Where had you come from?"

"My dears, we'd been dining near Bornlee Green. A dim general and his wife; and pretty heavy weather, by and large, we made of it."

"Rather late for a dinner party."

"With bridge afterwards, darling."

"I see. Tell me," Alleyn said, "have you seen or heard anything of Pyke Period since I left Baynesholme this afternoon?"

"No," said Bimbo, at once. "Why?"

Alleyn turned to Désirée, who raised her eyebrows at him. "And you?" he asked her.

"I ran in for a moment on our way to Bornlee Green. There was something I wanted to tell him. Bimbo waited in the car."

"Was it something about the letter we discussed just before I left Baynesholme?"

"Actually, yes." She gave him a half smile. "Sorry," she said. "I changed my mind. I told him."

"I don't know what anybody's talking about," Connie grumbled. She looked anxiously at Moppett, who had got herself under control and, with Leonard, stayed at the far end of the room, avidly listening.

"You're not alone in that, Auntie," said Moppett.

Bimbo said, loudly: "Look here, I don't know if anybody agrees with me, but I'm getting very bored with the turn this affair is taking. We're being asked all sorts of personal questions without the smallest reason being given, and I don't feel inclined to take much more of it."

"Hear, hear," said Leonard. Bimbo glanced at him with profound distaste.

"I fear, my darling," Désirée said, "you will have to lump it. Our finer feelings are not of much account, I fancy."

"All the same, I want to know. What's this about P.P.? Why the hell shouldn't you call in to see him? We might be living in a police state," he blustered, looking sideways at Alleyn.

"Mr. Dodds," Alleyn said, "any visit to Mr. Period during the last few hours is perfectly relevant, since, at about eleven o'clock this evening, somebody attempted to murder him."

There are not so very many ways in which people react to news of this sort. They may cry out in what appears to be astonishment, they may turn red or white and look ambiguous, or they may simply sit and gape. Bimbo and Désirée followed this last pattern.

After a moment Désirée exclaimed: "P.P.? Not true!" And, at the same time, Bimbo said: "Not possible!"

"On the contrary," said Alleyn, "possible and, unfortunately, true."

"Attempted to *murder* him," Bimbo echoed. "How? Why?"

"With a brass paperweight. Possibly," Alleyn said, turning to Désirée, "because you told him that I'd got the letter he sent by mistake to you."

" 3 "

Looking at Désirée, Alleyn thought: But I won't get any change out of you, my girl. If I've given you a jolt, you're not going to let anyone know it.

"That seems very far-fetched," she said composedly.

"Here!" Connie intervened. "Did you get a funny letter too, Désirée? Here—What *is* all this?"

"I'm afraid I don't believe you," Désirée said to Alleyn.

"You've no right to make an accusation of that sort," Bimbo cried out. "Making out people are responsible for murderous attacks and not giving the smallest explanation. What evidence have you got?"

"Since the damage has been done," Alleyn said, "I'm prepared to put a certain amount of the evidence before you."

"Damn' big of you, I must say! Though why it should concern Désirée—"

Alleyn said: "Directly or indirectly, you are all concerned."

He waited for a moment. Nobody said anything and he went on:

"It's too much to expect that each one of you will answer any questions fully or even truthfully, but it's my duty to ask you to do so."

"Why shouldn't we?" Connie protested. "I don't see why you've got to say a thing like that. Boysie always said that in murder trials the guilty have nothing to fear. He always said that. I mean the innocent," she added distractedly. "You know what I mean."

"How right he was. Very well, shall we start with that premise in mind? Now. Yesterday at luncheon, Mr. Cartell told a story about a man who cooked a baptismal register in order to establish blood relation-

ship with a certain family. Those of you who were
there may have thought that Mr. Period seemed to be
very much put out by this anecdote. Would you
agree?"

Connie said bluntly: "I thought P.P.'s behaviour was
jolly peculiar. I thought he'd got his knife into Boysie
about something."

Moppett, who seemed to have regained her com-
posure, said: "If you ask me, P.P. was terrified Uncle
Hal would tell the whole story. He looked murder at
him. Not that I mean anything by that."

"In any case," Alleyn continued, "Mr. Period was
disturbed by the incident. He wrote a short and rather
ambiguous letter to Miss Cartell, suggesting that his
ancestry did, in fact, go back as far as anyone who
bothered about such things might wish, and asking her
to forgive him for pursuing the matter. At the same
time he wrote a letter of condolence to Lady Bantling.
Unfortunately he transferred the envelopes."

"How bad is he?" Désirée asked suddenly.

Alleyn told her how bad Mr. Period seemed to be
and she said: "We can take him if it'd help."

Bimbo started to say something and stopped.

"Now this misfortune with the letter," Alleyn
plodded on, "threw him into a fever. On the one hand
he had appeared to condole with Miss Cartell for a loss
that had not yet been discovered, and, on the other, he
had sent Lady Bantling a letter that he would give the
world to withdraw, since, once it got into my hands, I
might follow it up. As long as this letter remained
undisclosed, Mr. Period remained unwilling to make
any statement that might lead to an arrest for the
murder of Mr. Cartell. He was afraid, first, that he
might bring disaster upon an innocent person, and,
second, that anything he said might lead to an examination of his own activities and Mr. Cartell's veiled

allusions to them. All this," he added, "supposes him, for the moment, to be innocent of the murder."

"Of course he is," Désirée muttered impatiently. "Good Lord! P.P.!"

"You don't know," Bimbo intervened with a sharp look at her. "If he'd go to those lengths, he might go the whole hog."

"Murder Hal, to save his own face! Honestly, darling!"

"You don't know," Bimbo repeated obstinately. "He might."

"Assume for the moment," Alleyn said, "that he didn't, but that he was in possession of evidence that might well throw suspicion on someone else. Assume that his motive in not laying this information was made up of consideration for an old friend and fear of the consequences to himself. He learns that I have been told of yesterday's luncheon party, and also that I have been given the letter that was occasioned by the conversation at the party. It's more than possible that he heard, on the village grapevine, that I visited Ribblethorpe Church this afternoon. So the gaff, he thinks, is as good as blown. With a certain bit of evidence weighing on his conscience, he sends his man here with a note asking you, Miss Ralston, to visit him. Wanting to keep the encounter private, he suggests a late hour. After a good deal of discussion with Mr. Leiss, no doubt, you decide to fall in with this plan. You do, in fact, cross the Green at about 10:45, and visit Mr. Period in his library."

"You're only guessing," Moppett said. "You don't know."

"You enter the library by the French windows. During the interview you smoke. You drop ash on the carpet and grind it in with your heel. You leave two butts of Mainsail cigarettes in the ashtray. Mr. Period tells you he heard someone whistling in the lane very late last night and that he recognized the tune. You and Mr. Leiss knew your way about the garden, I believe. To support this theory, we have the theft of Mr. Period's cigarette case—"

"I never," Leonard interrupted, "heard anything so fantastic. You don't know what you're talking about."

". . . Which you, Mr. Leiss, left on the sill, having opened the window with this theft in mind. Subsequently, it may be, the case became too hot and you threw it in the drain, hoping it would be supposed that Mr. Period had lost it there, or that the workmen had stolen and dumped it. Alternatively, you might have dropped it, inadvertently, when you altered the planks in order to bring about Mr. Cartell's death."

He waited for a moment. An all-too-familiar look of conceit and insolence appeared in Leonard. He stretched out his legs, leant back in his chair and stared through half-closed eyes at the opposite wall. A shadow trembled on his shirt and he kept his hands in his pockets.

Connie said: "It's not true: none of it's true."

Moppett repeated: "Not true," in a whisper.

"As to what actually took place at this interview," Alleyn went on, "Mr. Period will no doubt be willing to talk about it when he recovers. My guess would be that he tackled Miss Ralston pretty firmly, told her what he suspected, and said that if she could give him an adequate explanation he would, for Miss Cartell's sake, go no further. She may have admitted she was the whistler he heard from his window and said that she had come into his garden on the way home from the party to get water for Mr. Leiss's car-radiator, which had sprung a leak. I think this explanation is true."

Moppett cried out: "Of course it's true. I did. I got the water and I put the bloody can back. I remembered having seen it under the tap."

"After lunch, when you took Mr. Period's cigarette case off the sill?"

"Fantastic!" Leonard repeated. "That's all. Fantastic!"

"Very well," Alleyn said. "Let it remain in the realms of fantasy."

"If it's in order," Désirée said. "I'd like to ask something."

"Of course."

"Are we meant to think that whoever threw the fish laid the trap for Hal?"

"A fish?" Leonard asked with an insufferable air of innocence. "But has anyone said anything about a fish?"

Désirée disregarded him. She said to Alleyn: "I ought to know. I gave it to P.P. yesterday morning. He's dotty about pikes and this thing looked like one. He put it in the library. . . . Could I have an answer to my question?"

"I think the murderer and the paperweight thrower are one and the same person."

"Good," said Désirée. "That lets us out, Bimbo."

"I'm glad to hear it," Bimbo said with a short laugh. "Why?"

"Well, because neither of us has the slightest motive for hurling anything at P.P."

"Isn't he one of the trustees for Andrew Bantling's estate?" Leonard asked of nobody in particular.

She turned her head and looked very steadily at him. "Certainly," she said. "What of it?"

"I was just wondering, Lady Bantling. You might have discussed business with Mr. Period when you called on him this evening?"

Bimbo said angrily: "I'm afraid I fail entirely to see why you should wonder anything of the sort, or how you can possibly know the smallest thing about it."

"Yes, but I do, as it happens. I heard you talking things over with your dashing stepson at the party."

"Good God!" Bimbo said, and turned up his eyes.

Désirée said to Alleyn: "I told you. I called to own up that I'd given you his letter. I felt shabby about it and wanted to get it off my chest."

"What's his attitude about the Grantham Gallery proposal, do you know?"

"Oh," Désirée said easily, "he waffles."

"He'll be all right," Bimbo said.

"Just a moment," Leonard intervened. He still lay back in his chair and looked at the ceiling but there was a new edge in his voice. "If you're talking about this proposition to buy an art gallery," he said, "I happen to know P.P. was all against it."

Bimbo said: "You met Mr. Period for the first time when you got yourself asked to lunch in his house. I fail to see how that gives you any insight into his views on anything."

"You don't," Leonard observed, "have to know people all their lives to find out some of the bits and pieces. The same might apply to you, chum. How about that affair over a certain club?"

"You bloody little pipsqueak——"

"All right, darling," Désirée said easily. "Pipe down. It couldn't matter less."

"Not when you marry money, it couldn't," Leonard agreed offensively.

Bimbo strode down the room towards him: "By God, if the police don't do something about you, I will."

Fox rose from obscurity. "Now, then, sir," he said blandly. "We mustn't get too hot, must we?"

"Get out of my way."

Leonard was on his feet. Moppett snatched his arm. He jabbed at her with his elbow, side-stepped, and backed down the room, his hand in his jacket pocket. Alleyn took him from behind by the arms.

"You've forgotten," he said. "I've got your knife."

Leonard uttered an elaborate obscenity, and at the same time Fox, with the greatest economy, caused Bimbo to drop backwards into the nearest chair. "That's right, sir," he said. "We don't want to get too warm. It wouldn't look well, in the circumstances, would it?"

Bimbo swore at him. "I demand," he said, pointing a bandaged hand at Alleyn, "I demand an explanation. You're keeping us here without authority. You're listening to a lot of bloody, damaging, malicious lies. If you suspect one of us, I demand to know who and why. Now then!"

"Fair enough," said Désirée. "You stick out for your rights, duckie. All the same," she added, looking Alleyn full in the face, "I don't believe he knows. He's letting us cut up rough and hoping something will come out of it. Aren't you, Rory?"

She was inviting Alleyn, as he very well knew, to acknowledge, however slightly, that he and she spoke the same language: that alone, of all this assembly, they could understand each other without elaboration. He released the now quiescent Leonard and answered her directly.

"No," he said. "It isn't quite like that. It's true that I believe I know who murdered Harold Cartell. I believe that there is only one of you who fills the bill. Naturally, I'm looking for all the corroborative evidence I can find."

"I demand—" Bimbo reiterated, but his wife cut him short.

"All right, darling," she said. "So you've told us. You demand an explanation and I rather fancy you're going to get it. So do pipe down." She returned to Alleyn. "Are you going to tell us," she asked, "that we all had red-hot motives for getting rid of Hal? Because I feel sure we did."

"Contrary to popular belief," he said, "the police are concerned less with motive than with opportunity and behaviour. But, yes. As it happens you all had motives of a sort. Yours, for instance, could be thought to come under the heading of maternal love."

"Could it, indeed?" said Désirée.

"By God!" Bimbo shouted, but Alleyn cut him short.

"And you," he said, "wanted to invest in this project that Cartell wouldn't countenance. Judging from the unopened bills on your desk and your past history, this could be a formidable motive."

"And that," Leonard observed, smirking at Bimbo, "takes the silly grin off your face, Jack, doesn't it?"

"Whereas," Alleyn continued, "you, Mr. Leiss, and Miss Ralston were *directly* threatened, both by Mr. Cartell and, I think, Mr. Period, with criminal proceedings which would almost certainly land you in jail."

"No!" Connie ejaculated.

"A threat," Alleyn said, "that may be said to provide your motive as well, I'm afraid, Miss Cartell. As for Alfred Belt and Mrs. Mitchell, who are not present, they were both greatly concerned to end Mr. Cartell's tenancy, which they found intolerable. Murder has been done for less."

It was not pleasant, he thought, to see the veiled eagerness with which they welcomed this departure. Leonard actually said: "Well, of course. Now you're talking," and Moppett flicked the tip of her tongue over her lips.

"But I repeat," Alleyn went on, "that it is circumstance, opportunity and behaviour that must concern us. Opportunity, after a fashion, you all had. Miss Ralston and Mr. Leiss were on the premises late that night; they had stolen the cigarette case and the case was found by the body. The trap was laid by somebody wearing leather-and-string gloves, and Mr. Leiss has lost such a pair of gloves."

Leonard and Moppett began to talk together, but Alleyn held up his hand and they stopped dead.

"Their behaviour, however, doesn't make sense. If they were planning to murder Mr. Cartell they would hardly have publicized their actions by singing and whistling under Mr. Period's window."

Moppett gave a strangulated sob, presumably of relief.

"Lady Bantling had opportunity, and she knew the lay of the land. She *could* have set the trap; but it's obvious that she didn't do so, as she was seen, by Mr. Bantling and Miss Maitland-Mayne, returning across the planks to her car. She, too, had publicized her visit by serenading Mr. Cartell from the garden. Her behaviour does not commend itself as that of an obsessive maternal murderess."

"*Too* kind of you to say so," Désirée murmured.

"Moreover, I fancy she is very well aware that her son could anticipate his inheritance by borrowing upon his expectations and insuring his life as security for the loan. This reduces her motive to one of mere exasperation, and the same may be said of Mr. Bantling himself."

"And of me," said Bimbo quickly.

Alleyn said: "In your case, there might well be something we haven't yet winkled out. Which is what I mean about the secondary importance of motive. However, I was coming to you. You had ample opportunity. You retired to a bathroom, where you tell me you spent a long time bandaging your hand. You could equally well have spent it driving back to the ditch and arranging the trap. No, please don't interrupt. I know you were bitten. That proves nothing. You may also say that you took Mr. Leiss's overcoat to him. Were his gloves in the pocket?"

"How the hell do I know! I didn't pick his ghastly pockets," said Bimbo, turning very white.

"A statement that at the moment can't be checked. All the same, there's this to be said for you: if you are both telling the truth about your movements this evening, you are unlikely to have chucked the paperweight at Mr. Period's head. Although," Alleyn said very coolly, "the amorous dog chase might well have led you into Mr. Period's garden."

"It might have," Désirée remarked, "but, in point of fact, it didn't. Bimbo was never out of my sight."

"If that is so," Alleyn said, "it leads us to an inescapable conclusion."

He waited, and across the stillness of the room there floated small inconsequent sounds: the whisper of Fox's pencil and his rather heavy breathing, the faint rasp of Moppett's fingernails on the arms of her chair, and from somewhere within the house a scarcely perceptible mechanical throb.

"There remains," Alleyn said, "just one person to whom opportunity, behaviour and motive all point, inescapably. This one person presents certain characteristics: a knowledge of Mr. Cartell's movements, the assurance that at one o'clock the Baynesholme guests would have long ago left the scene, and access to Mr. Leiss's gloves. So much for opportunity. Behaviour. There are certain reactions. Everybody knows about Mr. Period's propensity for writing letters of condolence: he's famous for them. Now, suppose one of you gets a Period letter, couched in rather ambiguous terms but commiserating with you on the loss of somebody whom you saw fighting-fit the previous evening. What would you think? Either that he was dotty or that he had sent you the wrong letter. You might get an initial shock, but a few moments' thought would reassure you.

You would not, having gone to find out what it was all about and encountered a bewildered Mr. Period, turn deadly white and almost faint. But if you had murdered the supposed subject of the letter, how would you react? Suppose you had awakened in the morning with the remembrance of your deed festering in your mind and then been presented with this letter. Suppose, finally, that when you were being interviewed by the police, a second letter arrived, couched in exactly the same phrases. Wouldn't that seem like a nightmare? Wouldn't it seem as if Mr. Period knew what you'd done, and was torturing you with his knowledge? What would you do then?"

Connie Cartell had risen to her feet. She made an extraordinary gesture with her weather-chapped bandaged hand.

"You can't prove it," she said. "You haven't got the gloves."

At that moment a loud and confused rumpus broke out in the garden. There was a cry of frustration and a yelp of pain. The Pekingese leapt from Connie's embrace.

A body crashed against the French windows. They burst open to admit Pixie, immensely overwrought and carrying some object in her mouth. She was closely followed by Alfred Belt.

Alleyn shouted: "Shut those windows." Alfred did so and stood in front of them, panting noisily.

With an *expertise* borne of their early training, Alleyn and Fox seized, respectively, Pixie and Li. Alleyn thrust his thumbs into the corners of Pixie's slavering mouth.

Her plaything dropped to the floor. Alfred, gasping for breath, stammered: "In the garden, sir. Here. Ran her to earth. Digging."

Moppett cried out: "Lennie! Lennie! Look! They're your gloves!"

Alleyn said to Bimbo: "Catch hold of this dog."

"I'll be damned if I do."

"I do her," said Trudi.

She dragged Pixie from the room.

Alleyn stooped to retrieve the gloves. He unrolled them. The leather in the palms had been torn, and fragments of string hung loose from the knitted backs. The thumb of the left-hand glove was discoloured with blood. He began to turn it inside out. As he did so, Connie Cartell screamed.

It was a shocking sound, scarcely less animal than the canine outcry that had preceded it. Her mouth remained open and for a moment she looked like a mask for a Fury. Then she plunged forward and, when Fox seized her, screamed again.

The lining of the thumb showed a fragment of blackened and bloodstained cotton wool, and smelt quite distinctly of the black ointment used for girth-gall.

CHAPTER EIGHT

Period Piece

Mr. Pyke Period reclined on his library sofa, nibbling calf's-foot jelly and giving audience to Alleyn, Nicola and Andrew. He had just prevailed upon Dr. Elkington to allow him downstairs. Wan though he was, he might nevertheless have been suspected of enjoying himself.

"It's so utterly dreadful," he said. "One can*not* believe it. Connie! One knows, of course, that she has the reputation of a thruster in the hunting field, but I've always thought of her as just another of those fatiguing women who shout and laugh. Rather stupid, in fact."

"She is," Alleyn conceded, "a very stupid woman. But she has the cunning of her stupidity, I'm afraid."

"And all for that wretched girl! I fear," Mr. Period said, "that I may have precipitated matters, I mean, by suggesting that the girl should come and see me. The thing was, my dear fellow, I woke on that dreadful night and I heard that tune being whistled somewhere outside. And voices: hers and that appalling young man's. And when you described what must have been done, I thought they were responsible."

"But," Alleyn pointed out, "you decided not to tell me about this?"

Mr. Period changed colour. "Yes—for a number of reasons. You see—if it had only been intended as a trick—the consequences—so terrible for Connie. Oh, dear—*Connie!* And then I must confess—"

"You couldn't face the publicity?"

"No," Mr. Period whispered. "No—I couldn't. Very wrong of me. There . . . there was a personal matter . . ." He stopped and waved his hands.

"I know about the baptismal register," Alleyn said gently.

Mr. Period turned scarlet but said nothing.

Alleyn looked at Andrew and Nicola: "Perhaps," he suggested, "I might just have a word—"

"Yes, of course," they both said and made for the door.

"No!" Mr. Period quite shouted. They turned. His face was still red and his eyes were screwed up as if he expected a blow. "No!" he repeated. "Don't go! I am resigned. If I have to dree my weird I may as well dree it now. My nanny," Mr. Period explained with a travesty of his family preoccupation, "was a Highlander. I prefer, I repeat, that you should remain. Nicola, you lunched here, you heard the conversation? About— about the baptismal register? You remember?"

"Well, yes."

" 'Nuff said. But I felt sure that Hal was going to tell Connie and Connie would tell the girl and—and if I—indeed, when I saw her, the girl threatened—"

"Little beast," Nicola said heartily.

"Worse than that! I gathered they were prepared to use blackmail. And then, dear Désirée came in that evening and said, Alleyn, she'd given you that *unfortunate* letter, so—"

"So you felt you had nothing to lose?"

"Quite! Quite!"

"So you told the girl that unless she could explain their presence in the lane you would report it to the police."

"Yes. I said I felt it my duty to speak, in case

innocent people should be suspected. It was then she threatened to use—to make public . . . However! She was so impertinent and so brazen I lost my temper. I said I would ring you up at once. I quite shouted it after her as she went away. And then, you know, I *did* ring up, and—and then I don't know what happened."

Alleyn said: "What happened was this. Constance ·Cartell, on the hunt for her Pekingese, came into your garden. She probably caught a glimpse of her ward coming out by the French windows. She heard your final threat. She was terribly suspicious, indeed terrified, of you."

"Of Mr. Period?" Nicola exclaimed. "But why?"

"Because of the identical letters of condolence. She thought he suspected her. She had let me see the second letter, hoping to anticipate anything he might tell me by throwing suspicion on him."

"But how dreadful of her!" Mr. Period faintly exclaimed.

"She heard you shout that you were going to ring me up. You had your back to the window as you telephoned. The paperweight was on the table, near to hand. In an ecstasy of rage and fear for herself and her ward, she threw it at you and bolted. Everything she has done has been out of the unreasoning depths of her passion for that wretched girl. Her brother had threatened to bring a charge of theft against Mary, so Connie picked up Leiss's gloves from wherever they had been dumped in her hall and laid the trap for him. Afterwards, because the gloves were torn and stained with the stuff she put on her thumb, she buried them in her rubbish heap, which was due to be lit next day. She didn't wear gloves when she threw the paperweight. Her prints are there, quite clearly, along with several others."

"But—" Nicola began and then said: "Yes. Of course."

"Of course—why?"

"I was just remembering. They would be, anyway, because Mr. Period handed it round before lunch."

"I wonder if she's thought of that," said Alleyn.

He went over to Mr. Period. "You've had a horrid time of it," he said, "and I can't say the sequel will be anything but very deeply distressing, but as far as your private affairs are concerned, I don't think they will come into the case at all."

Mr. Period tried once or twice to speak. At last he said: "You are very kind. Too kind. I'm most grateful."

Alleyn shook his hand and left him. Nicola and Andrew saw him out.

Nicola said: "I've often tried to imagine what you were like in action. Now, I know. It's a bit sobering."

"I've been wondering," Andrew said. "Did you ever suspect me?"

"You?" Alleyn looked at the pair of them and grinned. "You didn't, it appeared, leave Nicola for long enough. And I'm damned if I go any further with this recital. Good-bye to you both." He went a few paces down the drive and turned. "By the way," he said. "I've been talking to Troy. She seems to think you're an acquisition as a pupil. I've seldom heard her so enthusiastic. Congratulations."

He waved his hand and left them.

Nicola looked at Andrew. "Congratulations," she said.

"Darling!" Andrew began excitedly, but she backed away from him. "No! Not now! Not yet. Let's wait. I must go back to Mr. Period," said Nicola in a flurry.

"I love you," said Andrew. "Isn't it astonishing?"

"It's heaven," Nicola cried and ran into the house.

Mr. Period was looking pensive and had the air of a man who has made up his mind.

"Nicola, my love," he said, still in a slightly invalidish voice, "it's just occurred to me that I really should explain about that business . . . in case there is any misunderstanding. The old Rector at Ribblethorpe was a dear old boy but a *leetle* eccentric. He christened me, you know. But would you believe it, he forgot to put my name in the register? I was a twin. He became so ga-ga, poor darling, that I'm afraid that when I discovered the omission, I was very naughty and took things into my own hands. It seemed the simplest way out," Mr. Period said, looking Nicola very straight in the eye. He gave a little titter. "But we won't put it in the book."

"No?"

"No," said Mr. Period firmly. " 'Nuff said."